Choices of Fate

S. Simone Chavous

Cover design by S. Simone Chavous

Editing by Kathy Krick of K² Editing

Proofreading by Kimberly Huther of Wordsmith Proofreading

ISBN: 978-0-9895701-1-4
eISBN: 978-0-9895701-0-7

Visit my website: http://www.ssimonechavous.com

Like me on Facebook: http://www.facebook.com/ssimonechavous

Follow me on Twitter: http://www.twitter.com/ssimonechavous

To my two girls, Cami and Isabella, for the endless inspiration, to Brian, for all of the love and support, and to my mom, Wanda, for always believing in me.

Contents

Prologue

Lucias gingerly opened the file that his first-in-command, Kaleb, had procured during his three-day trip to the Midwest, anticipating yet another dead-end in what felt like an endless search. He glanced over the notes, barely registering the words as his mind wandered to the delectable little meal that was waiting for him in the next room. It had been far too long since he last ate, especially for someone with his proclivities.

Then one little four letter word came into his field of vision and commanded his full attention. Carefully reading the surrounding sentence, he pulled one of the black X-ray films from the back of the stolen dental chart and held it up to the rather dim light of his quarters.

His perfect lips curled up into a wickedly satisfied smile. "This is most promising, my son. I assume you obtained all copies and related correspondence."

Kaleb responded, his eyes downcast. "Yes, Sire. My team scoured the doctor's physical files and computer server. A mining virus was uploaded to the system that corrupted all of the files and images related to that patient and removed all emails and Internet posts. We have verified that the request for advice he posted on the medical website was removed and the only respondent has been neutralized, along with the doctor and his staff."

"Excellent. I want you to choose your best man and send him back with your team to observe the family. I want to know everything there is to know about them before we move. There can be no mistakes. Everything we have been working toward depends upon this."

"My team is already in place and awaiting your instructions, Sire. I will fly out immediately to join them. "

"No, you are to stay here. If this is truly the child from the prophecy, the enemy knows your face and is no doubt watching."

"I do not understand, Sire. If the enemy knows, then why have they not taken the child?"

Lucias' eyes filled with anger as he spat, "You dare question me, Kaleb? I am your master, and I tell you what I want you to know and nothing more!"

He stood and began to pace in front of the desk as his rage dissipated. "However, perhaps it is time for you to know more."

He returned to his chair and removed the thin silver chain that hung around his neck. Using the small key that was attached, he opened the top drawer of the desk as he continued. "There is only one who would know of the child and it is a secret he would keep from everyone, even his own people. You know him well, considering he killed your only brother."

It was now Kaleb who was filled with rage as his thoughts turned back to that black day when he watched his brother fall at the feet of his enemy. Fighting the urge to question his master again, he held his emotions in check and responded with deference, "What would you have me do, Sire?"

Lucias placed the small velvet pouch on the desk and pressed his fingertips together in front of his face. "Wait. When the time comes, you will have your revenge and I will have the world."

CHAPTER 1 - *Baby Blues*

As she sat in the waiting room of Dr. Kline's office, Alexa finally lost the battle to hold back the tears that had been threatening to slide down her face for the last two weeks. She blamed it on the sleepless nights and the frustration of helplessly watching and listening to her sweet baby girl suffer, crying herself sick every night. It had nothing to do with Chloe's father; she was over that. Mostly.

A cute little tow-haired boy looked over at her from a child-sized chair in the play area across the room. He picked a little stuffed bear from the box of toys against the wall and ran past his mother and across the room to stand directly in front of Alexa and Chloe.

"Why are you crying?" he asked, looking to Alexa with concern in his hazel eyes.

She smiled slightly and swiped at the tears on her cheeks. "Oh, I'm just really tired and worried about my baby. I think she's sick and I don't know what's wrong. That's why we're here at the doctor's."

"Maybe this will make her feel better," he said, before stretching his little arm out to present the toy in his hand to Chloe.

Her eyes were squeezed shut as she continued to wail, so Alexa reached out and accepted the bear. "That's so sweet, thank you. I'm sure she'll really like it. What's your name, handsome?"

He grinned wide at Alexa, his two front teeth missing as he replied, "Jude William," before running back to his mother, obviously a little embarrassed.

Just then, the waiting room door squeaked open as a plump African-American nurse dressed in Mickey Mouse scrubs stepped through. Her name was Barb, based on the name tag attached above her left breast. "Ms. Ryan, the doctor can see you now." The nurse patted Alexa's shoulder and offered a sympathetic smile as Alexa passed through the doorway with her screaming nine-month-old in tow. Before the door closed, Alexa looked back at the sweet little boy, giving him a quick wink and sending him into a fit of giggles in response.

After an amazingly comfortable pregnancy and eight-and-a-half months of near bliss as a new mother, Alexa was completely blindsided by the rapid change in her daughter. Chloe had gone from crawling, babbling, and learning to walk, to nonstop crying and lying around without so much as attempting to sit up. She was refusing all solid food, instead opting to nurse so often that Alexa's nipples were raw and bleeding. Two trips to the emergency room in the middle of a couple of extremely bad nights and several visits to her regular pediatrician had led them to Dr. Kline. The man was considered to be something of a miracle worker when it came to dealing with inconsolable babies like Chloe, who were typically diagnosed as "colicky" and whose mothers were sent away with little more than a prescription for ear plugs.

"We're heading to exam room four on the left. Just strip her down to her underthings and bring her back out here to get her weighed."

Thanks to the screaming, Alexa could barely hear any of the nurse's instructions, but she'd done the drill so many times in recent weeks she was able to figure it out. She placed Chloe on the table covered with crinkly white paper, and unsnapped the pink and purple polka-dot jumper before pulling it over her head. Pulling two tissues from the box on a nearby counter, Alexa cleaned off Chloe's tear-soaked face and walked out into the hallway to join the nurse and put her on the scale. Once her movement settled down enough for a reading to pop up on the digital display, Alexa glanced down and felt her heart drop into her stomach. Chloe had lost another eight ounces since her last weight check, bringing the total loss to nearly a pound in the last two weeks. The tears that Alexa had managed to choke back, with the help of a kind little boy, started flowing once again.

Unflinching, the nurse gently passed Chloe back to Alexa and pointed them toward the exam room as she typed a few notes into her laptop. Once inside, she asked Alexa a few basic questions, measured Chloe, and then announced that the doctor would be in shortly. "Listen, honey. The best advice I can give you is to ask for help from wherever you can get it. Your mama, your friends. Anyone who says they'll keep the baby for you to get some sleep or get your hair done, you take advantage of it, child, ya hear?" Alexa nodded slightly. The words meant to offer encouragement only served to increase the deep ache in Alexa's heart.

There was no mother, no friends to speak of offering much needed help and advice. The only assistance since Chloe was born had come from an unlikely source, an unfathomably kind couple who lived next door to the house Alexa purchased in Fishers, IN. Alexa couldn't help but smile to herself as she thought of Jesse and Jill. She had lived there for several months and hadn't so much as waved at her neighbors but, shortly after she arrived home that first day with Chloe, the doorbell rang. When she opened the door, she was greeted by the cutest little spitfire of a woman and her teddy-bear of a husband, both with arms full of gift bags and trays of food. Overwhelmed by their kindness and embarrassed by her own conduct, Alexa apologized repeatedly for her unsocial behavior. Each time, the warm couple brushed it off and assured her that they were not offended and understood that she had a lot on her plate.

For the next week or so, Jill showed up every afternoon with a home-cooked supper, only staying a few minutes to gush over the baby. Both she and Jesse were really good about being helpful and friendly, without being intrusive or overbearing.

But for them and Chloe, Alexa was alone in the world, a painful reality she had grown quite accustomed to over the years. However, these last few weeks had begun to erode the protective wall she had built around her heart. She longed for someone to connect with, to lean on in these difficult times. Not so long ago, she thought she had finally found the one who would accept her, who would be there no matter what, but, like everyone else, he walked away.

As Barb started to exit the exam room, she turned back and looked kindly into Alexa's tear stained face. "After three easy babies, my youngest came along and knocked me right on my ass. This being your first, I can only imagine how scary this is for you, but don't you worry. Dr. Kline is the best. I've seen him soothe babies in crying fits far worse than this. He'll figure this out and get your sweet baby back to rights in no time, you'll see."

Alexa could only offer a half-hearted smile, unable to speak for fear of completely losing it and falling into yet another crying fit of her own. As she paced the room, trying desperately to console Chloe, she found herself sending up a little prayer that Dr. Kline could help her. Not usually one for prayer, she had always considered herself as more spiritual than religious, but at this point she found herself praying more often than not. Hell, she might even entertain calling in a priest to perform an exorcism if there was even a small hope that it would give her little munchkin some relief.

✧

After a brief reprieve, that had Alexa hoping her baby might finally be giving in to the exhaustion, Chloe's wailing kicked into high gear again. Bouncing her frantically as she turned to pace towards the door, Alexa let out startled yelp as she nearly walked straight into the man who had just entered.

"Ms. Ryan, I am terribly sorry if I frightened you. I did knock, but I suppose it would be a little difficult to hear a bulldozer coming through the wall over this little sweetheart here. I think we can safely say that her lungs are in working order."

Alexa lifted her gaze from Dr. Kline's chest to the charming smile that reached up to deep green eyes that were devastating, yet oddly comforting. To say he was handsome was a bit of an understatement.

He took a step back and extended his hand in greeting, "I am Dr. Elijah Kline."

After taking a moment to regain her composure, Alexa shifted Chloe to her left hip and shook the offered hand. The brief touch caught Alexa by surprise, but it was over before she could give it much thought.

"It's very nice to meet you, Dr. Kline. I can't thank you enough for squeezing us in on such short notice."

"It is no trouble. Most of my patients are referrals that require immediate attention, so my staff and I do all that we can to accommodate."

As he turned to wash his hands in the corner sink, Alexa took the opportunity to really look him over. At easily six-and-a-half-feet, of what Alexa guessed to be well-toned muscle, despite the lab coat that left a great deal to the imagination, Dr. Kline was an impressive man. If it wasn't for the flecks of gray in his chestnut hair, she would have placed him at around thirty years old. Of course, he had to be much older based on his profession and reputation.

He turned back to face them, reaching for Chloe, with an expression that implied his request for permission to hold her. As she handed the distraught baby to him, Alexa couldn't help but feel like she had met Dr. Kline before, even though that was impossible. There was no way she could forget a man like him, yet there was something about him that she couldn't quite place. A warm familiarity that immediately put her at ease and made her feel like everything was going to be all right.

Hell, there was a time when she might have actually been attracted to him yet, after everything that had happened in the last couple of years, she couldn't muster an interest for any man, no matter how good-looking or charming he might be on the surface.

"Now, Ms. Ryan, can you tell me when you first noticed a change in Chloe's normal routine and behavior?"

Opening her mouth to answer, Alexa halted in amazement as she looked over at Chloe in Dr. Kline's arms.

"Oh, my God. How did you do that? I think this is the first time in two weeks that she has stopped crying when she wasn't either asleep or nursing." Choking back a sob, Alexa continued shakily, "I don't understand. What am I doing wrong?"

Giving in to the exhaustion and frustration that had been weighing on her night and day, Alexa crumpled into a chair and sobbed into her hands.

Dr. Kline moved to stand beside the chair and placed a reassuring hand on her shoulder, as he let her cry it out for a few moments and Alexa's sobs turned into silent tears.

After several minutes quietly crying, Alexa snapped out of it and started to lift her head as a blaze of embarrassment began to color her cheeks.

Hastily swiping at the tears, she turned to face Dr. Kline and a seemingly happy Chloe chewing on his stethoscope as if everything was totally normal.

"I'm so sorry, Doctor. I don't know what came over me. I hardly ever cry, but lately it seems like that's all I do. I just feel so lost and helpless."

"Please, call me Elijah. There is absolutely no need to apologize. I promise you are not the first, nor will you be the last young mother to cry in my office. I tend to be something of a last resort when a pediatrician cannot come up with a traditional diagnosis. As was explained to you when you made the appointment, my methods are somewhat unorthodox and my fees are rather...hefty. We have our own lab on site and some of the most state-of-the-art diagnostic equipment in the state. That type of convenience does not come cheaply, but more than that I have found that the pricing of my services eliminates the patients who merely did a Google search before exhausting more traditional options. Of course, once we get through the initial consultation and determine that a patient requires further services, arrangements can be made to defer some of the costs."

Alexa merely nodded. The receptionist had explained most of that when she scheduled the appointment and had also mentioned that they did not accept any form of insurance. Having not had health insurance since she left her job shortly before Chloe was born, that wasn't a concern. When the receptionist indicated that they would require a large deposit before the visit, Alexa had been a little surprised but, for the first time, she was truly grateful for the large trust fund her parents left her that she'd only learned about on her eighteenth birthday.

When she left the attorney's office that day all those years ago, she felt anything but grateful. Abandoned, betrayed, furious, those words better described the emotions radiating from Alexa as she not-so-politely thanked Mr. Smith and stormed out of his office.

Snapping back to the present and feeling more like herself, with Chloe playing so contentedly on Dr. Kline's lap, Alexa finally answered his question regarding the change in Chloe.

"I think it started a little over two weeks ago. At first, she was just a little fussy around meal times. Within a few days, she was pushing away any solid foods that I would offer and crying constantly. The only time she doesn't cry is when she's asleep or nursing, which doesn't last long. She only sleeps in short spurts and I am so sore from the constant nursing and the biting that I can barely stand it long enough for her to calm down. I've tried everything to soothe her; warm baths, wearing her in a wrap, rocking, walking, bouncing, swinging, singing to her…nothing has worked for more than a few minutes at a time." Alexa considered the most troubling change that had occurred but, of course, that wasn't something she could mention to the doctor, or anyone else for that matter, so she only made a general reference to that issue. "I used to be so, um, intuitive about her needs, but I can't read her at all anymore."

Bouncing Chloe on one knee, Dr. Kline leaned over to the small counter and scribbled some notes on his pad. "When did you first introduce solids, and what did you offer?"

"I started her out around seven months with all of the recommended foods, orange and yellow vegetables, bananas, baby cereal. She did great with all of it. I didn't try anything new until she started refusing to eat, but she never does much more than let the spoon touch her tongue before she pushes whatever it is away."

"Did you notice any changes in her nursing habits before she started refusing solids?"

"Um, yeah, I guess so. She started biting me sometimes and was a bit rougher than normal. I took that as a sign that it might be time to start weaning, but she seemed to want to nurse more than ever."

Not one to be shy about such things, Alexa continued. "She really seemed to favor my right breast, but the nipple was so raw, and I even noticed it was bleeding some so I tried to only let her nurse on the left side for a while. She was so rough though, it wasn't long before that nipple was in pretty bad shape, too. I tried to express the milk by hand and feed her with a bottle or a sippy cup, but she won't take it that way. She only wants to nurse directly, so I've been doing my best to suffer through it."

As Alexa spoke, Dr. Kline remained quiet, nodding occasionally as he scribbled a few more notes and did a brief examination of Chloe as she looked up at him adoringly, seeming to love the attention. He looked in her ears, eyes, and mouth. Felt her glands and listened to her heart, lungs, and stomach.

"Ok, Alexa. May I call you Alexa?"

Nodding her agreement, she couldn't help but feel that spark of recognition again as he said her name.

"I would like to draw some blood to run some tests, if that's all right with you."

"Of course, whatever you need to do. I just want to help my baby."

Smiling at the sincerity in her voice, he added, "We will need some of your blood, as well. There are some genetic tests that can aid us significantly in narrowing down the possibilities as to what is going on with Chloe."

Again, she quickly agreed to do whatever was necessary, though it occurred to her that she couldn't remember ever having her blood drawn before. Actually, she didn't think she'd ever even been to see a real doctor. She never got sick and when she was pregnant, she opted for a midwife and a water birth at a birthing center. It didn't matter, he could have asked for one of her pinkies and she would have gladly sacrificed the appendage if it would get Chloe back to normal.

"Could you have her father drop by the office as soon as possible? We will need to collect a sample of his blood for the tests, as well."

Alexa felt the blood drain from her face as the doctor's request registered in her mind.

"Oh, um, I don't think that will be possible. He's out of the country, for work. I'm not sure when he'll be back." The lie came out easily. It was far simpler and infinitely less embarrassing than trying to explain the truth. At least the doctor hadn't presumed she was married, like most people did. Of course, that was probably only because she'd had to indicate her marital status on the paperwork she'd completed. Alexa had conveniently left the information about Chloe's father blank. Of course, she couldn't have provided most of the information even if she'd wanted to, since he had left her before she even knew she was pregnant.

"We'll run the tests that we can with your two samples. If we determine there is a need based on those results, perhaps we could make arrangements to get a sample of her father's blood shipped to us."

Alexa nodded her head in agreement, hoping that further tests wouldn't be necessary. She would cross that bridge when she came to it.

"If you will excuse me for a few moments, I'll get one of my nurses to come draw your blood. When you are finished, she will escort you to my office to discuss the next steps."

He stood and moved toward Alexa as Chloe reached out for her with a big smile on her face. It seemed like forever since she had seen her baby girl smile. Alexa scooped Chloe into a big hug as relief washed over her.

Dr. Kline reached for the door knob, looking back at them with a knowing smile on his face. "Everything is going to be all right,

Alexa."

She leaned her cheek against the top of Chloe's head and inhaled the sweet smell of her fine chestnut hair. Feeling her baby's body relax into her as she drifted off for a much needed and overdo nap, Alexa smiled back. Without even trying to dig into the how or why of it, she believed him.

CHAPTER 2 - *Girls' Night Out*

Standing in the exam room with her eyes closed, gently swaying back and forth while Chloe slept peacefully against her shoulder, Alexa's thoughts drifted back to the night her life changed forever. A year-and-a-half had passed, yet the memory and the pain were as fresh as if it had occurred only hours ago.

She was out for the first time in months at a happy hour with Jenny and Sarah, a couple of work friends. At least, they were the closest things resembling friends that she had at the time. Sarah was sweet and quiet, but she seemed to go along with whatever Jenny wanted. No one could really blame her, since Jenny was technically her boss and she was pretty awful to work for if she didn't like you. She was petty and jealous, especially of Sarah and Alexa. While she always put on a fake smile and said only nice things to her face, Alexa would overhear Jenny ridiculing her weight and general appearance behind her back. It had been that way since the first day she started in the tax group at Ernst & Young in Indianapolis. This night was no different.

I can't believe she is wearing that at her weight, though it would look amazing on me. Doesn't she own a mirror? Shit, I'll need to do an extra hour on the treadmill to work off all this food and alcohol tomorrow. At least sitting next to her makes me look hotter. Oh, my god, that guy staring over here is so fucking hot. Is he looking at me or Sarah?

Alexa rolled her eyes. She loved her outfit. The gray v-neck blouse with a hint of lace trim showed off just the right amount of cleavage and the flirty black skirt hugged her ample bottom perfectly. The wide red belt and red and black open-toed pumps added an ideal splash of color. She couldn't really blame Jenny. It's not like she would have ever said those things to her face. How could she know that Alexa could hear her thoughts?

She normally kept her shields up to keep from being bombarded by the thoughts of everyone around her. That skill had developed out of necessity shortly after her strange ability had emerged when she was a teenager. Strangers were the easiest to filter. It took a considerable amount of concentration for her to block out people she knew, particularly those she had spent a lot of time around. The better she knew a person, the easier their inner voice registered. With the cloud of alcohol covering her mind, it was damn near impossible to block close acquaintances. Especially with a loud broadcaster like Jenny, whose drunken thoughts were blaring loud and clear over the thump of the bass coming through the speakers in the crowded club.

This is why I don't drink, Alexa thought as Jenny's mind continued to interrupt what would have otherwise been a very pleasant buzz. At least Sarah was there.

I'll probably have to drag Jenny out of here tonight and get stuck paying for the cab again. I love Alexa's blouse, I'll have to ask her where she shops sometime. Better make sure Jenny isn't around. I don't know what her problem is, Alexa is so nice.

Sarah's sweet thoughts made Alexa smile. She didn't get those two being friends. Jenny was mean-spirited and overbearing. She wondered if she had only befriended Sarah in order to adhere to the old wisdom of "keep your friends close and your enemies closer". Based on her thoughts, she was even more jealous of Sarah than she was of Alexa. Sarah's sweet nature and exceptional beauty made her very popular with men, which Jenny couldn't stand since she was desperate to be the center of attention at all times. If it wasn't for Jenny, Alexa thought she and Sarah would probably be much closer.

Of course, Alexa never got too close to anyone. She knew better. Anyone who really got to know and spend time with her would eventually notice that she was different. It was so hard to hide all of her emotions when she could hear every thought going through her companion's head. Even if they didn't notice anything strange about her, she would ultimately push them away, as their innermost thoughts betrayed their true character.

Having a boyfriend was practically an impossibility. Alexa usually found herself completely disgusted within the first twenty minutes of any date she had ever been on. Either the guy was mentally fucking every other woman who walked by, or he was critiquing her body and all of the things that he could ignore just to get laid, just not if he wanted to seriously date her.

Holy fuck! He's coming over here. Does Sarah see him? Maybe I should get up and go to him before he gets all the way over. If I stake a claim it would be a violation of girl code for that little cunt to try anything. Shit, he's so hot!

Well, Jenny certainly wasn't wasting any time tonight.

Oh, wow, he's really cute. I wouldn't mind dancing with him tonight. Sarah's thoughts were considerably tamer.

At this point, Jenny was staring past Alexa, practically drooling as she flipped her thin, shoulder-length blonde hair while Sarah played with her straw nonchalantly, trying her best not to look at whomever had captured their attention from across the room. Alexa rolled her eyes and sighed.

She could have been at home, curled up on her comfortable old couch with a nice glass of pinot and her best friend lying beside her. So what if that friend had bad breath and liked to chew on her socks from time to time? Tilly was a great roommate and the faithful Great Dane made Alexa feel safe.

Taking the opportunity to make her escape unchallenged, while her companions were busy ogling some stranger, Alexa stood, making her excuses about having to get an early start the next morning even though it was obvious that the two women weren't hearing a word of it.

She grabbed her clutch and turned to make her way to the coatroom, walking right into someone in her hurry to get away.

"Excuse me, I'm really sorry," she blurted without even looking up.

"I am the one who is sorry that you are leaving. I spent the last ten minutes gathering up the courage to come and ask if you would let me buy you a drink."

Her breath caught as the stranger's accented voice registered in her mind and a tingling warmth gathered in her core and washed over her entire body. She turned to look up at him and felt her knees start to buckle as he swiftly wrapped his arm around her waist to steady her on her feet.

Where his voice had made her feel warm, his touch set her body on fire. Unable to speak, or remember her own name for that matter, she drank in the physical perfection of the man who seemed to be quite at home holding her.

His nicely tousled chestnut locks made him look like he had just rolled out of bed in the best way possible and were just long enough to make her think how good it would feel to run her fingers through them while he was pressed up against her so closely.

Moving her shameless stare down to look into his beautiful eyes that were somewhere between green and gray, she almost melted as the darkness of desire clouded them while he stared down at her lips.

Following suit, she gazed down to his full lips and felt her lacy black panties moisten as he wet his lips with his tongue and held on to the bottom one with his teeth.

Oh. My. God. She thought he was going to kiss her. A complete stranger who she had bumped in to literally fifteen seconds ago was going to kiss her in a crowded bar and, God help her, she had never wanted anything so badly.

As she held her breath, waiting, hell, practically praying that he would lean down and press his mouth to hers, he turned and pulled out the chair that she had vacated just a few moments earlier and eased her onto it, effectively snapping her back to reality.

The flood of Jenny's less-than-kind thoughts, which she had been oblivious to moments before, hit her like a slap to the face.

Why the hell is he talking to that fat bitch? Is he fucking blind? He must be looking for an easy lay. Lucky for him, he can do better than her if I have anything to say about it.

With that, Jenny patted the seat next to her at the end of the booth between her and Alexa.

"Why don't you join us?" she purred suggestively.

Without taking his eyes off Alexa, he slid into the seat.

"I'm Jenny and that's Sarah over there. What's your name, handsome?"

Still looking at Alexa and clearly addressing only her, he replied, "I am Ethan. What is your name, beautiful?"

Still a little thrown, and feeling a bit embarrassed about her reaction a few minutes ago, Alexa kept her eyes averted as she mumbled, "Um, Alexa."

Not to be dissuaded by Ethan's inattention, Jenny continued in what was obviously her "sexy" voice. "I feel like moving my body. Come on, uh, Ethan, was it? Dance with me."

"Thank you for the offer, but I was actually just about to ask Alexa if she would dance with me."

Alexa looked up at him through her thick black lashes. Was he serious? This guy was definitely out of her league. Not that she was unattractive; she was actually fairly confident about her appearance, despite constantly hearing how she has such a pretty face, if she would just lose some weight. Sure, she could probably stand to lose twenty pounds, but Alexa loved food and she was not the kind of girl who would starve herself just to fit some mold people tried to force on her. She was a real woman, with curves that she embraced and liked to show off from time to time.

Trying to get a read on what this guy's game was, Alexa relaxed her shields a bit, but she couldn't hear his voice. That was a first. She could feel his mind and the wave of desire that seemed to genuinely be directed at her, though his thoughts felt just out of reach, like they were covered by some sort of veil. Lowering her shields a bit further in an attempt to hear him, the cacophony of all the minds in the room started barreling in, forcing her to snap her shields back into place.

Her face flushing slightly from the exertion, Alexa felt a tiny bead of sweat trickle over her temple just as Ethan reached up and gently brushed it away with his thumb as he cupped her cheek.

With him touching her like that, everything else fell away. She could no longer hear Jenny, who was staring at her murderously or Sarah, who simply watched curiously with a slight smile on her face.

"So, how about it, Alexa? Will you dance with me?"

Overwhelmed by his touch and unable to find her voice, Alexa nodded as Ethan's hand left her face and slightly grazed her neck before he took her hand and led her through the crowd to the middle of the dance floor.

Just then, the upbeat song that had been playing ended and was replaced by a much slower song that Alexa had never heard before, but in that moment, she thought it was the sexiest song she had ever heard. The lyrics weren't being sung in English. It sounded exotic; African, maybe.

Ethan twirled her around, wrapped his arm securely around her waist, and pulled her body tightly against his as they began to sway slowly along with the music.

Alexa was overcome with the sensations his nearness evoked. She had never experienced anything so intense or consuming and she felt incredibly embarrassed by how strongly her body was responding to this stranger. She kept her head turned to the side, pressed up against his hard chest with her eyes closed in a vain attempt to get a hold of herself. Ethan brought his hand up and lightly traced the outline of her ear, continuing down along her jaw until he gently lifted her chin to bring her eyes up to his. The uncertainty she'd felt only a few minutes earlier was completely erased as she looked up into his smoldering eyes. She might not be able to hear his thoughts, but the attraction radiating between them was like a tangible force that surrounded them and shut out everything else.

"Are you single, Alexa?" God, she loved how he said her name.

She replied without hesitation, her voice barely above a whisper, "Yes."

He grinned down at her. "That is good. I would hate to have to break up a happy couple." The confidence implied by his statement was such a turn-on.

Her gaze shifted from his eyes to take in his sexy grin and she once again found herself wanting to kiss him.

Finally gaining some semblance of composure, Alexa stuttered, "Um, what about you?"

Ethan cocked an eyebrow at her. God, was everything he did sexy? "What about me?" he asked.

"Are you dating anyone?" She held her breath waiting for his response.

"No, of course not. I have not been with anyone in a very long time and I would never have approached you if I was not free to do as I pleased."

Something about the way he said that last part sent a tingle down her spine.

He leaned down and buried his face in the crook of her neck. His hot breath grazed her skin as he breathed her in.

"You smell amazing, delicious even," he whispered.

He brushed the tip of his tongue faintly across her neck as if he just couldn't resist one little taste. Alexa shivered, as goose bumps spread all over her body.

Lifting his head to look into her eyes again Ethan whispered, "You are so beautiful, Alexa."

Not really accustomed to compliments, a blush colored her cheeks as she glanced away from his intense stare.

He brushed his thumb over her heated cheek. "This makes you look even more beautiful, but why do you look away? Have I offended you?"

Alexa couldn't help but giggle a little. Of all the liberties he had taken during their extremely short acquaintance, calling her beautiful had to be the least offensive.

"No, of course not. It's just that I'm not used to compliments, I guess."

"Well, that breaks my heart. Feel it, it is breaking as we speak." He pulled her hand up and placed it over his heart, then leaned down and whispered in her ear. "You should hear how beautiful you are every day of your life."

Alexa had never felt so turned on in her entire life.

Just then, the song ended and another up-tempo number started.

"How about I buy you that drink now?" Ethan suggested.

"Sure, but I actually just want some ice water."

Ethan pulled away from her and started toward the bar, still holding her hand. Her body felt the loss of his nearness immediately and she unconsciously stuck out her bottom lip in a little pout.

As they neared the bar, he turned to her with a knowing smile on his face as he asked, "Why do you look like someone just stole your lollipop?"

The reference made Alexa think of all the things she could be licking, causing her to stumble and fall into someone sitting on a stool at the bar.

"Hey, watch it you fat cow! You made me spill my beer!" he spat as Alexa jumped back a few feet.

Before Alexa could even process the vile words the drunken asshole had just spat at her, Ethan had him by the throat down against the bar.

"Apologize. Right. Fucking. Now." Ethan's voice remained calm, but the rage pouring off of him was palpable. The man struggled against his grip, gasping for air that wasn't coming, though to look at Ethan he could have just been casually leaning against the bar, based on the amount of effort he seemed to be putting into it. Wow, he was strong.

It all happened so fast. Standing there in shock, Alexa's mind was assaulted with the feeling of pure terror rolling off the man. He thought he was about to die. The force of it knocked her to her knees as she gripped her head between her hands, but no sooner had she hit the floor then the pressure waned significantly.

"Alexa, are you all right?" She glanced up to see Ethan, the concern evident in his eyes as his gaze examined her for the source of her pain. How had he managed to get to her so quickly looking as if he hadn't just been chocking the life out of some goon who was well over two-hundred-and-twenty pounds?

"I'm fine. Sorry, I guess I just got dizzy. Too much to drink maybe." That was a reasonable excuse.

She looked towards the man crumpled against the bar coughing and attempting to get to his feet. His eyes were fixed on Ethan's back, obviously terrified as he started edging his way towards the exit. Now that he was standing up, Alexa noticed the large dark wet stain running down his pants. His beer had spilled over the bar; this was something else. He had actually pissed himself.

Shit, I'm sorry, I'm sorry, I'm sorry! Oh, fuck! What the fuck is wrong with that guy? Please, God, just let me get out of here and away from that psycho freak!

Regaining her composure and completely sobered up, Alexa snapped her shields back in place to block the man's panicked thoughts.

Ethan was still watching her intently as he helped her stand.

"Are you sure you're okay, Alexa?"

"Yes, I'm fine. That was my fault, I'm so clumsy. You shouldn't have done that." The last part came out in a whisper as she looked down towards his feet.

"No one will ever speak to you that way again." His words sounded a lot like a promise. One that she was certain he could back up after what she had just witnessed. The display should have raised all kinds of red flags. She should be afraid; he was a complete stranger after all, but fear was the last thing she felt. His protectiveness excited her.

He took her hand and headed after the escaping man who had only made it a few yards away.

The man's eyes widened with fear at their approach as he stammered, "I, I'm sorry, man. I'm just drunk, I didn't mean anything. Just let me leave and I'll never come back here again, I swear."

"Apologize to the lady." Ethan's voice was calm, controlled; yet the undertone of rage was evident.

The man didn't hesitate. "I'm really sorry, ma'am. I didn't think before I opened my big mouth. I had no right to speak to you that way." His eyes darted to Ethan, searching for approval of his apology.

"Uh, it's ok. Sorry I bumped into you."

With that, Ethan nodded and the man quickly crossed the remaining distance to the exit and disappeared into the night. He hadn't even bothered to stop and retrieve his coat on his way out and it was the middle of December.

Alexa noticed a couple of big bouncers making their way through the crowd towards her and Ethan.

"You want to get out of here, go somewhere a little quieter where we can talk?" Ethan asked.

She should have said no. He was a stranger, a dangerous stranger if the last few minutes were any indication, but with his beautiful eyes staring down at her she gave the response that was in her heart as a bright smile lit her face.

"Sure."

CHAPTER 3 - *Just a Little Pinch*

"Ms. Ryan? Ms. Ryan?" Barb whispered as she gently tapped Alexa's shoulder, snapping her back to the present.

"I knocked before I came in, but you didn't respond. Are you okay?"

"Oh, yes, I'm fine. Guess I just zoned out for a minute." Alexa smiled down at Chloe still sleeping in her arms, and then looked back up at the kind nurse. "With everything in the last couple of weeks, I haven't really had any peace and quiet to just think, so I guess my mind decided to take full advantage of the opportunity."

"I certainly can't blame you for that. I told you Dr. Kline is a miracle worker. It's hard to believe that's the same child I saw earlier. I hate to have to do this, but we need to get her blood sample now. Yours, too."

"Of course; can you do mine first? At least give her a few more minutes of rest. God knows she needs it."

"Absolutely; if you can just shift her over a bit and give me your free arm."

Alexa did as instructed. As the nurse swabbed the inside of her elbow with alcohol, she started noticeably shaking.

The nurse raised her eyebrows slightly. "Afraid of needles?"

"Um, no, I don't think so. Well, I don't know, I've never had to think about it. I guess I'm nervous because I don't know what to expect."

"Really? You mean you've never had your blood drawn? Never had a shot before?"

Alexa shrugged her free shoulder slightly. "Not that I can remember. I recall hearing something about there being bad reactions to vaccines in my family or something, so I was opted out of the mandatory stuff when I was a kid. There hasn't really been any reason to have my blood drawn. I never get sick."

"What about when you were pregnant with Chloe? Your doctor would have wanted to run some tests early on, check your iron levels, etcetera."

"No, I actually decided to use a midwife and have a water birth at a birthing center. I wanted as little intervention as possible. She always came to my house for my checkups and the pregnancy was really easy. I felt amazing the whole nine months. I didn't have any morning sickness or other problems to speak of at all."

"Well, you sure are brave, and lucky! I had all four of mine naturally, though that wasn't really by choice. Back when I was young that's just how it was done, but you can bet I would have taken the drugs if they offered 'em to me." She chuckled as she swiveled on her stool and grabbed the syringe that was waiting on the nearby tray. "All right, honey, I've been doing this for a whole lot of years and I'm damn good at it, if I do say so myself, so don't you worry, you'll barely feel a thing, just a little pinch. Look away, I'll count to three and then do it, okay?"

Alexa shook her head and looked away.

"Ready, one...okay, it's in there, told you it wouldn't hurt much."

Alexa turned to look while Barb snapped the first collection tube in place. "I thought you said you were counting to three?"

Barb gave her a playful wink. "I've learned over the years that it hurts a lot less when people aren't anticipating the pain. Most of it is in our heads, you know."

After filling up another tube, the nurse removed the needle and placed a small cotton swab and Band-Aid on Alexa's arm. Just then, Chloe started rooting around towards her free arm like she wanted to nurse. Alexa shifted her over and turned her head the other way. After a few moments she was still again.

"Ok, now comes the hard part. I hate to say it, but I'll warn you this one is probably going to hurt you a lot more than your own did. I'll be quick and, if we're really lucky, she won't even wake up."

Amazingly, Barb was right. Chloe barely stirred while her blood was drawn.

"Now, I'm going to go run and check these samples into the lab down the hall, then I'll come right back and show you the way to Dr. Kline's office."

Alexa considered trying to put Chloe's jumper back on, but not wanting to push her luck, she decided to leave her in just her onesie. It was the middle of summer, after all, and quite warm out. True to her word, Barb was back before Alexa could even get all of her things loaded into the diaper bag.

"Here, let me carry that for you since you've got your hands full already. Just follow me this way." Barb grabbed the full diaper bag and expertly slung it over her shoulder as they headed out the door.

They proceeded down the long hallway, past several more exam rooms, a restroom, and an intersecting hallway that seemed to go for quite a while in both directions. While they were walking, Alexa was able to take in the facility in a way that she hadn't been able to when she was so busy trying to console Chloe. Everything was clearly state-of-the-art. She saw signs for the lab, X-ray and ultrasound, treatment, and even a cafeteria. The décor was clean and modern, yet warm and comforting, much like Dr. Kline himself.

At the end of the hallway, they turned left and came to a small waiting area.

"You can just have a seat here. Dr. Kline will be with you shortly. If I don't see you again before you leave, you have yourself a good day and take care of that sweet baby, ya hear?"

Barb placed the diaper bag on one of the empty chairs and patted Alexa's shoulder before heading back down the hallway.

Alexa eased into another empty chair, trying not to jostle Chloe too much. As she glanced at the time on her cell phone, she thought this had to be some kind of record. Chloe had been asleep for nearly forty-five minutes. She hadn't slept that long in over two weeks.

Sitting there, she took a moment to take in the area, noticing a security keypad on the door to Dr. Kline's office.

That's weird. I wonder what he's hiding in there.

Alexa laughed at herself for being so suspicious. He probably just stored confidential patient records in there, maybe some prescription pads or samples from pharmaceutical reps that he didn't want falling into the hands of some receptionist with a drug-addict boyfriend. Still, it made her very curious to learn more about the good doctor. She had kept her shields up initially, but now she was determined to listen in on Dr. Kline briefly.

Just then, the door swung open.

"Alexa, please come in. I'm glad to see Miss Chloe is getting in a nice little nap." He smiled at her warmly as she brushed past him and entered the spacious office.

The room was huge, with bookshelves lining two of the walls while pieces of art, that Alexa could only assume were very valuable, lined the others. One piece in particular caught her eye. It was of a man, and even though he was standing in the open, she couldn't really see him when she was looking directly at the painting. It was like he was behind some sort of veil, quite an interesting visual effect. When she looked off to the side, she could swear it looked exactly like...him.

Of course it looked like him, even after all this time she still saw him everywhere. Every man going around a corner or leaning in a dark alley was him. She felt him everywhere, but he was never really there when she looked again. Her mind had been playing cruel tricks on her for all these months, and she had learned to ignore it, but something about the way the man in the painting was standing with his head cocked to one side was so familiar.

"Well, Alexa. So far, Chloe seems to be the picture of health. Even with the recent weight loss, she is still well within the normal range for height and weight. Of course, we never want to see a child her age lose weight, so while we are waiting for the results of your blood work I would like for you to try these supplements. Give her one ounce right before each nursing. You can try giving it to her by bottle or spoon-feed it to her."

Turning her attention to the small package Dr. Kline had slid across the desk, Alexa picked up one of the containers examining the contents. The liquid was a milky brownish red color.

Inquiring about the ingredients of the mixture, Alexa lowered her shields to hear Dr. Kline's thoughts. She was met with telepathic silence as he said aloud, "It's my own formula of vitamins and minerals with some beet juice. It should soothe Chloe and help her to gain back some of the weight she lost."

Usually when Alexa lowered her shields, she was flooded with the thoughts of anyone nearby. She sat there for a moment in silence and searched with her mind for Dr. Kline's stream of consciousness. As she probed with her ability, she was met with an almost physical presence in Dr. Kline's mind that was blocking her from truly hearing him. She could sense his intentions, like hearing a person's tone of voice through a wall without being able to decipher the actual words and was certain that he meant well. But she couldn't hear him. That had only happened one time before since her ability manifested over ten years ago. Ethan.

"Alexa, did you hear me?"

She had been so focused on listening in on his thoughts that she had missed whatever he had been saying to her aloud the last few minutes.

Thinking quickly she replied. "No. I apologize; I'm just so tired I can

42

hardly focus."

She thought she noticed a flash of recognition in Dr. Kline's eyes just then, but it was gone before she could be sure it had ever been there at all. No one knew about her ability, but in that moment she felt like the good doctor knew she was searching his mind. Of course, that was impossible.

Ok, Alexa. You really are tired. Get a grip.

"I understand, Alexa. If we are lucky, Chloe will go down and get a good night of sleep tonight once her belly is full. Then you can catch up on your sleep, as well. The lab results should be ready by tomorrow afternoon, so I would like to see you both back here then to discuss the findings. Can you come in at three?"

"Oh, yeah, of course we'll be here."

"Excellent. I will let the receptionist know. Here is my card with my personal cell phone and pager numbers. Please contact me if there are any problems before then."

As she took the card, and slipped it into the diaper bag, he continued. "Alexa, please understand that you can contact me at any time, day or night, no matter how small or trivial you believe your concern to be. I am at your complete disposal until we get Chloe on the right track."

He placed his hand reassuringly on her shoulder. Taking advantage of the physical connection, Alexa attempted to peer into his thoughts one last time, but again heard nothing. She could feel that his intentions were sincere and she trusted him to help her, though she didn't understand why his thoughts eluded her telepathy. Why did he remind her so much of the man she had been trying so hard to forget?

"I can't thank you enough for your help. You've already made such a difference, though I admit I haven't the slightest clue how you did it. Care to share your secret?" Alexa raised her eyebrows and smiled inquisitively.

Dr. Kline chuckled. "Let us just say I have had many years in practice to hone my bedside manner. I cannot take all the credit; most likely, Chloe was so exhausted she would have fallen asleep for anyone."

Alexa sensed he was holding something back, but decided to let it go as he escorted her back to the main reception area. They confirmed her three o'clock appointment for the next day and she and Chloe were on their way.

Miraculously, Chloe stayed asleep through getting in her car seat and most of the thirty-minute drive back to their home in Fishers. With about ten minutes to go, Alexa glanced in the rearview mirror of her 2009 Lexus LX 570 to see Chloe starting to stir in the light-up mirror she had installed in back so she could see her while driving.

When Chloe began fussing, Alexa switched the satellite radio over to Kids Place Live, hoping for one of their favorites to sing along with and keep her occupied for the last few minutes of the drive.

Singing the last line of "Down By The Bay" as the garage door came down, Alexa cut the engine and rushed to get Chloe unloaded. She wanted to get her in the house and fed before whatever magic Dr. Kline had used wore off completely.

Stepping into the laundry room/entryway, Alexa looked around at the mess of clothes she hadn't gotten around to washing, along with various other items she'd carried in and set on the utility table. She had a bad habit of dropping things there and forgetting about them until she passed them the next time she came home, usually with her arms full, so many things had sat there for weeks. Making a mental note to give the room some much needed attention after Chloe went to sleep, Alexa opened the next door and stepped into the kitchen, where they were greeted by a very excited Tilly whose tail was wagging so hard it shook her entire body.

"Hey, Tilly Wiggles, look who's home!"

As was customary, she bent down with Chloe and let Tilly inspect her thoroughly. Chloe giggled as the giant dog's whiskers tickled her face and she gave her a quick lick. It always made Alexa smile, the way Tilly would dance around anxiously until she was allowed to check the baby. The last two weeks had been hard on her, too. While Chloe was crying, she would pace around the house anxiously whining. She hardly ate anything and had obviously lost some weight as a result.

"Don't worry, big girl. I think everything is going to be okay now." Alexa stood and gave her a good scratch behind the ear before making her way around the island of cabinets to the sliding glass door that led out to a spacious patio and intricately- landscaped backyard. She flipped up the latch and used her left foot to kick up the wooden dowel rod that she used for a little extra security, before letting Tilly out for some overdue exercise. If left to her own devices, the four-year-old Great Dane would probably never leave Chloe's side.

Unable to resist, Alexa stepped outside to take a quick walk around her own private oasis. She paused at her favorite spot, an Amish-made freestanding hammock she had picked up in Shipshewana, which was positioned next to the koi pond, complete with a soothing waterfall that had often lulled her to sleep when she relaxed there during her pregnancy.

Giving Chloe a big kiss on the cheek, Alexa turned and headed back along the stone path to the house. Once inside, she pulled the package of supplements that Dr. Kline had given her from the diaper bag and retrieved a clean bottle from one of the cherry cabinets. Setting the container on the black granite countertop, she used her free hand to twist off the top and emptied in an ounce of the milky liquid. She twisted the nipple on securely and presented it to Chloe, saying a silent prayer that she would take it. She refused it as first, but Alexa was persistent. She squeezed the nipple and smeared a little drop of the mixture on her lips to let her get a taste. Once she did, she latched on and gripped the bottle with both hands, gulping the rest of it down in record time.

Feeling encouraged, Alexa placed the empty bottle in the sink and walked out of the kitchen into the great room where Chloe, like usual, looked up and pointed to the skylights at the top of the cathedral ceiling. Before the chaos of the last couple of weeks, she often liked to stand beneath the glass and look up for birds that sometimes passed over. After pausing for a moment, they continued down the hallway to the nursery that adjoined the master bedroom. She laid Chloe on top of the padded changing table/dresser and pulled a pair of Winnie the Pooh pajamas from the top drawer. Quickly stripping off her clothes, Alexa looked down at a calm and quiet Chloe and flashed her a big grin. Chloe began to squirm and giggle in anticipation, knowing what was to come as Alexa inched closer to her exposed belly, her smile growing even wider before she pounced, blowing a loud raspberry against Chloe's soft skin. The resulting laughter was music to Alexa's ears and a sound that had been missing from her life for two deceptively long weeks.

Though she was overjoyed at Chloe's improved mood, she knew it was probably a bad idea to continue playing and getting her riled up. She had taken a nice nap earlier, but it was already after six and she was in desperate need of a nice long night of sleep, as was Alexa.

After quickly changing her diaper and slipping on her pajamas, Alexa picked her up and moved to sit in the rocking chair positioned below a colorful moon and stars decoration that hung from the ceiling. She sat back and lifted her shirt, offering her breast to Chloe as she sang the first words of "Dream A Little Dream". She cringed a little in anticipation of the pain that she had come to associate with nursing, but cried a few grateful tears of joy as Chloe latched on and nursed gently while they rocked slowly as Alexa continued to sing the words of one of her favorite songs.

Stars shining bright above you.

Night breezes seem to whisper, I love you.

Birds singing in the sycamore tree.

Dream a little dream of me.

Say nightie-night and kiss me.

Just hold me tight and tell me you'll miss me.

While I'm alone and blue as can be,

Dream a little dream of me.

Alexa looked around the little room at all of the cute baby animal faces surrounded by soft pastels that adorned the walls. It had taken her nearly a week to complete the intricate jungle mural and she was quite proud of it. Though she had chosen a very practical career, her heart had always been in art. She laid her head back on the chair and smiled as she continued to rock and sing, enjoying the quiet for the first time in weeks.

CHAPTER 4 - *A Night at the Zoo*

"Where are we going?" Alexa asked as she strolled alongside Ethan who had been holding her hand since they left the crowded club.

"Well, first we are going to my car," he said smiling.

"I don't know if that's such a good idea," she replied, worrying her bottom lip.

"Listen, Alexa, I understand, you do not know me, but for whatever it is worth, I would never let anything or anyone hurt you. I just want to spend some time with you, to get to know you better. I cannot really explain it; I am just drawn to you in a way I have never experienced before. From the moment I laid eyes on you I knew I had to know you, to be near you."

Maybe she was being foolish, but Alexa felt it, too. The moment she first heard his voice, she was lost.

She smiled up at him, deciding for once in her life to take a chance, to put herself out there. "Ok, so first to your car, then what?"

"Have you ever been to the zoo?"

Well, she certainly hadn't expected that.

"Wow, um, no. I've lived in the area for like seven years, but I've never made it there. You know, I keep meaning to go, I love animals so much, it's just, I never seem to have the time."

Ethan stopped and grinned at her as he lightly ran his thumb over her hand. "Well, Alexa. I think it is time we remedy that situation."

She looked up at him then furrowed her brow as a thought occurred to her. "Wait, it's almost eight. Is the zoo even still open?"

"It is open until nine from Thanksgiving until the New Year, and I happen to know a few people. We can stay later, if we like."

"Huh, a man with connections, I like that." She smiled up at Ethan and squeezed his hand playfully.

She didn't know him at all, yet this all felt so comfortable; so natural. And the chemistry was undeniable. Even now, walking in the cold December air, she could feel the electricity of his touch running up her arm and touching her in places she'd never even known existed. Maybe this man was what she had been waiting for all this time as she went through the motions of her life without being connected to any of it. Perhaps he was what was missing.

The thought was terrifying, yet exhilarating.

"Wow, is this your car?"

They had stopped alongside a slick black Maserati convertible.

"Yes." Ethan looked down, seeming almost embarrassed. "It was a rather impulsive purchase. My tastes are not usually so…flashy."

She laughed lightly. "I know exactly what you mean. I bought a Lexus right out of college to celebrate my new job. Granted, it was used, just a year old, though. Considering that I'm an accountant and very practical, it was definitely out of character. I didn't have any student loans and I'd managed to save quite a bit of money working while I was in school, so I figured, what the hell."

Not to mention, she had a hefty trust fund left by her parents, but she never touched that money. She was too angry to think about it most of the time.

"An accountant? Really? I certainly would not have guessed that."

"Really, why not?" she asked curiously.

Ethan turned her so that her back was against the side of his car and eased her towards it until she was pressed against the cold side. He let one hand rest lightly on her side, right at the base of her coat and just at the top of her hip while he brought the other up to cup her cheek as he looked into her eyes.

"I guess I blame it on the stereotype to which I have grown accustomed. When I picture an accountant, I see a nerdy little man with glasses and a pocket protector. Trust me when I say, you have entirely shattered that perception."

Slightly embarrassed by the compliment and feeling overwhelmed by her body's response to his closeness, Alexa looked down as she said, "Well, I don't usually wear glasses, just contacts, but I definitely am a nerd." She smiled shyly and chanced a look up at Ethan.

Ethan's gaze shifted to her lips as she spoke and his eyes darkened. "You are the most beautiful, sexiest woman I have ever laid eyes on, Alexa."

His mouth was mere inches from hers and she could feel his hot breath caressing her lips as he spoke, sending shivers all over her body.

"Are you cold?" he inquired, still staring at her lips and already knowing the answer. Even though it was freezing outside, the intense heat that was passing between them was almost enough to make him sweat, if that was something his body actually did.

"No, I'm fine." What was she saying? She was outside, in the dark, with a strange and probably dangerous man pressing her up against his car on a freezing December night. But even considering all of that, she had never felt warmer, or safer, or more alive for that matter, in all her life.

"Alexa, I know this probably seems very strange to you, but I have never felt anything like this before. Please tell me you are feeling it, too. That there is something extraordinary happening between us."

There was a pleading in his voice and his eyes as he said the words that took her breath away. She was shocked by his sincerity and openness. Though she still couldn't hear his thoughts, she was certain that he meant what he was saying to her. Knowing that in her heart she wanted her to scream her response, instead it came out in a quiet whisper as she looked up at him and said, "Yes, Ethan. I do, I feel it, too."

There was so much she wanted to ask him. Before she could get another word out, Ethan closed the short distance between them and demandingly crushed his mouth against hers. Though initially shocked by his forcefulness, Alexa quickly melted into Ethan's kiss. As she relaxed against him, his kiss softened and he gently traced the seam of her lips with his tongue. When her lips parted slightly, his tongue delved into her mouth, brushing against her own as he mimicked the action with his hips.

Alexa felt her already damp panties flood with moisture. Ethan's hand that had been resting on her hip slid down under the edge of her coat and back up to find her bare skin. A lustful moan escaped her throat as he lightly traced circles along her waist and back as he continued to explore her mouth.

Breaking away, Ethan placed his forehead against Alexa's as he panted, attempting to get a hold of himself before things went too far. "God, you taste so good."

Breathless herself, Alexa took a moment, listening to Ethan's pained breathing before she asked, "Why did you stop?"

She could feel his conflict in her mind. His body clearly did not want to stop, based on the rather intimidating hardness she felt pressing into her stomach before he moved away.

He took a deep, fortifying breath, trying to compose himself and then said, "Well, sweetheart, we are in a public parking lot, so I have to stop sometime."

Alexa felt the color rise in her cheeks. What had gotten into her? She was acting like some wanton teenager and, when he said the words, she realized she had no intention of making him stop. She was fairly certain he could have laid her down and taken her in the thin layer of snow that was still on the ground without a word of protest exiting her lips.

It was the alcohol. Of course it was, at least that was the story she was going to stick to as she attempted to regain some of her pride, even though she had sobered up a while ago. Just as she opened her mouth to explain as much, Ethan pulled out his keys and said, "Besides, we have a date." He kissed the tip of her nose and smiled. "I have a feeling you are going to love the zoo at night."

The next thing she knew, they were speeding along Washington Street heading for the zoo. As they were driving, he reached over and took her hand without saying a word. She couldn't help the euphoric smile that spread across her face as she looked out the window, hiding her face from Ethan, trying to appear unaffected.

I can't believe it! Oh, God, it's all happening too fast, but he is just so amazing, and the way I feel, it's like my soul has been crying out for him my entire life and now that he has answered I am lost. He is different than anyone I have ever met. I am different just being near him. Maybe this is it, maybe this is my chance. He is what I have been waiting for, what I have been missing my whole life.

Her heart started to race as she considered the implications of her thoughts. She had been waiting so long, convinced she would never meet anyone, yet here was this gorgeous man whose mind was gloriously silent. Her unsuccessful romantic past wasn't due to a lack of trying. There had been several men in previous years. No, they were boys in comparison to Ethan. Boys who had clumsily pawed at her, trying to lift up her shirt or pull down her pants while they thought about how big her ass was or what excuse they were going to give to escape as soon as they had gotten what they wanted. At first, those types of thoughts caught her off-guard. After a time, she came to expect it and, as a result, no guy ever made it past second base. Eventually, she started to avoid dating altogether.

"Hey. Are you still with me?" Ethan asked, noticing her dazed expression.

Alexa turned to look at Ethan and she was struck all over again by how attractive he was.

"Yeah, sorry, guess I was daydreaming."

A crooked grin lit up his face as he looked at her. For the first time, she noticed his dimples. How had she missed those before? Maybe she hadn't really seen him smile anywhere with enough light for her to notice. As if he wasn't already the most ridiculously appealing man she had ever seen. He had to have dimples, too.

She was thinking about kissing each of those dimples when Ethan announced their arrival at the zoo.

Though feeling uncertain about the speed with which everything was happening between her and Ethan, she was truly excited about their little excursion. Just a few weeks ago she read about a new addition to one of the exhibits, a dolphin named Orin, and she kept telling herself she would finally make the effort to visit the zoo and see him. She had fallen in love with dolphins as a child, but her interaction with them was limited to what she saw in books and online. The guardians at the group home rarely took any of the children outside of the compound, especially Alexa.

They approached the admissions window, where an attractive young blonde sat. She looked up and her jaw nearly hit the floor as she gawked at Ethan. Her expression quickly changed when she noticed Alexa next to him. Alexa didn't need telepathy to know exactly what the woman was thinking. What was a man like Ethan doing with a woman like Alexa? She couldn't blame her, since she sort of wondered the same thing, but never being one to look a gift horse in the mouth, Alexa was going to enjoy as much of Ethan as she could get. When they reached the window, a man stepped up behind the clerk and greeted Ethan personally.

"Hello, Mr. Kellar. Please come through this way. It's such a pleasure to see you again. If you, or your lovely guest, require anything during your visit, please let me know."

Alexa looked up at Ethan, curiously. He smiled down at her shyly and whispered in her ear.

"I donated some money to the zoo this year."

The feel of his warm breath flowing across her skin made her shiver.

He gave her a quick smile and released her hand to step over and speak privately with the gentleman. It must have been a lot of money, because Alexa was fairly certain this man was the president of the zoo based on a photograph she had noticed in the news a while back. She let down her shields just a bit to hear the man and confirm her theory. Oh yeah, it was a lot of money and he was indeed who she suspected. She couldn't help but wonder how a man as young as Ethan had the means to donate so much. If it wasn't for the expensive car, she wouldn't have guessed him to be wealthy at all.

While he looked great, nothing about his appearance really indicated money. In her profession, Alexa had come across a lot of men who liked to flaunt their wealth and she had learned to spot some of the obvious signs. Flashy watch, expensive shoes, dropping not-so-subtle hints, etcetera. As he continued to make small talk with the man who greeted them, Alexa took a moment to survey Ethan's appearance. Under his black leather jacket, he wore an open charcoal button-down over a plain white t-shirt tucked into gently frayed designer jeans which rode low on his trim hips and hung down over a pair of black bike-toe loafers. Her pulse began to quicken as she stood there evaluating him.

As if he sensed the change in her demeanor, Ethan looked over and caught her staring. His eyes darkened as his perfect lips formed a sexy lopsided grin. Alexa looked away, laughing at herself for being so easily affected and pulled out her iPhone to keep herself occupied while she waited.

As she scrolled through posts and information on the zoo's website, it dawned on her that Ethan would probably have similar thoughts about her if he ever found out about her finances. She lived on the salary from her job and nothing more; everything else had remained an untouched secret, but it was there and she would have to deal with it someday.

It occurred to her that she had no idea what Ethan did for a living, or anything else about him, for that matter. She was definitely curious; she wanted to know everything there was to know about the gorgeous man who had unexpectedly walked into her life. They would have to get to all that later. Right now, she wanted to try something different, to live in the moment for a change. So she pushed all of her questions and concerns aside, and made the decision soak in and savor this whole experience with him.

While she was lost in thought, Ethan slipped up behind her and slid his arms around her waist. "So which animals would you like to see first?"

"The dolphins," Alexa replied without hesitation.

"Sounds like a plan," Ethan said before he turned to the zoo president and asked, "Can you set up an up-close visit with the dolphins?"

"Of course, Mr. Kellar. If you'd like, we can even arrange for you to get in the water with them. I believe we even have wet suits that you can use."

Alexa squealed with excitement.

Ethan laughed, "I guess that means we definitely want to get in the water."

Alexa couldn't even begin to hide her enthusiasm. She was absolutely thrilled. Ethan grabbed her hand as they followed the gentlemen down several pathways and into an employee entrance of the Marsh Dolphin Theater.

"If you could wait here a moment, Mr. Kellar, I'll fetch one of the trainers to get you suited up and escort you to the enclosure."

Once they were alone, Ethan turned to Alexa who was fidgeting enthusiastically. "This is just a guess, but I get the impression that you are a little excited," he smiled warmly as he teased, admiring her sweetness.

"I've always wanted to swim with dolphins. It's kind of silly, but when I was a little girl, I found this book about them in the library where I grew up that I checked out and sort of, uh, never returned." She glanced at him nervously, realizing that she just admitted to being a thief, even if it had been when she was little. Seeing only amusement and warmth in his expression, she continued. "I hid it under my bed and would take it out at night and look at all of the pictures whenever I had a bad day or was feeling lonely. I didn't really have the best childhood, and whenever things got really bad I would imagine that I lived alone on a deserted tropical island with a beautiful lagoon. I would swim there with a pair of young dolphins that got separated from their family, just like me."

Surprised with herself, Alexa looked over at Ethan. "I've never told anyone that before. It's a little embarrassing, but that dream got me through some hard times."

"Do not feel embarrassed, you have a beautiful imagination. I am sorry that you ever had to feel so alone." He wrapped his arms around her and pulled her close, placing a chaste kiss on her lips. "You can tell me anything, Amor. I want to know everything about you."

Alexa felt a rush of elation hearing his desire to know about her and the term of endearment, even if it was in another language. She had taken some Spanish classes in high school and, though she wasn't entirely fluent, she understood a lot of the language. Her elation was quickly followed by a twinge of guilt, knowing there was one thing about her he could never know. Her ability had to remain a secret. That was a lesson she had learned the hard way and it was one she would not soon forget.

Just then, the trainer walked in and they were suited up and climbing into the dolphin enclosure before she could give it another thought. They spent nearly an hour feeding and interacting privately with the dolphins. Alexa felt as giddy as an eight- year-old as they were introduced to each dolphin and learned the commands to get them perform a wide variety of tricks. She looked over at Ethan several times during the experience, feeling awed at how much his enthusiasm seemed to match her own and grateful to him for allowing her the opportunity.

She couldn't believe how much her life had changed in a matter of a few hours. Though it was overwhelming and quite surprising, she had never been happier.

They climbed out of the water and went into their designated areas to change back into their clothes. Alexa couldn't stop smiling as she stood there ringing her hair out with one of the towels the trainer provided. It was well past the zoo's closing time by then, so Alexa rushed to get ready to leave, not wanting to further inconvenience the staff that had been so kind and accommodating. As she exited the women's locker room, Ethan surprised her by grabbing her around the waist and lifting her into his arms as if she weighed no more than a leaf. That was most certainly a first for Alexa.

As he cradled her in his arms, she smiled up at him with her arms around his neck and boldly pulled herself up to press her mouth against his as he moved them towards the exit.

Ethan smiled inwardly at her forwardness and at how good it felt to have this woman next to him. After all this time, he felt a glimmer of hope. This was his chance to escape the fate that had been forced on him the day he was born. This was his choice, she was his choice.

Gently setting her down without breaking their contact, Ethan deepened the kiss as he backed her up against the door. He ran his hands up her sides and she tightened her arms around his neck, struggling to get closer to him. A desperate moan escaped her throat as he outlined her lips with his tongue. He growled lowly in response and pressed his hips against her, making her aware of how much he was enjoying their time together.

Feeling how large he was against her, Alexa felt a twinge of fear which was quickly replaced by excitement. She had waited so long and now, after just a few hours with Ethan, she knew why. She had been waiting for him. Realizing that, she began to kiss him more fiercely, running her hands through his hair and grinding her hips against his thigh. Just as she started to contemplate making love to him on the floor where they stood, someone cleared their throat behind them.

"I'm terribly sorry, Mr. Kellar, but it is well past closing and we need to lock up this building and set the alarm."

It was the same gentleman who had greeted them earlier in the evening.

Seemingly unfazed, Ethan pulled away from Alexa before briefly pressing his mouth against hers again.

"Of course, we really appreciate the extra consideration you have given us tonight. It was an amazing experience." He winked at Alexa and smiled broadly as she felt a blush creep across her cheeks, realizing he wasn't referring to the time with the dolphins.

They made their way to the exit and stepped outside to begin the walk back to Ethan's car. With wet hair, the already-cold air was almost unbearable and Alexa's teeth began to chatter just a few steps out the door. Ethan took off his leather jacket as they kept walking and tossed it around Alexa's shoulders. She opened her mouth to protest, but he beat her to it.

"Do not worry about me, I have on two shirts and my hair is already dry."

He grabbed her hand and held it the rest of the way, not letting go until after he'd opened the car door for her and she was seated inside. He hurried around to the driver's side, hopped in, started the engine, and reached over to turn on Alexa's seat-warmer. As the car warmed up, Ethan just sat there watching Alexa for a moment before he asked, "Did you enjoy our date, Amor?"

Feeling incredibly nervous and totally lost in thought about all the things she hoped would happen between her and Ethan, she didn't even hear his question as she turned and looked into his beautiful green-gray eyes. Before she could talk herself out of it, she took a breath and leaned in to press her lips to his, taking the lead for the second time that night, determined to take things where she desperately wanted them to go.

As she started to kiss him with greater passion, he pulled away slightly as he brushed her cheek with his thumb, "I will take that as a yes. Am I driving you to your car or your home?"

Getting ahold of herself enough to consider his question she replied, "Oh, yeah, home. I took a cab to the club tonight since I knew I would be drinking."

Ethan smiled, pleased with her caution and sense of responsibility. Those were qualities she would need in order to be with someone like him, to survive in his world.

"You will have to tell me where home is, or at least give me the address to enter into the navigation system."

Most of the short drive to her home was spent in silence as she tried to work up the nerve to actually ask him to spend the night. She felt pretty confident that that was where things were going, since she could sense his lust with her ability, and she had felt the physical evidence of it more than once, but she had no intention of leaving it to chance.

Come on Alexa, get it together, you're twenty-five years old, you can ask a man to go upstairs.

As they got closer to her apartment building, she was pulled from her thoughts when he asked her to verify the directions coming through the speakers from the computerized GPS voice.

A few moments later, they arrived at her apartment building and he pulled the car into a space right in front of the entryway that was miraculously vacant. She usually had to park on the other side of the lot by the dumpsters. As Ethan removed his seatbelt, but left the car running as he reached for the handle to get out and open Alexa's door, she blurted, "Do you want to spend the night with me?"

Her cheeks immediately flushed with color. She'd never done anything like this before and she had certainly never been so bold with a man.

Ethan took a deep breath and sighed. "I don't think that is a good idea tonight."

"Oh, ok. Well…goodnight, then." Alexa struggled to say the words as her voice cracked in embarrassment. She was mortified. After feeling so confident, the disappointment was immense.

She reached for the handle to flee to the safety and comfort of her apartment. Before she could make her escape, Ethan hit the door locks and reached over to grab her hand as she struggled to unlock the door, again trying to fight back the tears of humiliation.

"Alexa, please wait." He took another deep breath, struggling to restrain himself, yet not wanting her to leave feeling like he didn't want her when that was so far from the truth. He wanted her so badly he could hardly stand it, but if he was going to take this chance he had to be sure. "Listen, you have to know how much I want to come up. I do not think I have ever wanted anything more in my life, but it is best if we wait. There is so much we need to talk about, learn about each other before taking such a step. I do not want to rush you and I want you to know me, to really know me and what you want before we go further."

He moved his hand up to lightly grip her chin and turn her face towards him, seeing a lone tear sliding down her cheek.

"Oh, Amor, please do not cry. You must trust me. Please trust me; I only wish to protect you. I do not wish to see you sad." As he said the words, Ethan knew it was not only her he was protecting. He had guarded his heart his entire life, determined to be the master of his own destiny. So when he left Alexa tonight, he would visit the place he had avoided for many years. He would go see…her.

He leaned over and kissed away the tear on Alexa's cheek and lingered there, breathing shallowly, and she closed her eyes. Before he could think better of it, his mouth was slanting over hers again. She immediately opened to him and his tongue slipped inside, lightly teasing hers. He kissed down the line of her jaw to her neck, then abruptly pulled away and pressed himself back against the door of his car panting, as if he couldn't get far enough away at the moment.

She opened her eyes to see him looking as if he was in pain. Not knowing what to think or say, she instinctually opened her mind and was met with a feeling of struggle like she had never felt, but once again she couldn't hear any clear thoughts. As she reached out to him, his face changed and the torment that she felt was replaced with what she could only describe as conditioned restraint.

"I am sorry, Alexa. Please understand that this is incredibly difficult for me." He leaned in and placed his forehead against hers. "I want you so badly right now, in this moment, but I want you forever more. That is why we must wait."

Well, shit. Hearing that just made her want him even more. Maybe it was all just a line of bullshit, some kind of reverse psychology to get her in bed. It was working.

Forgetting her embarrassment, she leaned her face up and pressed her mouth against his yet again, then pulled away and said, "Please, Ethan," another kiss, "please, I want to be with you tonight."

Before she could blink, he was over the center console kissing her fervently as he pressed his knee between her legs, sending a jolt of arousal through her.

And just like that he pulled back, hovering over her and looking into her eyes while she panted with desire.

"Alexa, I cannot come up with you tonight." Her expression became one of hurt and confusion, until he continued, "But, I am going to make you come with my mouth. I must taste you."

His words and the hunger in his eyes were almost enough to send her over the edge.

And then he crushed his mouth against hers, sliding his tongue inside as a promise of what was to come when he moved between her legs.

Ethan gently teased her breasts through her shirt, rubbing his thumbs over the hard nipples, circling, then gently pinching each one before he slid his hands down under her skirt. He grabbed ahold of her lacy black panties as he pulled her body towards him and slowly slid them along the trail of kisses he was placing along her inner thigh. Once he reached her knee, he lifted slightly and pulled her panties all the way off before returning to kiss his way back up her thigh while she trembled in anticipation.

Then he hovered above her, so close that she could feel his hot breath on her sensitive flesh as he stared down at her sex which was glistening with her arousal. He stayed there for what seemed like an eternity, intimately admiring her perfection before he finally swiped his tongue up along her wet lips, relishing the taste of her sweet juices like a desert soaking up a first rain after a long drought. The intense, unfamiliar sensation made her buck her hips up pressing harder against his skilled mouth. In response, he reached one arm underneath and around her waist, laying the other across her stomach to pin her down as he sucked relentlessly on her sensitive clit while she squirmed with pleasure.

It wasn't long before she started to feel flushed all over her body as an intense pressure was building in her core. She had touched herself, many, many times. It never felt anything like this. She tried to back away, to ease the intensity, but Ethan was relentless. He held her even tighter as he sucked on her delicate flesh and then slid his tongue down and plunged it inside her as her body exploded around him, pouring her sweetness out into his eager mouth.

He continued to hold her and lap up her delicious nectar as her body quaked with her orgasm.

He stayed there, savoring ever tremor until her body finally stilled. Then he shifted her back into her seat, grabbed her panties off the floor and tucked them into his pocket before he hopped out of the car and jogged around to open her door.

He held out his hand as Alexa grabbed a hold and stumbled out on very wobbly legs.

He led her up to the doorstep and pulled her towards him as he leaned down and gently kissed her as if he hadn't just ravaged her with his mouth.

As he pulled back, she licked her lips and felt her arousal building again as she tasted herself on her lips.

"Goodnight, Alexa. I'll be in touch soon."

And with that, he turned and was gone.

CHAPTER 5 - *The Doctor's Call*

Alexa was startled awake by Tilly barking insistently at the patio
door. She had apparently dozed off while nursing Chloe since it was
nearly dark and had started to rain. Chloe seemed unaffected by the
racket and remained asleep as Alexa transferred her to her crib,
covered her with a pink chenille blanket and flipped on the baby
monitor before she made her way back down the hallway to the
kitchen.

She slid the door open for Tilly who rushed in and shook off,
spraying water all over before dashing to curl up in her bed in front of
the fireplace. The shivering dog looked at Alexa expectantly, causing
her to chuckle as she walked over and flipped the switch to ignite the
gas fireplace. Though it was the middle of summer, the rain had really
cooled things down so she decided she'd give Tilly a couple of
minutes to warm up as penance for leaving her outside in the rain.

Locking the door and positioning the dowel rod, Alexa leaned her
back against the wall and took a deep breath. She both hated and
loved dreaming about him. Despite her best efforts, the only dreams
she ever remembered seemed to be about him. Most of the time they
were more like memories from the limited time they were together,
occurring in such vivid detail that she could smell his delicious scent

when she awoke. Some were so real she would awaken in the throes of an intense orgasm, panting and dripping with sweat. Even in her sleep, she was powerless to control her body's response to him. Other times, she would dream of him watching her as if she was looking over his shoulder seeing herself go about her day. No wonder she couldn't stop thinking about him; he had hijacked her subconscious.

Her stomach growled and she glanced at the clock on the microwave. It was almost nine, probably a little too late to eat, but she was suddenly starving and realized she hadn't had anything since her light breakfast consisting of some fresh fruit and toast with almond butter.

I'll just have something really light, she thought, strolling to the refrigerator.

Avoiding the temptations of the other shelves, she immediately pulled open the vegetable crisper and took out a head of lettuce, a tomato, and a cucumber. She grabbed a knife from the counter and got out the olive oil, balsamic vinegar, and some herbs to make a light dressing.

She removed a large salad bowl and placed it next to the cutting board in the middle of the island countertop and began slicing up the vegetables. Halfway through the cucumber, the phone rang, startling her and causing the knife to slice into the top of her left thumb. She instinctually stuck it into her mouth and began to suck as she reached for the phone. Her mouth was flooded with the metallic taste that she had never really minded, letting her know the cut was fairly deep.

Before she could read the display to see who it was, she heard Chloe whimpering over the baby monitor. Taking the phone with her, she headed for the nursery still sucking her bleeding thumb and glanced down at the display. It was Dr. Kline's office.

Her heart started to pound.

Oh, God. Please.

She paused in the hallway, bending over and placing her hands against her knees, still holding the phone that she was terrified to answer. It was well past office hours; a call at this time could only mean something bad.

No, maybe it's just an automated call to confirm our appointment tomorrow. She tried to reason the panic away, but before she could fully convince herself, she looked down and saw the drops of blood pooling at her feet.

Chloe's whimpers were rapidly evolving into a full-blown cry and the phone continued to ring.

Alexa attempted to remain calm and made a detour into the bathroom on her way to the nursery. She would have to let the call go to voicemail. If it was an appointment confirmation, she could listen to it once she got everything under control. If it was something worse, well, she didn't really want to think about that right now.

She quickly rolled out a few sheets of toilet paper and wrapped them around her bleeding thumb, applying pressure to the rather deep cut with her index finger. The makeshift bandage would have to do until after she attended to Chloe.

The phone stopped ringing just as she entered Chloe's bedroom. It was dark enough outside that the automatic nightlight had come on, though there was still enough natural light coming through the open blinds for her to see Chloe standing in the crib with her arms outstretched as she continued to wail.

Alexa scooped her up and swayed back and forth with her, singing softly as they moved to the rocker.

She started to lift her shirt for Chloe to nurse and cursed under her breath. She forgot about the supplement. Hoping that Chloe was tired enough to simply nurse and go back down for the night, Alexa decided against taking the time to retrieve a bottle of Dr. Kline's special elixir.

She sat back attempting to get Chloe latched on to her left breast, but Chloe seemed to find the makeshift bandage on her thumb far more fascinating and kept trying to pull on it and get it into her mouth.

Just as Alexa decided to just switch her to the right side, the phone started ringing again. Taking a breath, she looked down at the display. It was Dr. Kline's office again and there was no voicemail from before.

The panic returned and started to overcome her, but she decided in that moment, no matter what it was, no matter how awful or hard, she would be strong for her sweet baby.

With that, she swallowed the large knot in her throat, hit the 'on' button and said in her most calm and cheerful tone, "Hello, this is Alexa."

"Alexa, hello, it's Elijah."

"Um, who?" she replied, slightly confused.

"Elijah, Dr. Kline. I'm calling about Chloe's test results."

She had forgotten that he asked her to call him by his first name. She should have realized immediately when there was no telepathic chatter coming over the line.

"Of course. Doctor, I'm sorry, Elijah, please tell me, how bad is it?" Before he could respond she continued. "It's really bad isn't it? I mean it's late, your office has to have closed hours ago and you're calling personally, so just spit it out!" So much for remaining calm.

"It's all a matter of perspective, Alexa. In my opinion it is miraculous, considering her age."

"I don't understand. What does that mean? Is Chloe sick? Is she, oh, God, is it something," she paused almost afraid to ask it out loud, "life threatening?" Alexa was on the edge of the chair, gripping Chloe tightly with her left hand as she waited for his reply. Her entire life hung on his next words.

"No, she is not sick, Alexa, not in the slightest."

Alexa sighed as she let go of some of the tension she was feeling and leaned back.

"Oh, thank God!" The relief and gratitude washed over her.

He just called to tell me the good news so I wouldn't worry.

"Alexa, there is more. I must speak with you, in person, as soon as possible. Tonight, if there is any way you can."

"What, why can't you tell me whatever it is now? Is something wrong or not?" She was practically yelling and started getting worked up again as she realized her feeling of relief had been premature.

"There were some, abnormalities, in your blood work. Alexa, please, I need you to trust me. There are some things that you need to see to understand, that is why we must speak in person. I know it is a lot to ask, but I need for you to have a little faith. I am only trying to do what is best for Chloe."

The doctor's choice of words renewed that nagging feeling of familiarity that she had felt in his office earlier.

Alexa looked down at Chloe, trying to make sense of everything. She had been so distracted by the phone call that she hadn't noticed that Chloe was no longer nursing, yet had remained completely quiet. As her mind started to process what she was seeing, she tried to pull her thumb, the one that she had cut deeply only minutes before, from Chloe's mouth. As she pulled, Chloe's hands gripped on more tightly, holding her thumb in her mouth with an unusual amount of strength while she continued to suckle. Completely horrified, Alexa felt a sharp pain and yanked harder, freeing her thumb from Chloe's mouth and her hand from her tiny grip. The action caused Chloe to giggle, her mouth wide, revealing her bloodstained tongue and teeth. Alexa stood and placed Chloe on the floor. Taking another look at the mess of blood, her first thought was to get a towel to wipe the dark liquid from Chloe's mouth before she swallowed it, and then she saw them. Two new, and rather unusual, teeth. Canines that were abnormally long and had not been there earlier in the day when Alexa had last seen the inside of Chloe's mouth.

She simply stared as the phone slipped from her hand and banged against the floor, sliding under the crib.

Alexa remained frozen in place staring at Chloe, with blood, her blood, dripping down her little chin as she reached for her favorite Ernie doll. The faint sound of Dr. Kline's voice finally pulled her focus away and Alexa scrambled to her knees to retrieve the phone. Once she had it back in her hand, she put it to her ear and remained on the floor, sitting with her back against the crib as she looked at

Chloe who had stood up and was walking toward a tub of toys in the corner. As far as Alexa knew, Chloe had only just learned to crawl before their lives got turned upside down two weeks ago. Now she walked as if she'd been doing it for months.

"Alexa? Alexa, are you there? Is everything all right?"

By some miracle, Alexa found her voice through the shock and managed to sound somewhat normal. "Um, yes, yes, I'm still here, I, I just dropped the phone."

"Can you meet me here, then, or should I come to you?"

"We'll be there in thirty minutes."

Alexa hurried to the bathroom and quickly bandaged her injured thumb to stop the bleeding and cover the puncture marks left by Chloe. She then grabbed a towel, wet it a little in the sink, and returned to the nursery to wipe the mess from Chloe's face and then the floor. Thank goodness for hardwood flooring that was easy to clean. As she removed the last remnants of blood, Tilly appeared and, sensing Alexa's anxiety, walked over and leaned into her leg. Alexa rubbed the top of her head. "It's okay, girl, everything's okay," she said more to reassure herself than anything else.

She scooped Chloe up, and as much as it pained her to admit about her own child, held her at a bit of a distance out of fear. She was so frazzled by everything, she forgot to grab the diaper bag before heading out the door to the garage.

As she loaded Chloe into the car, never taking her eyes off of her, Alexa ran through the possibilities in her mind. She lifted Chloe's top lip to get another glimpse of her new teeth, feeling both curious and terrified. How would she explain this to Dr. Kline, or anyone for that matter? To her relief, and confusion, they had miraculously disappeared.

Okay, the most likely explanation was that she was having a nervous breakdown, had completely lost her mind, and had imagined the whole thing.

Maybe I'm schizophrenic, that comes on later in life, right? In your twenties. Or maybe I'm just hallucinating? It really wasn't hard to seriously consider that possibility. She had been hearing voices in her head for over a decade, so perhaps she wasn't a telepath; maybe she was just crazy.

Alexa closed the back door, took a breath and rushed around to hop in the driver's seat. She looked back at Chloe who was strapped into her car seat and starting to doze of as if nothing out of the ordinary had occurred.

The most comforting scenario was that this was all just an elaborate dream. Alexa had realistic dreams all the time. She was probably at home in bed the night before their appointment with Dr. Kline, making this entire crazy occurrence up in her subconscious mind.

Of course, that didn't explain the throbbing pain that she was feeling in her arm where she continued to pinch herself. Nor did it account for the marks on her thumb.

In that moment, Alexa decided she would just have to figure it out somehow. No matter what was going on, Chloe was her child and she would do whatever it took to help and protect her. As afraid as she was for Chloe and herself, she knew she needed help, so she hit the button to open the garage door, took a deep breath, gripped the steering wheel, and backed down the driveway to make her way to the only source of help that she could think of. Dr. Kline.

While part of her actually hoped that she was certifiably crazy, Alexa knew deep down that it was all real. Just like she had known that night. She had spent months trying to convince herself it had been a dream, but she had always known the truth. Perhaps that was why she hadn't completely fallen apart when her nine-month- old baby started drinking her blood. Or when she noticed the two new teeth that had popped up in minutes. Or the puncture marks on her thumb. Or when Chloe got up and walked as if she had been doing it for months.

Some part of her had always known, always expected something extraordinary from Chloe. Of course, she had assumed it would just be the telepathy that she had already witnessed that Chloe would inherit from her. She had spent so much time and energy focusing on trying to get over Ethan that she completely blocked out, or at least ignored, what she knew had happened that night. What she knew he was capable of. Just thinking of it made the spot on her neck throb and sent a little jolt between her thighs.

CHAPTER 6 - *An Unexpected Gift*

The morning after their trip to the zoo, Alexa watched with disgust as the trashy waitress strutted away after taking their order. She had practically offered herself up to Ethan for breakfast while Alexa considered kicking her in the throat. Like a true gentleman, Ethan simply ignored her advances and placed his order, keeping his attention completely focused on Alexa.

"I think you should move in with me," Ethan said as he smiled broadly at Alexa across the table, showing off his adorable dimples.

She started to choke on the drink of orange juice she had just taken, as her eyes widened in surprise.

In a flash, Ethan was next to her patting her back as she regained her composure. His warm hands on her back certainly weren't helping with that.

"Are you all right, Amor?"

"Well, um, that depends. Did you seriously just ask me to move in with you?" She lifted her wrist to check the time on her nonexistent watch before looking up at him. "Considering that we met, oh, I don't know, about twelve hours ago, that would be beyond crazy. So the logical conclusion is that I imagined it and am suffering some kind of mental break."

Ethan chuckled as he slid back into his seat. "Too fast? It's just, I thought about you all night. I couldn't stop thinking about you long enough to concentrate on anything else. It is incredibly distracting. I will never be able to get anything done, so I thought the best solution would be to have you with me as much as possible."

Reaching into the pocket of his jacket, he pulled out a long black velvet box. "I have something for you." He slid the box across the table, while Alexa just continued to stare down at it, completely shocked and uncertain what to expect.

When would he possibly have had time to get her a gift? Tentatively, she picked it up and pried it open slowly, gasping at its contents.

"Oh, my God, Ethan. I, I don't understand, when did you do this? How did you find this? It's so beautiful."

Ethan stood and removed the platinum necklace from the box, moving to help Alexa put it on.

"So you like it?" he asked, smiling broadly as he brushed her hair to the side and dropped the delicate pendant, composed of two intricately-carved dolphins, against her chest. They had white diamond eyes and were facing the center, holding a ring from which dangled a rather large solitary blue diamond.

Alexa's initial thought was that she couldn't accept it. It was obviously real and must have cost a small fortune.

As if he had read her mind, after securing the clasp at the back of her neck and pressing a gentle kiss on the tender skin, he said softly into her ear, "Please do not say you cannot accept it. Since I am certain you have already decided to crush my heart and refuse my offer of cohabitation, for now," that part in a tone implying it was inevitable, "then you must accept my gift to soothe my ego."

"Ethan, it's just so perfect, but it's too much. I don't deserve this."

He placed his hands on her shoulders and with his mouth so close she could feel his warm breath on the sensitive skin behind her ear as he spoke. "Amor, you deserve everything. And that is precisely what I intend to give you. I only ask for one thing in return. A promise. You must promise to wear this always. You can adjust where you clasp the chain in the back to hide it beneath your clothes if you wish, but you must never take it off. Please promise me this."

He then began kissing the back of her neck along the trail of the chain, sending little shivers down her back. That was so not fair. She would have promised anything with his lips touching her like that. A low moan escaped her throat followed by her whispered response. "I promise."

With that, he pulled her out of the chair wrapping his arms around her waist, pulling her close and burying his face in thick waves of her hair that was still gathered to one side. "Thank you, Amor."

If she was being honest, as absurd as it was, her refusal of his original proposal wasn't completely heartfelt. In fact, she probably would have run off to city hall and promised to love, honor, and obey if he had requested it. After a moment, he took her hand and slid back into his chair, placing their joined fingertips on the tabletop, grinning triumphantly.

God, he was beautiful. From his sexily tousled hair to his full sensual lips, he was perfect. And his eyes, so deep and soulful; Alexa felt at once lost and at home looking into their depths.

Reluctantly, Alexa pulled her hand away from his grasp and ran her fingertips over the cool metal of the dolphin pendant on her skin, gently grasping the diamond for a moment before looking up. "When you called this morning you said we needed to talk and last night you said you want us to learn about each other before we took the next step. I told you a lot about myself, but I know so little about you, so tell me. Tell me what I need to know about Ethan Kellar." Once again, Alexa pushed with her mind, concentrating and seeking Ethan's stream of consciousness. Again, she hit a barrier, just like the night before.

Ethan ran a hand through his hair as he sighed and leaned back in his seat. He wanted to be honest with her, about everything, yet he was so afraid of how she would react and what it would mean. His secrets were not his alone and there would be consequences of revealing them if she were to choose to reject him.

Sensing his conflict, Alexa placed her hand over his again in an attempt to comfort him. The contact sent a bolt of electricity up their arms. His eyes, which only moments before were filled with concern, were now clouded with a passion that matched her own.

Pulling his hand back slightly to gather his thoughts, Ethan cleared his throat and said, "My life is very complicated. It is difficult to explain. There are things that could make our relationship… challenging."

"What things? Your work, your family?"

"Yes, both of those things."

Again being practical, Alexa decided to approach the issues head on.

"Okay, so first tell me what it is that you do."

"I work for my family, for my parents, managing the family foundation." That explained the large donation to the zoo.

Right then, Alexa really wished she could hear Ethan's thoughts. She could feel that he was being evasive, but still trusted him despite that fact.

"Wow, so you must be very close."

Ethan clasped his hands in front of him and stared down at the table. "Actually, no, we do not speak often. In fact, we have not spoken or seen each other in many years. I keep them updated on foundation business via email or through couriers who deliver documents and get signatures when necessary. It is very complicated. They have certain expectations of me that I have no desire to live up to, especially with regard to my romantic attachments, but I went to see my mother last night, after I left you."

Alexa started to relax some; this wasn't such a big deal. So he was concerned about his parents' disapproval of her. She couldn't quite place his accent. Maybe he was from a culture where parents weighed in heavily on their children's choice romantic partners. It was old-fashioned, but not unheard of.

"So, how did that go?" she asked, feeling extremely anxious waiting for his response.

"Far better than I had hoped." He looked up into her eyes. "I think my mother has finally accepted that I want something different than what was planned for me; my father, too. Now they seem to only desire my happiness and they were quite pleased when I told them about you. I cannot wait for you to meet them." He smiled, but it didn't quite reach his beautiful eyes. "My sister may prove to be more difficult to convince. Her views are rather, traditional. She believes that one's duty must come before all other things."

Alexa reached out for his hands again, feeling her heart pound and blood rush from the contact. Just being near him, she was in a constant state of arousal. When they were actually touching, the rest of the world seemed to fall away.

He looked up at her for a moment like he wanted to eat her alive, but quickly put himself in check and said, "There is more I must tell you." He was determined get it all out in the open, to give her the freedom and knowledge to choose. The one thing he had fought so hard his entire life to gain for himself. He deliberately picked this mediocre restaurant that was never busy and selected a seat by the back exit so he could quickly diffuse the situation and get her out without drawing too much attention if she freaked out.

Alexa moved her hands back and placed them in her lap deciding that she should be honest with him as well, or at least as honest as she could be without sounding like she had completely lost her mind. The only other time she tried to tell someone about her telepathy she ended up in the psych wing for two weeks.

"Ethan, wait. There is something I need to tell you first." She swallowed hard, gathering her nerve. Just thinking about saying the words aloud sent blood flowing into her cheeks.

Ethan looked at her curiously. Well, this was a surprise. He was so wrapped up in his own secrets that he hadn't considered she might have some of her own.

Then so quietly he may not have been able to hear if he were merely human, Alexa said, "I've never had a boyfriend or anything."

He continued to look at her, a confused expression covering his face. "That is hardly a concern, Amor. I have never been seriously involved with a woman. My life has been far too complicated and I never found anyone who was worth effort, until I met you." He pulled her hand up to his mouth and placed a gentle kiss against her knuckles.

She couldn't help smiling at that, but her sober expression returned as she went on. "Yeah, but I have to assume you've been with women. You know, um, sexually."

Alexa wanted to crawl under the table.

Ethan's eyes widened as the realization hit him. "You are a virgin?"

Her cheeks felt like they were on fire. She nodded almost imperceptibly without raising her eyes. All the awful things she had heard boys think about her over the years came rushing back. Not that she thought Ethan was like them; she already knew he wasn't and somewhere deep within her heart she felt, with absolute certainty, that they were meant for each other. But she wanted to please him so badly and she knew her inexperienced fumbling would be a far cry from what someone like Ethan was accustomed to in the bedroom.

Too afraid to meet his gaze, Alexa reached out with her ability to gauge his reaction. What she found caused her to snap her head up to see his face. The intensity of the passion she saw in his eyes robbed her of breath. A cracking sound pulled her attention down to his hands that were gripping the table so hard it seemed to be giving way to his harsh touch.

She had never felt such extreme want in her life. If she'd had the presence of mind to consider it, she would have regretted her choice to wear a skirt, as there was so much moisture between her thighs it was certain to drip down her legs as soon as she stood.

Through gritted teeth, Ethan practically growled, "We need to leave, now."

"Don't you want to eat? The waitress should be back with our food any minute."

"Oh, I intend to eat my fill and then some," he said huskily as his lustful gaze burned into her. Alexa swallowed hard and stood feeling the evidence of her arousal coating her inner thighs. Ethan was immediately behind her, guiding her through the back exit with his hand on the small of her back.

"Fuck, Amor, I can smell how much you want me," he breathed against the back of her neck. She probably should have felt mortified, but hearing that made her impossibly wetter. If he kept this up, she wasn't going to be able to walk. Once they were outside, Alexa started to ask where they were going. Before the first syllable escaped her mouth, Ethan had her pressed up against the wall, his mouth moving desperately against hers.

Just as she started to melt into his forceful kiss, giving in to her deep desire, he pulled back, placing his forehead against hers. "I'm sorry, Alexa, I should be gentle with you, but I cannot control myself when I am so near to you."

She placed her hand against his cheek and looked into his stormy green-gray eyes. "Ethan, I want to be with you. I want you to be my first, any way that you want to take me. I've waited far too long for this. I didn't know it before, but I was waiting for this, for you."

The pleading in her eyes broke his heart, yet it was the lust that he saw there that set him on fire. As much as he wanted to wait, to be gentle, to tell her everything first, he knew the battle was lost. He had to have her. That was all that mattered in that moment.

His mouth crashed down upon hers again, his tongue darting in, exploring and savoring every line and curve.

Giggling came from off to Alexa's right. She was more than willing to ignore it and the fact that they were in a very public place in the middle of the day, but Ethan reluctantly broke away and grabbed her hand, tugging her towards the parking lot.

"We will take your car, I can drive," he said in a rather clipped tone. Alexa didn't mind, she could feel how hard he was struggling to contain his desire which only made her own increase.

Ethan remained silent and kept his hands tightly on the steering wheel the entire drive to Alexa's apartment. She didn't complain; she was so nervous and excited she really wouldn't have known what to say if he tried to talk to her. The anticipation was brutal. Her body was practically humming with need.

Though he had probably violated about a dozen traffic laws to do it, they arrived at Alexa's place in record time. Alexa opened her door and stepped out, turning to meet Ethan and head up the stairs to her unit, but she was met with Ethan's hard body pressing her against the car before she could even close the door.

Perhaps if he hadn't been kissing her like that and if she couldn't feel his rock hard erection pressing into her stomach, she may have wondered how he had gotten there so fast.

Still kissing her, Ethan lifted Alexa up and she wrapped her legs around his waist, all too aware of the fact that the only thing between her and his hard stomach was her rather flimsy little thong.

Before she knew what had happened he was asking for her keys. Completely dazed, she glanced around. They were already at her door on the third floor. She didn't even know they'd climbed the stairs.

"You already have my key ring; it's the one with the black rubber lining," she said as she grabbed his bottom lip between her teeth. She was surprised by the husky sound of her own voice and her increasing boldness. She liked this side of herself.

Ethan growled as he pulled her body even tighter against his own and dug into his own pocket to retrieve the key to her door.

Before he slid the key into the lock he paused and placed his fingers under Alexa's chin, lifting her lust-filled eyes to meet his.

"Are you certain, Amor? Is this what you want?" Ethan knew he had to give her a chance to change her mind before he was alone with her inside. Once they crossed the threshold, he had no hope of being able to stop.

"Yes, please, Ethan! I've never wanted anything more in my life."

Heat appeared in his eyes as he took in her words. The sound of his name on her lips was more than he could bear. In a flash, Alexa felt the cold leather of the couch beneath her as Ethan's body pressed into her, his mouth thoroughly claiming hers.

Then sound of their entrance brought Tilly barreling out of the bedroom, tail wagging as usual, until she caught sight of Ethan and began to bark frantically.

Ethan released Alexa's mouth and sat up. "Friend of yours?" he joked as Alexa jumped up and shooed the giant dog out the door to the balcony.

"Sorry about that, I must have been too distracted to tell you I have a dog," she said as she made her way back to the couch. Without another word, Ethan grabbed her, slung her back underneath him and kissed along her jawline to her neck where he paused, letting out a low groan before moving down to kiss the exposed flesh of her collarbone.

"Lose the clothes." His voice came out far more forceful than he intended. He was struggling with everything he had to keep the beast inside him leashed.

He reluctantly moved back enough for Alexa to obey as he pulled his own shirt over his head in one swift motion.

Alexa greedily drank him in as she fumbled with her own shirt. Her eyes falling on the beautiful tattoo that covered the left side of his chest and snaked down his side, her body clenched with need at the sight and she imagined running her tongue along every intricate line and swirl of the dark pattern. With one final tug, she pulled her shirt over her head and tossed it on the floor with Ethan's.

She reached behind her to unfasten her bra, but before she could complete the task Ethan was on her again, his face between her breasts. In one swift motion, he tugged with his teeth and pulled her bra off completely, adding it to the growing pile of clothes on the floor.

Ethan gazed down at her full breasts and hard pink nipples hungrily, and growled. "My, God, you are so beautiful."

Alexa's cheeks heated slightly, more from arousal than embarrassment. She had never been so naked in front of a man before. Ethan's gaze was like a physical touch, heating her skin wherever he looked. The pure want in his eyes erased any insecurity she might have felt.

He ran his hands down from the tops of her shoulders, over her breasts where he circled each tight nipple with his thumbs before preceding along her stomach and out to her hips. He hooked his fingertips under the waist of her skirt and panties and slowly pulled them down her legs and off. He sat up on his knees and devoured her completely naked body with his eyes while he slowly unbuckled his belt and pants.

Alexa couldn't take her eyes off what his hands were doing. He stepped on to the floor, pulled down his zipper and bent over, sliding his pants off. He stood upright again and Alexa gasped, her eyes popping wide in surprise as she took in the sheer size of his throbbing cock.

Holy shit.

Without thinking about it, she slid back slightly on the couch as she looked up to see Ethan with a worried expression on his beautiful face.

He sat down and reached for her hands, pulling her into a sitting position, then grabbed her face and kissed her deeply before pulling back to say, "Do not be afraid, Amor. I will be as gentle as I can. I will not lie to you, at first there will be some pain," he paused and began trailing kisses down her jawline and onto her neck before continuing, "then so very much pleasure. I promise you. Do you trust me?"

His voice sounded different now, his accent a little thicker maybe and so ridiculously sexy. Alexa looked into the deep pools of his greenish-gray eyes and felt her fear melt away. She wanted this so badly, and though she barely knew Ethan, she trusted him implicitly. Her ability, though not fully effective with him, provided her with great insight into a person's character and intentions. Ethan was a good man, and though they had only met the night before, he cared for her, deeply. Of that she was certain, so she let go and nodded.

Ethan stood and pulled her up with him. "Where is your bedroom?"

She pointed down the hall and he immediately scooped her up, kissing the sensitive spot behind her ear as he carried her to her room. When they arrived he stood at the edge of the large bed and turned her in his arms, placing her legs around his hips and capturing her mouth in another deep kiss.

He felt the moisture from her hot flesh dripping down his abs and groaned loudly, letting her slip further down on his hips, placing his hard length between the soft cheeks of her ass.

A low moan escaped her throat and her hips bucked into him instinctually from the contact.

Ethan lightly bit her bottom lip as he ended the kiss and laid her back on the bed using his well-muscled thigh to spread her legs wide. He then turned his focus to her breasts. Taking a moment to appreciate the sheer perfection of them, he lightly slid his fingertips down the middle of her chest and gently traced around the shape of each ample mound. Alexa trembled beneath his touch.

God, so responsive, so beautiful, he thought as he took the first hard nipple into his mouth and suckled. Alexa moaned loudly, arching into his mouth.

It was as if there was a direct line from her nipple to her most sensitive core. Every flick of his tongue sent a jolt straight down and had her panting, raising her hips up, searching for release.

Sensing her need, Ethan moved his hand down to stroke her soft wet flesh as he continued working his mouth on her nipples. He slid his fingers over the small strip of soft curls and between her lips. Groaning at how wet she was, he slipped the tip of one finger gently inside her, testing, teasing.

"Amor, my God, you are so tight." He had to fight the intense urge to immediately plunge his throbbing cock deep inside her. He knew he needed to prepare her, be gentle to make it good for her. And he needed to keep his most primal side in check. She would bleed; he had to remain in control.

Ethan began to kiss down the middle of her body, stopping above her navel, dipping his hot tongue inside before continuing down. Still stroking her insides with his fingertip, he flicked his tongue over her swollen clit. Her hips shot up as she moaned, pushing her fingers into his hair as she tried to get even closer to the sensation of his mouth.

He smiled at her eagerness as he sucked her sensitive flesh into his mouth and pushed his finger further inside.

"Oh God, Ethan, that feels so good," she whimpered, feeling her climax building. Impossibly, it was even better than the night before in his car, being able to move freely, feeling his bare skin next to hers.

Her legs began to quake uncontrollably as the pressure built and subsided over and over with each movement of his tongue and fingers. Just as she was about to fall over the edge, Ethan stopped. Alexa's eyes snapped open and she squirmed, desperate to end the exquisite torture. She opened her mouth to protest, but before she could utter a word Ethan's covered her mouth with his, slipping his tongue inside as he began sliding his throbbing cock up and down her overly sensitized flesh.

She fell over the edge as the waves of orgasm washed over her body. While she was still at the peak of her release, Ethan pushed inside of her in one swift motion and stilled.

She gasped and dug her fingernails into his back. Her climax continued through the discomfort of being filled for the first time. Ethan remained still with his face turned away, panting and wrestling desperately with the beast within him to remain still and ignore the delicious scent filling the air.

Finally, after several minutes he began to move, feeling that he had regained control. His strokes were slow and measured. He turned his face to Alexa and brushed her long brown hair away from her eyes as he stared down at her.

"Open your eyes, Amor." She obliged and was taken aback by the emotions she saw swimming in the depths of his beautiful eyes. It all felt so amazing; she was overwhelmed and felt tears building as her own emotions welled up in response.

"Aye, fuck, does it still hurt? Do you want me to stop?"

Alexa quickly shook her head. "No, no, I'm sorry, no. I didn't mean to cry, this is just so, so amazing. I'm just overwhelmed, happy."

He sighed in relief and smiled down at her as he started to move again. The pain had subsided and she felt another orgasm building.

Ethan filled her so completely. She couldn't help feeling as if he was made just for her. Though she was initially grateful that his thoughts were blocked, in that moment she wished that she could hear him. She wanted to be connected to him in every way possible.

She started to cry out as another climax crashed down upon her. Ethan covered her mouth and swallowed her moans as his own orgasm tore through his body and his essence poured out inside her.

As their rapid breaths began to slow he remained there on top of her, enjoying the connection while she gently stroked his hair.

Alexa's hand stopped and her body stiffened suddenly.

Ethan pushed up slightly to look down at her concerned expression.

"What's wrong, Amor? Are you hurt?"

She swallowed, hard. "That was so stupid, we didn't use anything. I'm not on birth control, Ethan."

He chuckled and rolled off her to the side and pulled her into his arms. "Do not worry, Amor, I cannot get you pregnant."

She turned her face towards him. "How do you know that, are you, um, sterile?"

"In a manner of speaking, yes."

She looked at him, thoroughly confused. "What does that mean?"

He couldn't get into too much detail without revealing everything, and now was not the right time, so he decided to go with a simplified version of the truth. "There are genetic anomalies in my family that make procreation rather…challenging. Certain steps would need to be taken for me to even attempt to have a child, so you need not concern yourself."

Alexa could sense that there was more he wasn't saying, but she was too relieved and it felt so good laying there in his arms that she decided to let it go, for now.

They spent the day locked away in Alexa's bedroom, talking and making love. She was exhausted, but Ethan seemed to have an unlimited supply of energy. Not that she was complaining, she had never been happier, and he was doing all the heavy lifting.

It was well after the sun went down when she woke to Ethan kissing a trail down her back.

"Alexa, Amor, are you awake?"

She moaned lightly in response. Having just woken up, Alexa's shields were completely down and she could feel Ethan's need. They had made love multiple times over the course of the day and into the evening, still he wasn't sated. Each time they were joined, she sensed that he was holding back something.

"I love you, Alexa. I have waited such a long time for you, and I know with everything that I am and have ever been that I love you."

Alexa gasped, overwhelmed and elated. Feeling bold, empowered by his declaration, she turned, rolled Ethan onto his back and climbed on top of him. She reached behind her and stroked his thick stalk as she looked down at him, searching, wondering what he needed from her.

She raised herself up and placed his wide crown at her wet and rather sore opening. She slid down slowly, gazing at Ethan until he filled her completely once again.

With him buried to the hilt, she leaned down and spoke softly against his ear.

"Ethan, I love you, too. I am yours. Everything I have, everything I am, is yours. Take whatever you need from me. I will do anything for you."

He groaned hearing her sweet words and let his eyes drift to the soft thrum of her pulse at the base of her neck just inches away from his mouth. He knew when she offered herself to him like this she didn't understand the implications. His baser self, his beast, didn't care. He needed to possess her fully. Just thinking the thought, he felt his fangs lengthen in anticipation. And then her body clenched around him, squeezing his cock like a vise and he lost the last bit of his control. He licked along the length of her vein causing it to rise to his call and, closing his eyes, he struck.

Alexa didn't understand what was happening. It was if her pleasure had increased exponentially but instead of building from her core it was flowing down from her neck where Ethan was kissing her. As the waves of the mind-blowing climax started to subside she felt Ethan's body go rigid and suddenly felt incredibly drowsy. The feeling was unnatural, like she was covered with a shroud and being pulled underwater. She began to panic and felt Ethan pull away from her neck, felt the sting of, oh, God, his fangs retracting. And then it was dark.

Ethan paced the room as Alexa slept, trying to understand how he had missed it. The moment her blood hit his system he knew his mistake. She was the one. The girl from the prophecy whom he had spent the last two-hundred years trying to avoid. He roared up at the ceiling, knowing that he wouldn't wake Alexa, having placed her under a trance the moment he realized his error.

This can't be! She doesn't have the mark. The prophecy was very specific about the mark on the right side behind the ear. My mother confirmed it last night.

He strode over to Alexa and turned her to look at the right side of her head as she slept. Even in his state of distress her beauty overwhelmed him. He examined the skin behind her ear, wondering if the mark was simply too faint to notice, but there was nothing visible on her skin. He gently ran his fingers through her hair to move it up and examine farther down on her neck when he glimpsed a dark spot on her scalp about an inch back from her hairline. Gently parting her hair, he sighed and climbed into the bed to hold her while she slept. He felt a tear slide down his cheek as he pulled her body close and let the trance lift. This would be the last time he held her and his heart ached with the loss.

Alexa awoke early that morning and smiled as she stretched lazily, reaching for Ethan before the images of him biting her neck came crashing through her mind. She grasped for her neck and scrambled off the bed to the mirror.

"Oh, thank God," she sighed with relief. It must have been a dream. Though, as her thoughts turned to Ethan, that spot on her neck began to tingle. She glanced down to see she was dressed in her favorite t-shirt and a pair of boy shorts. She didn't even remember getting dressed. In fact, the last thing she remembered was making love to Ethan and him biting her, which had clearly been a dream. She thought hard, trying to grasp the memory of the last real thing that had happened the night before. It was so odd, she hadn't been drinking, yet she felt as if she had blacked out.

Glancing around the room, she couldn't find any sign of Ethan. She opened the door and walked out into the hallway, calling out to him, but the only response came from Tilly who was pawing at the door to the balcony.

"Sorry, girl. I didn't mean to kick you out for the whole night. You probably need to go for a walk, huh?" She turned back into her room and grabbed a pair of comfy jeans, sliding them on as she head towards the kitchen to get Tilly's leash. As she approached the counter, she saw the note.

Alexa,

I do not know what to say to you now that will make this easier. Please understand that I would never intentionally hurt you, and everything we felt is real, though you may find that very hard to believe at present. My only wish is to protect you. That is why I must leave. I wish I could explain, but it would only make things more difficult. You deserve the chance to choose your life, a normal life that would never be possible with me. Please remember your promise. As much as you may hate me for this, I am begging you to keep it. You have my heart now and forever.

E

Alexa felt light-headed. The note slipped from her hand and floated to the floor as she crumpled to her knees.

CHAPTER 7 - *A Desperate Search*

After sitting in stunned silence for several minutes, Alexa hopped up and grabbed her iPhone. She scrolled to Ethan's name and clicked on it, heart pounding as she waited for the ring that didn't come. A recording came on notifying her that the line was no longer in service.

Alexa put the phone down and forced herself to venture outside only briefly to walk Tilly before she grabbed the note and crawled back in bed. She read it repeatedly, going over every line in detail.

What does he think he needs to protect me from?

She went over every moment she had spent with Ethan, remembering the feeling of conflict she had sensed at times.

That was about his family, his parents, and he said they had come around after he visited them, didn't he?

But she had felt it after that, right before she told him she was a virgin. She had been so anxious about telling him that she didn't give him a chance to finish what he wanted to tell her.

A normal life? What a joke! I've never had a normal life. How is he giving me a choice? He is taking my choice away; he decided this all on his own without even talking to me!

Tilly stayed by her side as Alexa remained silent in thought, occasionally laying her large head across her stomach, silently offering comfort as she had always done. When she brought home the gangly and extremely clumsy ten-week-old Tilly over three years ago, Alexa hadn't known how important the Great Dane would be in her life. Somehow, the dog's company and affection had made Alexa's loneliness bearable the last few years.

Alexa climbed out of bed and paced around her apartment, unwilling to accept this. She had to find him, not only for an explanation, but to convince him he was wrong. She knew they were supposed to be together, with every fiber of her being. He wanted to give her a choice. Alexa already knew it wasn't her choice to make, and it wasn't his, either. Their hearts had made it for them. Looking back, Alexa realized she had been in love with Ethan from the first moment they met. It was as if their souls had already known each other for a lifetime. Time was insignificant, loving each other was inevitable. It was fate.

She nervously twisted the diamond hanging from her necklace and an idea came to her. Ethan had donated money to the zoo. She didn't know where he lived, but someone at the zoo would have his information; they would need to send him a letter to document the donation for tax purposes.

She quickly dressed and took Tilly for another short walk before hopping into her Lexus and driving to the zoo. As she approached the entrance, she was surprised to see the same girl from that night at the window.

The girl looked up at Alexa, recognition and something similar to disgust evident in her expression.

"Hi, I don't know if you remember me," Alexa lied, "I was here the other night, with Ethan, uh, Mr. Kellar. I was wondering if I could speak with the gentleman who escorted us into the zoo for a moment."

"You mean the president and CEO? May I ask what this is about?" she asked in a less-than-polite tone.

"Um, well, it's kind of private."

"Well, Mr. Ross isn't here yet. He won't be around for another couple of hours. Is there something I could help you with?"

Alexa stood there for a moment as other patrons filed around her to the next admission window. Hell, what did she have to lose?

"I was wondering if you could give me some information...on Mr. Kellar. I lost my phone and it had his number in it and he, uh, he left his watch in my car. It looks expensive, so I really want to get it back to him as soon as possible. So he doesn't worry, you know?"

"Hmm, well, I'm terribly sorry," her voice dripped with sarcasm, "but we can't release any personal information about our patrons." She had a satisfied sneer plastered across her beautiful face. Unable to help herself, Alexa listened in, hoping the girl would think of something that could help her find Ethan.

I knew it! There is no way Ethan Kellar was really with her. I mean, look at her. She's a freaking mess and he can have any woman he wants. Hell, he didn't even seem to notice me at the zoo's charity ball and I looked a-mazing. He has to be gay, that's the only explanation. In all the times I've seen him he's never been with a woman, except her.

Alexa snapped her shields back in place. Clearly, this girl wasn't going to help her find Ethan, and the last thing she needed right now was to hear how far out of her league he was. She was, however, grateful to hear that Ethan hadn't been dating anyone else recently.

"Yeah, well, thanks anyway." Alexa didn't wait for the snotty girl to reply before turning and heading back to her car.

After she climbed inside and closed the door, Alexa leaned her head back against the soft leather seat and sighed.

Now what, Alexa?

Since nothing immediately came to her, she decided to head home, open a bottle of wine, and take a nice hot bath.

Sliding into the warm water, Alexa immediately felt some of the tension in her body start to dissipate. She took a large gulp from the glass of cabernet sitting on the edge of the large jacuzzi tub and picked up her pen. Trying to be organized and practical, she was an accountant after all, she had brought a pen and notepad into the bathroom to brainstorm ideas for locating Ethan. Keeping herself occupied and focused on a task helped to dull the ache in her heart that resulted from Ethan's absence.

The process was actually soothing. She began listing various ideas, the first, and most obvious, of which was a Google search. Of course, someone like Ethan wouldn't simply have his home address and phone number listed in the white pages, but maybe she could find something about where he worked.

There's probably a website for his family's foundation that would have an office address, maybe a business contact number.

Alexa bit her lip anxiously as she considered what she would say when she found him.

She gripped the dolphin pendant in her fingers, finding comfort in the tangible representation of her relationship with Ethan.

Straightening her spine slightly with determination, she turned back to the search and her notes.

If the Internet search proved fruitless, she would try going to the club where they met and asking around. Surely he had been there before, and a man like Ethan didn't go unnoticed. As a last resort, she would return to the zoo and attempt to get a personal meeting with the president, but she really didn't want to risk facing the bitchy blonde again and looking like a desperate stalker.

Feeling confident in her plan of attack, Alexa slid a little further into the water and really started to relax. She picked up the remote to the iHome on the vanity and clicked on the first song in a new playlist on her iPod that she made the night she met Ethan. She had searched for hours looking for the song that they had danced to, the lyrics were in another language, she believed it was African, but never found it. She did, however, find a variety of other songs that made her think of Ethan, which comprised the list that was now flowing through the room.

As she lay there, listening to the slow, sexy beats and soulful lyrics, she started to think about how it felt being in Ethan's arms on the dance floor that night. She closed her eyes, touching the spot on her neck that had started to tingle and thought about Ethan's mouth there against her skin. She moved her fingers down along her neck between her breasts, coming back up to circle each of her hardening nipples. All the while, she kept imagining her hand was Ethan's skilled mouth. She continued down, sliding her hand under the water and slipping her fingers between the engorged folds of her pussy. Her hips bucked up involuntarily when she grazed over the sensitive bundle of nerves that was begging for attention. With all the tension and emotion of the day, it was only a few moments before the powerful climax flooded her body. The sexual release prompted another kind of release and Alexa suddenly started sobbing uncontrollably as all of the emotions she had been holding at bay came crashing down.

Alexa awoke the next morning feeling confident and determined. She dressed for work quickly in a smoke-colored Armani pantsuit and black patent leather Manolo Blahnik pumps. It was one of her favorite ensembles, and definitely one of the benefits of being single and living in a city with a low cost of living.

She decided the night before that she would put off her search until after work, hoping that, given the time, Ethan would come to his senses and be waiting at her apartment when she returned.

She hadn't even gotten her computer booted up before Jenny sauntered into her office, a long list of questions and thoughts about Ethan bouncing around in her head.

Did she go home with that guy? Why would he pick her and what the hell happened up at the bar? I wonder if she fucked him. What's so fucking special about her? Shit, I love those shoes.

"Hey, Alexa, what happened to you the other night? I don't know if you saw, but I guess there was a fight or something up at the bar, and we couldn't find you after that."

"Yeah, I saw. There was some drunk guy at the bar starting trouble, and I took that as my cue to head home. Don't you remember? I was already about to leave before that guy came over." Hoping to avoid further inquiry from her coworkers, Alexa thought it best to act as if nothing had happened with Ethan. "Anyway, Eli, or Ethan, or whatever his name was offered to get me a cab. He did, and then I went home."

"Oh, well, did you give him your number or anything? Did he ask you out? I mean, come on Alexa, I know you're like shy, or don't date or whatever, but that guy was seriously hot. You had to be interested."

Alexa crossed her legs as she turned in her chair to face Jenny. After all, she was Jenny's superior and they weren't really friends, even if Jenny tried to fake it. These questions were completely inappropriate in the office. "Listen, Jenny; I appreciate your concern, but my personal life is just that, personal. I prefer not to discuss it at work and I really have a lot to do today, as do you."

Fucking bitch, Jenny thought before saying. "Oh, yeah, sorry, I was just curious, you know?"

Alexa replied coolly, "It's fine. I appreciate you including me in social activities, but let's just keep things professional while we're in the office, okay? How are you coming along with the TCH Industries tax work-papers? I would like to review those in the next day or two so we can meet the client's deadline."

Oh fuck, I haven't even started that. "They're coming along fine. I'll have them to you tomorrow or Wednesday to review."

"Great. Thanks, Jenny."

Alexa turned to her computer without waiting for Jenny to say anything further. She felt a great deal of satisfaction putting Jenny in her place after the way she'd treated her Friday night and for all the nasty things Jenny had thought about her over the years. She usually didn't hold any of it against her. Jenny was actually the senior employee by two years and really took it hard when Alexa passed her up.

Alexa had moved up extremely quickly, making manager after only three and a half years with the firm. Being a telepath definitely had its perks. Of course she was incredibly smart, but knowing what was expected without being told went a long way.

The rest of the workday passed without incident. At exactly five o'clock, Alexa opened up her Internet browser and typed "Ethan Kellar" in the search field. After quickly browsing through the search results, her confidence began to wither. Nothing jumped out at her.

She continued to browse through several pages of results, finding nothing useful. After about an hour running various searches, Alexa slammed her laptop shut, packed up and headed out, deciding she would just have to drive to the club and ask around.

Alexa walked into the building and headed straight for the bar to a bartender that she recognized from that night. The place was surprisingly busy for a Monday night.

The girl looked up from wiping down the bar as Alexa approached and took a seat. "What can I get you, hon?"

"A glass of cabernet, thanks."

"Coming right up." She quickly returned with a glass that she filled from a bottle of one of Alexa's favorite labels. "Hey, weren't you here Friday night?" she asked as she pushed the glass towards Alexa.

"Um, yeah, I was. Work happy hour," she said before taking a healthy sip of wine.

"That boyfriend of yours sure was something. I probably shouldn't tell you this, but I have to admit I was a tiny bit jealous. I had been serving him drinks for a while, and flirting pretty hard, but he didn't seem to notice me and then he saw you come in and there was no talking to him after that. Can you hold on a sec?" she asked as she moved down the bar to a guy who was flagging her down without waiting for a reply. After serving him a beer, she returned to Alexa. "You're a lucky girl; he was a great tipper and in my experience only really nice guys tip like that when they're not trying to get in your pants. That's just my luck; I only seem to attract assholes." She laughed.

Alexa took another sip of wine. "Actually, he's not my boyfriend. I just met him that night. That's kind of why I'm here. I was wondering if you knew anything about him."

"You're shittin' me! Really? I would have put money on you two being a couple, especially after what he did to Jim for running his big mouth at you. That douchebag is a regular and is constantly hitting on me, like non-stop," the red-headed bartender recalled. "You'd think he would at least give me a decent tip once in a while if he ever hoped I'd actually go out with him. Sorry, though, I'd never seen your hottie before and I haven't seen him since."

Fucking great. Alexa though to herself.

"Thanks anyway," Alexa said before downing the rest of her wine.

"Listen, I don't know what happened with you two and I'm not trying to be nosey or anything, but that guy was seriously into you. I see a lot of shit working here, and he was not the kind of guy who is just looking to hook up."

Alexa gave her a half-hearted smile, laid a five dollar bill on the bar and headed for the door. When she stepped out onto the sidewalk, she let out an audible sigh as she considered her last option.

Maybe she won't be working.

After a short walk, Alexa reluctantly climbed into her car and headed to the zoo.

When she arrived at the entrance, she was grateful that the girl from before wasn't anywhere to be seen. Steeling her nerves, she approached the admissions window and asked to speak to Mr. Ross. The attendant looked surprised, but then nodded and disappeared for a few minutes before returning with Mr. Ross in tow. The friendly gentleman came out to greet her enthusiastically.

"Such a pleasure to see you again, Miss….?"

"Ryan, Alexa Ryan."

"Yes, of course, I apologize. I don't believe we were properly introduced the other night. Are you here with Mr. Kellar again?" he asked as he looked around curiously.

"No actually, that's why I'm here. Mr. Kellar and I are, um, fairly new acquaintances. I had his number but I somehow managed to lose my phone and he left something rather valuable in my car that I would really like to return to him." Alexa hoped the lie would be more effective on Mr. Ross than it was on his catty employee.

"Since we haven't known each other very long, I don't know where he lives or how to contact him to return it. When we were here he mentioned that he'd donated some money to the zoo and I was hoping that you could give me his address from your records." Alexa placed her hand on Mr. Ross' forearm, hoping to convince him to go against protocol and give her the information.

"Ms. Ryan, I'm terribly sorry, but I couldn't help you if I wanted to. Mr. Kellar only provided an address for a post office box when he signed up for his membership and made the donation."

"Oh. Well, do you know the name of his family's foundation?"

"Again, I'm sorry, but to tell you the truth, I really don't know anything about him at all. I had never seen nor heard of him before when he showed up at the zoo's charity ball a few months ago and made the largest donation in our history. He even requested that his generosity remain anonymous to the public."

"Well, thank you for your time, Mr. Ross. I'm sorry to have bothered you."

"It is no bother, Ms. Ryan. Please come back any time."

CHAPTER 8 - *Life Resumes*

Nearly a month later, Alexa still hadn't been able to find any trace of Ethan. It was like he had never even existed. Each morning before that, she woke up hoping he would show up at her door apologizing and professing his undying love, and each night when he didn't, she would sink a little further into despair.

This morning was different. She had finally given up. When she opened her eyes, she simply wanted to close them again and remain asleep forever. She saw Ethan in her dreams and now she knew that was the only way she could be with him.

Despite her pain, Alexa laughed at herself. *I have become one of those pathetic women I always made fun of.* Not having any close friends, other than Tilly, she had a lot of time to read and watch movies. For years, she had scoffed at the women in the stories who immediately fell hopelessly in love with men who would disappoint them. It had always seemed so ridiculous to her that after a brief encounter, they would be in love, unable to live without this man they barely knew. Now here she was, living it. But in those stories, the men came back. For those women, there was a happily ever after.

It was a Thursday, and of course she was supposed to work that day, but she just couldn't bring herself to get out of bed. She grabbed her iPhone and typed a quick email to work letting them know she was sick and wouldn't be in for the remainder of the week. A four-day weekend was just what she needed.

A few minutes later, when Tilly pushed her out of bed demanding to be let out, she regretted the little white lie she had just told as she actually got sick and vomited all over her bedroom floor, unable to make it into the bathroom in time.

She stumbled into the bathroom, rinsing out her mouth before getting a towel and some cleaner to take care of the mess. She often complained about how cold the hardwood floors got in the winter, but this wasn't the last time she would feel grateful about how easy they were to clean compared to carpet. Feeling one-hundred percent better physically, but emotionally exhausted, she wearily slipped on some sweatpants and a sweater and headed out with Tilly. Watching the big dog relieve herself, it dawned on Alexa that she really needed to pee, immediately.

With Tilly in tow, she sprinted up the stairs and back into her apartment, not even bothering to remove Tilly's leash before she rushed into the bathroom. Sitting there, Alexa reached for the toilet paper finding there was none left on the roll. She really was in a funk. She was not the type of person to use the last of the toilet paper and not replace it. She leaned over and opened the cabinet below the vanity to fetch a roll, moving a full box of tampons out of the way to get to it.

Then it hit her.

Oh. Shit.

She finished up quickly and rushed out to grab her phone from her nightstand, immediately opening the calendar app. She started scrolling back through the days, looking for the notation she always made for the start of her monthly visitor. Before long she had scrolled back over seven weeks with nothing.

She scrolled forward back through the days, hoping she had simply missed where she had marked it.

No, there's no way. He said he's practically sterile! She hadn't sensed a lie from him; then again, she had sensed that he loved her, and look how *that* turned out. Maybe her telepathy was on the fritz. He was the first person she couldn't actually hear, maybe that meant her intuition about him was blocked, too.

Seven pregnancy tests and a trip to the gynecologist later, Alexa finally accepted that she was pregnant. With Ethan's baby. The lying bastard.

But she wasn't really mad. Suddenly the hole that he had left in her heart felt full again. She took all of the love she felt for Ethan and poured it into the tiny life growing inside of her. All of the anger disappeared and was replaced with gratitude. Their encounter was brief, but she had really loved Ethan, he had loved her, and their love gave her this incredible gift. For that, she was grateful.

After the first trimester, Alexa felt absolutely amazing. She felt strong, vibrant, and alive. Better than she had ever felt in her life. The only problem she noticed was that her telepathy was far more sensitive and it took far more energy to block people out.

Everything was progressing perfectly, according to the home midwife Alexa hired. She left her one-bedroom apartment in Indy and bought a nice little house about thirty minutes away in Fishers, Indiana. She didn't know the sex of the baby so she kept the nursery neutral. Each night, she would sit in a rocking chair in the nursery, silently imagining what it would be like to sit there with her precious baby in her arms. Then one night, something miraculous happened. She heard her baby for the very first time.

It wasn't really words, more like flashes of thought, images of what the baby could see and feel from within the comfort of her womb. It was the most beautiful experience of Alexa's life. From then on, she kept her shields down when she was at home alone, wanting to soak up every bit of information from the miraculous life that had been growing in her belly for the previous five months. Alexa grabbed her swollen belly, looking down in awe of the miracle that was her baby. There was a lot she didn't fully understand, considering her baby didn't yet think in language, but she could sense its emotions and moods, see what it saw. She knew her baby didn't like it when she ate spicy food, or when she slept on her right side. She knew it loved when she sat in the rocking chair and sang. Doing just that one evening, she realized her baby was a girl when she saw the images of her looking down at her cute little legs.

Starting the next day, she began reading through all the baby girl names in a book she had purchased the month before, making notes next to names that the baby seemed to like until she came across the name Chloe. When she read that name aloud she immediately felt the baby's love for it. Unable to help herself, Alexa wondered if Ethan would like the name, too.

Efan?

Alexa's hand shot up to her mouth as she gasped and looked down at her belly in complete shock. That was the first real word she had received from her unborn baby.

Oh, sweetheart, Ethan was mommy's friend, but he is gone now. Mommy loves you so much, Chloe.

Alexa felt the tears streaming down her face.

Wuv Mommy.

The next few months flew by. Chloe's mental vocabulary grew each day and the ability to communicate telepathically allowed Alexa to bond with her so completely. Her lifetime of loneliness and secrets was over. Of course, she feared for Chloe and the hardships she would face being a telepath. Alexa's ability didn't manifest until she was a teenager. She had no idea what it would be like for Chloe as an infant, toddler, and pre-teen being able to hear every thought of the people around her.

As Chloe developed, Alexa had to learn to shield her thoughts about Ethan or not think about him at all if Chloe was awake, as hard as that was. She still felt him everywhere, and often thought she saw him. Despite the hurt he had caused her, she couldn't help but feel grateful to him for giving her Chloe.

Mixed in with all that was amazing about her pregnancy, there were some challenges. Once Alexa had started showing, the rumors at work began to fly. She did her best to block out everyone's thoughts, but since her delicate condition had heightened her telepathy, it was far more difficult.

As her due date approached, Alexa made the difficult decision to leave her job to stay home and raise Chloe, truly appreciating her trust fund for the first time. With her being a telepath, she couldn't risk putting Chloe in child care and having her ability discovered.

Chloe arrived on a warm, sunny afternoon late in September. Seven pounds, eleven ounces of pure joy of which Alexa had never know the like.

Over the next eight and a half months, Alexa watched Chloe grow, facing the typical trials of motherhood and being met with the unique challenges of parenting a telepath.

She worked diligently to keep Ethan out of her thoughts, an impossible task with his eyes staring back at her every time she looked at Chloe. But she managed to hide that part of herself away, locked up in a far corner of her heart that she only allowed herself to visit when she was alone in the quiet of the night.

And then one seemingly normal morning, Alexa's world came crumbling down around her. She walked into Chloe's room, mentally saying good morning as she gathered a few stray toys from the floor. Receiving no reply, she looked at Chloe and spoke aloud.

"Good morning, angel."

Chloe smiled wide, but still no response.

"What's wrong, sweetie, you don't feel like talking to Mommy?"

Chloe looked at Alexa curiously, and cooed aloud, but mentally there was silence. Lowering her shields completely, Alexa searched for Chloe's mind, her heart crashing down into her stomach at what she found. Silence.

CHAPTER 9 - *Late Night Appointment*

Alexa pulled her car into the parking lot in front of Dr. Kline's building. It was completely empty and the building was dark, except for the front porch light and one other inside that Alexa assumed was in Dr. Kline's personal office.

Chloe was awake and smiled brightly at Alexa as she started to unstrap her. Alexa checked again to be sure that the new teeth she had seen earlier were no longer visible and breathed a sigh of relief when she confirmed that they were in fact hidden. A normal person might have taken their absence as an indication that they had imagined the night's earlier events. Alexa wasn't exactly normal. She had spent the thirty-minute drive going over the details of what she had witnessed in her bedroom and could only come up with one explanation. It wasn't really that hard for her to believe, hell, she was a telepath after all. As far as the world around her was concerned, telepaths didn't exist, either. She wasn't quite ready to say the word, but in her heart she knew what Chloe was, and she loved her all the same.

As she approached the door to Dr. Kline's building, a feeling of dread washed over her.

Oh, God, the abnormalities in Chloe's blood, what if he knows what she is? what if her teeth come back?

In all her consideration on the drive over, she hadn't thought about what she would do if Dr. Kline, or anyone else, discovered the truth about Chloe. If she had learned anything in her lonely pathetic excuse for a childhood, it was that people don't like different.

She considered leaving, calling the doctor and making some excuse, but what if he already knew? When she thought back to their phone conversation she realized he had seemed almost, excited. She tried to remember exactly what he said. She had been so distracted with Chloe, it was a little fuzzy.

She could have stood there arguing with herself for hours trying to decide what the right thing to do was, but she kept coming back to one important truth. She trusted Dr. Kline. Her intuition told her to trust him.

My intuition was wrong once before. Her heart squeezed tight with the thought. She had trusted Ethan and he left her, breaking her heart with a scribbled little note in her kitchen.

Then it hit her like a slap in the face.

That's what he wanted to tell me; that was the conflict I felt. Is that why he left? Was he afraid to tell me?

Of course he was afraid to tell her the truth about himself. Alexa felt a little twinge of guilt; she hadn't even considered telling Ethan her secret.

Before she could dwell on it further, the door in front of her swung open revealing Dr. Kline's smiling face. He was dressed casually in a pair of jeans and a plain grey T-shirt.

As seemed to be protocol when she was near him, Alexa instantly felt at ease, but was afraid to speak, worrying that once she opened her mouth everything in her head would spill out and she desperately needed to play it cool, find out what the doctor knew.

"Thank you for coming in at this late hour, Alexa." He glanced around outside before continuing. "Please understand that it was necessary. Follow me and everything will be explained."

That seemed like an odd way to phrase it. She held Chloe close as she stepped past him through the door, but Chloe had ideas of her own. She immediately tried to lean away from Alexa reaching out to the doctor, opening and closing her little hands as she whined. This absolutely lit up the doctor's handsome face as he reached out to take Chloe in his arms.

"What a little traitor," Alexa joked, trying miserably to sound exasperated. It warmed her heart to see Chloe interact with the doctor and further confirmed her trust in him.

He held Chloe with one arm as he closed and locked the door, and then quickly entered a code into the keypad off to the right, changing the light on it from green to red.

Without another word, he started walking and Alexa followed him through the lobby, down the long hallway to his office. When she walked through the door, she saw the strange painting of the man who reminded her so much of Ethan out of the corner of her eye, yet refused to look at it. She couldn't think about him right now.

Dr. Kline walked to the edge of his desk and turned to face Alexa, leaning back expectantly. Confused, and realizing it was probably pointless, Alexa lowered her shields. As soon as she did though, as expected, she was met with silence. However, two other important things were evident. There were three distinct minds around her, and they were all blocking her in the same way.

Before she could fully process the information, he spoke.

"Hello, Amor."

Hearing that voice, Alexa's body immediately betrayed her as fires that she thought long ago burned out ignited with a rampant fury. Her skin flushed, heart rate increased, and she felt the moisture pooling between her legs. Without turning or acknowledging him in any way, she closed her eyes taking a deep breath, willing herself to stay composed. Her mind was racing as she calmly walked to stand directly before the source of that voice.

Alexa stared at him for what seemed like forever, realizing that he was even more beautiful than she remembered. Then she raised her hand and slapped him right across his perfect cheek, once, twice, three times, before he finally caught her by the wrist. His hand touching her bare skin sent lust coursing through her veins, which only enraged her further. Employing her free hand, she attempted to slap him once again, but he grabbed that wrist as well, pushing both of her arms together behind her back and pulling her body against his.

She struggled against his grip, spewing every expletive she'd ever heard at him while he remained quiet, waiting for her to calm. When she finally gave up the struggle, it was as if all the walls she had built up over the months, all the hurt, the confusion, the anger, the love, everything she had ever felt came crashing down and she collapsed into the comfort of Ethan's strong arms, sobbing uncontrollably and without shame.

Ethan released her wrists and pulled her closer, gently stroking her hair while she cried.

"Shhh, shhh, I know, Amor. I know."

After crying for a long time, Alexa started to calm. Still sniffling, she whispered against Ethan's chest, "You left me. How could you leave me, Ethan?"

He gently placed his fingers under her chin to lift her face up as he spoke. Looking into his eyes, she saw so much pain and regret. And love.

"I only left to protect you, Amor. I thought if I stayed away, you would be safe."

"You could have told me the truth. I would have accepted anything you had to say."

Just then Chloe cooed across the room. Alexa looked over to see her sitting happily on Dr. Kline's lap, playing with some blocks on his desk. Shame washed over her. She had let her feelings for Ethan and his sudden reappearance overshadow her concerns about Chloe.

Ethan's grip tightened, causing Alexa to look back at him as she attempted to move towards Chloe. She stopped, trying to swallow the knot growing in her throat as she watched tears streaming down Ethan's beautiful face. His gazed was fixed on Chloe.

"Oh God, Ethan." Her own tears began to flow again. Doing what felt right, Alexa took Ethan's hand in her own and started pulling him towards Chloe, to meet his daughter for the very first time.

As they neared, Chloe looked up, smiling broadly, the greenish-grey eyes that she had inherited from Ethan fixed on him curiously. A flicker of recognition flashed in those eyes and she smiled broadly, opening her arms to him in a request to be picked up.

Ethan looked over to Alexa, uncertain of what to do. "It's okay, she wants you to pick her up," she said reassuringly. Somehow, seeing this, Chloe meeting her father for the first time, eclipsed everything else.

He picked Chloe up, pulling her into his arms, an expression of complete wonder lighting his beautiful eyes. Alexa glanced over at Dr. Kline, who had remained silent since they arrived in his office, surprised to see a tear rolling down his chiseled cheek. She was more confused than ever and could feel the questions bubbling up inside her, but she pushed them back, not wanting to take anything away from this moment for Chloe or Ethan.

Chloe was clearly examining Ethan, tilting her head from side to side as she looked at him, being a little silly as if she was trying to ease some of the tension in the room. Her eyes turned to Alexa as she put her tiny hand on Ethan's face and proudly said, "Dada."

Alexa gasped and looked to Ethan, whose expression was one of utter delight.

"That's her first word," Alexa said, pulling Ethan's attention to her for a moment.

"I can't believe it, how could she know?" Ethan inquired, not really expecting an answer, as he sat down on the floor with Chloe never taking his eyes off of her.

That was a good thing because Alexa wasn't about to offer one just yet. She knew Chloe had seen him in her mind. Despite all of her effort to block her thoughts of him from Chloe, enough had leaked through for her to recognize him. And now, apparently, she could talk.

Alexa remained silent for several minutes, waiting and watching as Ethan and Chloe sat on the floor quietly staring as if they were trying to soak up every bit of each other.

When she couldn't stand it any longer, the questions that had been swirling in her mind from the moment she heard his voice started pouring out. "Ethan, what are you doing here? Why did you lie to me? Why did you leave?"

Ethan gestured towards the doctor. "He called me. I am here for you, Amor. And Chloe." He smiled down at his daughter who was still staring at him adoringly, before looking up at Alexa, his expression confused. "When did I lie to you?"

She pointed at Chloe. "Um, let's see, where should I start. Maybe when you made me believe that I could trust you, that you loved me! Or how about when you told me you couldn't get me pregnant! We were together one night, and poof! Here she is, so how do you explain that? And wait, Dr. Kline, or I mean, Elijah, how could you possibly know who Ethan was or how to get a hold of him? I never put his name on anything."

"Perhaps we should start with something else and come back to that. We have a lot to share with you tonight, Alexa. Most of it will be very difficult for you to understand or even believe, but you must trust that we only want to help and protect both you and Chloe. Do you trust us?"

Alexa again began to feel at ease as Dr. Kline spoke. What was up with that? She nodded slowly, indicating her trust, and just wanting some answers.

"Perfect, let's begin with Chloe," Elijah continued. "First, let me reassure you that she is perfectly healthy, better than healthy even. She is very special, Alexa; one of a kind, in fact. The difficulties that led you to my office in the first place are the result of changes that Chloe is going through. She is growing, rapidly, both physically and mentally. Based on what I found in her blood, she is maturing at three to four times the rate of an average human child."

The words falling upon her ears should have sounded crazy, unbelievable, but Alexa knew it was true. She had witnessed it over the last day with Chloe's sudden recovery and miraculous walking.

Alexa turned to Ethan and Chloe, her gaze landing upon her daughter. She looked so happy and normal there in her daddy's arms. Shifting her focus to Ethan, in his eyes she saw so much love and understanding. He was Chloe's father, despite everything in the past. Alexa knew she needed to trust him, with everything.

"At home tonight, before we came here, I cut myself. I was bleeding and, and…."

"Chloe bit you."

Alexa's eyes shot to Elijah in astonishment. "Yes, how could you have guessed that?"

"That is part of who she is now, part of why she is special. But there is more, correct?"

Alexa once again looked to Ethan, hoping for some sort of guidance, some indication of what she was supposed to do here. Her telepathy was her most closely guarded secret. She had concealed that part of herself for so long and the thought of revealing it caused a light sheen of sweat to cover her forehead.

Ethan stood up with Chloe and took a step towards her, placing his hand on her shoulder. "Amor, I love you and I love Chloe. I will never let anything happen to either of you as long as I live. You can trust us, you must trust us."

She clenched her hands into fists at her side and looked down at the floor. Sighing, she opened her eyes and looked up at Chloe who gave her a big smile of encouragement.

"I think she can read minds. I think she is a telepath." Alexa searched Ethan's face for some sign of shock or disbelief, but none appeared. Instead he looked at Chloe and leaned to place a kiss on her cheek causing her to giggle with delight.

Turning to Elijah, she continued deciding to just get it all out before she lost her nerve. "Up until two weeks ago, I could hear her thoughts. We would talk to each other, telepathically. Then it just stopped, I couldn't hear her anymore and everything else started to change."

"Well, that is interesting. Telepathy is a very unique and powerful ability, though not unheard of amongst our kind. I can only assume, based on the fact that you are still confused, that you cannot read my mind or Ethan's?"

"Yes, you're right. Ethan was the first person I ever met who I couldn't hear, even when I really tried to listen in." She chanced a glance at Ethan to see him with a slight, sexy smirk on his face that sent a little rush through her body. How could he still affect her like that with everything else that was going on?

Turning back to Elijah she said, "Chloe was the second, and you were the third. Your minds are all the same in the way they feel to me. I guess it makes sense for Chloe to be like Ethan, but what is the connection with you?"

"Well, in this case we are all related, but to be honest, I do not believe that is why you cannot hear our minds."

"Wait a minute, are you two brothers, or cousins or something?" She looked between the two men, acknowledging what should have been obvious to her before. They did look a lot alike. That was why she had thought Dr. Kline seemed so familiar when they first met.

"Actually, no, Alexa. Ethan is my son."

She started to laugh. "Yeah, ok, is that supposed to be funny? You have different last names, and you can't be more than five or ten years older than him, if that." Before he answered, she already knew how it was possible.

"As a matter of fact I am nearly five-hundred years older than him, though without the aid of a little well-placed hair dye, we would probably appear to be even closer in age than you have guessed," Elijah responded, glancing at his son, "and despite my protests, Ethan changed his last name many years ago. I suppose he hoped it would protect the family in some small way."

"Are you telling me you're all immortal?" Alexa asked feeling somewhat disoriented, her legs beneath her starting to feel like Jell-o. Even though she already knew what Chloe was, what Ethan was, and now what Dr. Kline must be, too, it was still unbelievable to hear it confirmed.

"Not exactly immortal. We can be killed, but we have the potential to live a very, very long time."

Her thoughts immediately shot to all the stories and myths that she had read when she was younger, all of the movies that she had loved, obsessed over even, believing them to be make believe, but always wishing that world was real. And in that moment, no longer able to deny the truth, she finally let herself think the word before saying it aloud.

"You're vampires."

CHAPTER 10 - *Secrets Revealed*

It was dark. Alexa considered opening her eyes, then remembered that she had been with Ethan and she wasn't quite ready to let go of him to wake up and go back to life without him.

What a crazy, beautiful dream that was. She thought as she turned to snuggle into her bed hoping to go back to her dream. Instead of her soft comforter, she found she was nestled in a pair of strong, muscular arms. Her eyes snapped open to take in Ethan's beautiful face looking down at her with concern and fear in his eyes. It hadn't been a dream.

Taking in her surroundings, she realized she was still in Dr. Kline's office, on the sofa in the back. Chloe was sitting across the room on the floor with Elijah, playing contentedly with some colorful blocks.

She sat up and turned her focus back to Ethan, her heart doing flip-flops at having him so near, having him back in her life, no longer only in her dreams. Seeing the uncertainty in his expression, she reached up and touched his cheek, pulling him towards her and pressing a soft kiss against his full lips. She wanted him to know that she accepted him, every part of him.

She probably should have been afraid. She probably should grab Chloe and run. They were vampires, after all. She almost wanted to laugh at how ridiculous it sounded in her own mind, that vampires were real, yet she couldn't deny it after what she had seen from Chloe that night. Knowing what she did about her own preternatural abilities, she didn't want to deny it. Strangely enough, knowing this about Ethan, about Chloe, it all made her feel at home, normal.

Her thoughts drifted back to the night Ethan had grabbed the man at the bar, how fast and strong he'd seemed. And the next morning how quickly he had carried her up the stairs. And the bite that still made her neck tingle whenever she thought about it.

All of it made so much more sense now and she had to admit that on some level she had always known something was different about him. Maybe that is what drew her to him in the first place. She knew all about being different, about not being accepted for who you really are. Looking at Ethan, she realized she was a little afraid. Not that she or Chloe were in danger, but that she would lose him again.

She pulled back slightly to look at Ethan again. "Did I pass out?" Her voice sounded rough and scratchy to her own ears. Ethan reached over to the end table and retrieved a glass of water which he moved to her lips. She gulped it down gratefully.

"Yes, just for a few moments. I understand if you are afraid, but Alexa, Amor, please do not fear me." He gently stroked her hair as he continued. "I would never hurt you and I will never lie to you. When I told you that I could not get you pregnant that night, I believed that to be true. If you had been almost anyone else in this world, it would have been true, but you are very special, just like our daughter."

His eyes turned to Chloe, who was in his father's arms and he smiled. His expression was full of pride and adoration for his baby girl.

"So it's true then? You *are* a vampire?" Though she knew the answer,

126

Alexa needed to hear him acknowledge it out loud.

"Yes, Amor, that is the common term. The definition that humans associate with it is, somewhat inaccurate. Our people…"

"I'm not afraid of you, Ethan. Not at all," she blurted, interrupting him. She needed to tell him, before he revealed anything else; he had to know that she did not fear him. She loved him, though she wasn't quite ready to voice that particular sentiment again.

Ethan smiled fully for the first time in what seemed like forever, revealing the deep dimples that Alexa couldn't resist. At least it was the first time since that morning he walked out of her apartment. These many months had been absolute torture for him, more than she could ever know.

Overwhelmed with what could only be described as gratitude, he placed a chaste kiss on her forehead, breathing in the sweet scent of her hair before looking into her eyes and continuing.

"Our people, vampires, began with what we now know was a genetic mutation many, many centuries ago. We are still partly human, but the gene enhances many things in our kind. The myths you have probably heard are fairly accurate about a great deal of our abilities. We are much stronger and faster than humans and have acute hearing and sense of smell. We heal rapidly and live far longer than any normal human who has ever existed. To my knowledge, in the last one thousand years none of our kind has died naturally."

Ethan searched her eyes, trying to gauge her reaction.

Alexa had to fight to repress the smile that threatened to spread across her face. Ethan was nervous; she could sense it with her ability, and the speech he had just given sounded rehearsed, like he had been practicing what to say to her over and over again.

She schooled her features and nodded, encouraging him to continue.

"Like humans, we vampires are all very different and have individual abilities and talents. There are those who are blessed physically, while others are great artists or scientists. And there are some who possess preternatural abilities, though those talents are somewhat rare."

Alexa considered all of that for a moment before asking, "What about you," she said looking at both Ethan and his father, "do you two have any special abilities?"

Ethan sighed and looked away. "Yes, my father has power over emotions; he can soothe or incite the feelings of others in most circumstances." Well, that explained why Alexa felt so at ease around Elijah. "And I can influence the minds of both human and vampire-kind by suggesting or altering thoughts, so long as they are not shielding themselves, which is something most of our kind are taught to do at a young age." Ethan continued as he chanced a glance back at Alexa, searching for the question he anticipated in her eyes, but he found none. Still, he had to be sure she knew. "I have never tried to influence your thoughts in that way, Amor, you must know that." Alexa smiled reassuringly. "But, I did use a talent that is common to all of our kind on you once."

Her smile faded. "What does that mean exactly?"

He stood and started to pace. "I am so very sorry, Amor, I should never have crossed that line without your permission. That night, when you gave yourself to me, I lost control. You were laying there beneath me, so beautiful, so vulnerable, so open, and I could no longer suppress my craving. I took your blood." He watched her carefully as he spoke, expecting her anger which never came.

Instead, she asked, "What is it like, craving blood?"

He felt relief in his heart. "I have never attempted to explain it before." He pondered for a moment. "I supposed it starts off with a nagging feeling, more intense than hunger. It is a need that builds slowly at first, and becomes more intense the longer we go without drinking blood. Feeding from the vein is very pleasurable; it can be very sexual, very sensual. Many couples feed on one another for this reason." His eyes darkened with need and he began stroking the side of Alexa's neck which was now tingling, causing her panties to dampen.

Ethan's nostrils flared as he smelled her arousal and closed his eyes, breathing it in deeply, savoring the scent as it slid down his throat and set his blood on fire.

"Are you craving blood now?" she asked, sensing his desire and secretly wishing they were alone so that he could ravage her neck and her body again right then.

"I am craving you," he replied huskily, leaning close so that his breath tickled her ear.

"I remember how it felt when you bit me," she whispered as her cheeks flushed from the memory.

"You remember that?" he asked, pulling back slightly to look at her, sounding genuinely surprised. "You are more powerful than we anticipated."

"Why wouldn't I remember?" she asked, feeling confused. "To be honest, I had convinced myself it was just a dream, but I never really

129

believed that, and when Chloe bit me tonight, it confirmed what I already knew in my heart. It was all real."

"Yes, it was real, Amor. I attempted to remove the memory. The talent we all possess, it is to alter the memories of the humans we feed upon, to make them forget, to protect the secret of our kind. And our saliva contains an enzyme that speeds healing, removing any marks in only a few minutes. I should have tried to make you forget that you had ever met me, but I could not bear the thought. I am too selfish. I should have realized it would not work on you. You are so special." He stroked her cheek with his fingertips, looking down at her reverently, taking in every detail of her flawless face.

She leaned into his touch. "How am I special, Ethan?"

"In so many ways, Amor. But what I speak of is in your blood, your genes. You are human, but you are also vampire. I tasted it the moment your blood touched my tongue."

"And it was evident in the sample of your blood that I tested," Elijah stated, surprising Alexa. She had forgotten he was even there and had not noticed him move across the room with Chloe securely in his arms. The enhanced speed would take some getting used to.

"I don't understand; how can that be? I'm not a vampire. I'm not very fast or strong. And I definitely don't drink or crave blood." She was almost laughing, it seemed so ridiculous. "Perhaps there was an error with my blood work."

Elijah responded, "There was no error. I ran the tests multiple times on both samples that we collected. On a genetic level, you are exactly like us. Physically, you are something else, perhaps something more."

"Tell us, when did you first realize you could hear the thoughts of others?" Elijah questioned.

"I think I was maybe thirteen or fourteen," she said, trying to remember exactly how old she had been.

"So, around the time you went through puberty, then?"

She nodded.

"That is when our people begin to change. Our children are nearly identical to human children until that time. We are not certain what triggers the transformation. With the onset of puberty comes the need to consume human blood and, shortly thereafter, enhanced speed, strength, and other abilities become evident."

Alexa stood abruptly, leaving the comfort of Ethan's warmth for the first time since she woke up and her heart immediately protested, but she needed a clear head for this.

"Let me get this straight, you're saying that I'm a vampire? Me, Alexa Ryan?"

"Yes, in every way that matters, you are vampire. Why you do not display the typical traits, we cannot be certain." Elijah glanced toward Ethan before continuing. "But one thing that is sure, based on the properties of your blood, you have the potential to be one of the most powerful beings our kind has seen in the last one thousand years. Perhaps it is time to discuss what you know of your parents."

CHAPTER 11 - *Alexa's Past*

Thinking of her parents took Alexa back to that day. Put her back in that chair sitting across from Mr. Smith in his office at Smith, Stone, and Waters.

It was her eighteenth birthday. Earlier that day, Ms. Johnson, the coordinator at the group home (which could more accurately be described as a compound), called Alexa into her office to process the paperwork for her to move out and into the dorms at Indiana University in Bloomington. Alexa felt that it was more like her release than a simple move.

Being extremely bright, Alexa had completed her education in the compound's school system before her seventeenth birthday, but she was forced to remain there for another year until she was legally considered an adult. As they were finishing up, the stout woman handed Alexa an envelope.

"I was given this with specific instructions to present it to you on this day. A car service has been retained to drive you to your destination and is waiting outside the gate as we speak."

There were no tears, no hug from the woman who had raised her for most of her life. Ms. Johnson had always treated Alexa like a job, an assignment to be completed, nothing more. She made sure her basic needs were attended to, but avoided any further interaction. Perhaps she was afraid of Alexa's ability, perhaps she was just that cold. Either way, Alexa would never know.

A few hours later, she was greeted by a rather attractive receptionist at the law firm that specialized in estates and trusts and escorted to the office in which she was now sitting.

"Ms. Ryan, it is so nice to finally meet you, my dear. Your parents enlisted my services many years ago to administer the trust that they left to you. "

Alexa looked over the rather plain man as he entered the room, briefly shook her hand, and took the seat behind the desk.

"I'm sorry; my parents left me a trust fund?"

"Yes, the fees for the group home where you were raised were taken out annually; however, you are still quite well off, as you can see. As of today, you have unlimited access to the funds."

He slid a piece of paper that turned out to be a K-1 from the trust across the table, followed by a copy of its most recent tax return, a set of financial statements, and a small sealed envelope. The interest on the K-1 alone was more than enough to cover all of her college expenses for the next four years.

"Oh, my God." Alexa stared at the papers, her mouth hanging open in disbelief.

"You are a very fortunate young lady, Ms. Ryan."

Alexa almost laughed. The last thing she would have called herself before that day was fortunate. Her childhood had been so lonely at the group home. She was never allowed to leave the grounds and, because of her ability, she didn't have any real friends anymore. Anyone she was close to figured out that something was wrong with her eventually, not that she ever talked about it.

She had told the resident counselor once, who dismissed it at first, but when Alexa started repeating all of the chubby man's thoughts back to him, he became extremely agitated and then downright afraid of her. He locked her in his office and ran off to fetch Ms. Johnson. The robust woman came in, looking somewhat ruffled and, without even glancing directly at Alexa, she grabbed her arm and led her to a flight of stairs and down into the basement which contained several rooms that would be better described as cells. She escorted Alexa into one, then backed out and closed the door.

"I'm sorry to do this, but you must learn this lesson absolutely. You are never to speak of the things that caused this again. I do not want to hear a word of it. You will stay here, alone for two weeks, at which time you will return to your room and go back to your normal studies. You will not mention any of this to anyone or you will come back here for a month. Have I made myself clear?"

Alexa nodded and Ms. Johnson turned and walked back up the stairs without another word. She turned around, examining the room, finding a toilet and sink in the corner, a table and chair in the middle, and a small cot off to one side. There was one small window high up in the back, whose light was mostly blocked by what appeared to be a bush outside. For the next two weeks, the only person Alexa saw was an attendant who brought her food three times a day. The young man simply walked up to the door and slid a tray through the slot. He never spoke to or even looked directly at her.

At the end of two weeks, Ms. Johnson came, unlocked the door and silently led Alexa back across the grounds to her quarters. Once inside, she simply stated, "Remember this, it will help to keep you safe. You must conceal that part of yourself from everyone."

After that day, Alexa never again mentioned her telepathy to another soul and she began to withdraw from everyone. It was too difficult to hear people's innermost thoughts and pretend that everything was just fine. With time, she learned to harness her talent and shield her mind from the constant flow of external thoughts, but by then she had already been labeled as a freak among the kids living there, so she spent the remaining years of her time there essentially alone.

Now, sitting in Mr. Smith's office, listening to him speak of her parents made her heart ache in a way it hadn't in many years. If only she could remember some small part of them. All she knew was their names, William and Rebecca Ryan. She was told that they perished in a house fire that destroyed everything, while an eighteen- month-old Alexa had miraculously survived, being found wandering alone outside by a neighbor. There were no surviving relatives to take her in, so after a brief stint in a foster home she had been placed in the care of the Beaumont Children's Home in Evansville, Indiana.

"Did you know them well?" Alexa asked, feeling a slight sting in her eyes at the hope of learning something real about the only people in the world who once loved her.

"I'm afraid not; I only met them once when the trust was set up fifteen years ago."

"I'm sorry, what did you say? That's impossible. My parents died before I was two."

"Hmm, let me see." He pulled back Alexa's copy of the trust tax return, glancing at it briefly before pointing to the date in a small box on the first page. "No, that is correct; the trust was established on this date, which is just a few weeks over fifteen years ago."

Alexa sat there completely stunned. What did this mean? She reached into her bag, retrieving the folder of paperwork Ms. Johnson had given her. Behind a copy of her birth certificate was a general information record which included the date of her admission to the group home, over sixteen years ago.

Oh, come on, I don't have time for this shit. You're rich now, you little bitch. Just get out of here so I can get back to that hot new secretary upstairs.

Alexa's eyes shot up to the falsely-smiling face of Mr. Smith. All of the emotions that were barreling through her mind must have weakened her shields. Hearing the evidence of his true character in his thoughts, she thought better of pressing the issue further and risking revealing anything to the little weasel. She took a deep breath, pushing down the emotions swelling up inside her and reinforcing her shields before continuing.

"Oh, I guess I was wrong about the dates," she lied. "So is that it then?" she inquired calmly.

"Yes, everything you need to access your money, in addition to photo identification, of course, is in that envelope. It's been a pleasure, Ms. Ryan. Here is my business card. Please do not hesitate to call if you have any questions." He stood and motioned towards the door. "Would you like me to escort you out?"

"No, please don't trouble yourself, Mr. Smith, I can find my own way," she replied starkly, taking the proffered business card and tucking it into her bag with no intention of ever using it. With that, she turned and rushed out of the office.

Back in the town car, the reality of what she had just learned hit her like a bulldozer. Her parents were alive when she entered the group home. She wasn't orphaned, she was abandoned.

"To the campus in Bloomington now, miss?" the driver questioned.

"No actually, I'd like to make a stop at the public library first."

"Very well, miss."

Alexa spent the next few hours poring through old records, looking for information about her parents. She looked at every newspaper article she could find involving fires the year that she entered the group home, but none matched what she had been told. She searched through birth records and obituaries and still came up empty. It was as if they had never existed. But if it had all been a lie and she had been abandoned, why the trust fund?

Leaving the library even more confused than when she'd entered, Alexa decided then and there that she wasn't going to waste anymore of her life living in the past. For whatever reason, her parents hadn't wanted her and there was nothing she could do about that. She was resolved to move on with her life. She was finally free to do as she pleased for the first time in her life and she was going to take advantage of the opportunity.

Like hell if I'll use any of their money. They didn't want me; I don't want or need their money.

Strengthening in her resolve, Alexa sat up a little straighter. She had a couple of weeks before classes started to find a job. After scoring a nearly perfect score on her SATs, which she had of course taken at the compound, she had been awarded a full scholarship to Indiana University, which included room and board in the dorms. Due to her ability, she had declined to stay on campus since she would have to room with at least one other student and opted to pay for her own apartment nearby. The resident counselor at Beaumont had provided a report exempting her from the freshman requirement of living on campus.

Four years later, she graduated with a 4.0 GPA, a business degree from the prestigious Kelley School of Business, and a job offer from the tax department of one of the top accounting firms in the country.

"So, you never found any further information about your parents?" Ethan asked, pulling Alexa's focus back to the present.

"No. I didn't look for them after that day. I figured they didn't want to know me, so was no point trying to find them. If I actually managed to locate them or learned that they had died after abandoning me, I would just have to relive the disappointment and rejection."

Ethan stroked her arm reassuringly. "Amor, I do not believe your parents abandoned you."

"I agree with Ethan," Elijah stated.

Alexa looked back and forth between the two incredibly handsome men. "What are you talking about? Are you saying my parents are alive?"

For whatever reason, even though she'd easily accepted everything that had been revealed to her so far, this information was the hardest to process. Not waiting for a reply, she spoke her thoughts as they came to her. "Of course they are; if I'm really a vampire, so are they." Alexa fought to contain the emotions that were welling up inside her.

"But, why? How could they just leave me all alone in that place?"

"To protect you, Alexa, from the war," Elijah said gently.

CHAPTER 12 - *The War*

"Many vampire couples, my wife and I included, have taken extreme steps to protect their children from this war. Some were placed with human families to hide until their powers emerged. Other families went into hiding, leaving the comfort and community of their vampire colonies to live in solitude. Some even enlisted the help of witches, at least those who could find a witch who was willing to consort with vampires."

Ethan placed his hand on Alexa's chin and gently turned her to face him. "I promise you, Amor, once you and Chloe are safe, we will find out what happened to your parents." She nodded slowly.

After giving her a moment, Elijah continued, "There exists a very old and powerful vampire, known as Lucias. Nearly seven hundred years ago, he started a movement, demanding that members of our race rise up and take our rightful place as the dominant people of this world, with him as the ruler, naturally. He and his followers see humans as inferior beings, meant to be slaves to our kind. Of course, the majority of our people saw him as a fanatic and refused to support his cause. After all, we are all partly human and are such a small minority that we fear complete annihilation if we were ever to be revealed to the humans. We are much stronger, but they outnumber us several thousand to one."

"Still, despite the insurmountable odds, Lucias and his group went on a rampage, attacking and killing humans for sport and all the while searching for and capturing young vampire females to breed children that he could raise to follow him. One taste of the blood of a carrier reveals the presence of the gene. They would wipe out entire villages in a matter of hours."

"It was during that same time that the black plague struck, wiping out millions of humans, which provided an excellent cover for the activities of Lucias' group. However, our people were not completely immune to the disease. It was not lethal to those of our kind, but any member of our race who ingested the blood of an infected human began to change, becoming stronger and faster. However, the increased strength and speed came at a price. This is what birthed some of the myths about our kind. The infected were sensitive to sunlight and silver and required blood daily. Over time, infected members of the race developed a nearly insatiable bloodlust, often attacking other members of the race in an attempt to quench their thirst. Those who were attacked also became infected."

Alexa sat there, eyes wide as she leaned into Ethan, completely engrossed in Elijah's recounting of the race's history.

"It was during that time that the group now known as The Agency was formed to police our people and contain the infected. Unfortunately, and despite exhaustive efforts to find a cure, it soon became obvious that the only timely solution was to terminate the diseased. Thus was born the Elite, a group of specially-trained warriors brought together with the sole purpose of eliminating the infected before they destroyed us all. Nearly all of Lucias' followers perished in those times and he remained quiet for many years. So long, in fact, that many seemed to forget or forgive his previous misdeeds, accepting him back into our society with open arms. So many had been lost in those dark times, it seemed we could not afford to cast any aside as we attempted to rebuild and move forward. Then, close to three hundred years ago, the disappearances started."

"Lucias?" Alexa asked as she now sat on the edge of her seat, with Chloe playing happily on the floor beside her and Ethan gently stroking her back.

"Yes. Of course, we did not know he was responsible in the beginning. It started off slowly, one or two at a time, spread out around the world. It took weeks to get news about the other colonies back then, so no one realized that the incidents were related. The missing were always teenagers who had recently undergone the transformation. In retrospect, it was very clever to target the newly changed who were easily influenced and whose disappearances would not raise too much suspicion."

"Like human teenagers, our kind can be quite temperamental during that stage of life and it was almost a tradition for them to run off from their families in an attempt to assert their independence and explore their new powers. Ethan was particularly challenging during that time," he smirked in his son's direction. "However, they would always turn up after a few months, maybe a year, of being on their own, but this was different and they were staying gone much longer without word."

"A year on their own? I can't fathom letting Chloe just leave like that. Why didn't anyone search for them?"

"Ahh, yes. Well, parents of our race have a bit of an advantage in that department. We can sense our descendants through the blood bond that exists. The more closely related we are, the stronger the sense. So even though these children were gone, their parents always had a general idea of where they were and that they were safe. Then one day, fifty children who had not yet undergone the transformation were all taken in what turned out to be a well-coordinated and patiently planned attack."

"The bond does something else, as well. Elder members of a family can strongly influence the actions of their descendants. In fact, the bond with a very old member of the race, like Lucias or myself, can be so powerful that any direct command given cannot be disobeyed. To do so would cause unbearable pain. As you can imagine, that kind of power is easily abused. Lucias has used that bond to enforce his will and build the most lethal and loyal army imaginable."

"For the last three hundred years, our people have lived in fear. Lucias has been far less conspicuous in his quest for power, no longer openly slaying humans and there has not been a disappearance in nearly twenty years. However, there have been rumors about a new kind of soldier under Lucias' command. Those who claim to have seen them speak of enhanced abilities, movement so quick they are difficult even for vampire eyes to track. There are whispers that they are infected, that Lucias has discovered a way to control the virus that plagued our kind so long ago and use it to his advantage."

"But our people have not been idle. The Elite have spent these many years recruiting and training new members to battle Lucias' forces when the time comes. And The Agency has implemented training programs in all of the remaining vampire colonies around the world, teaching our people to fight, to protect themselves."

"So where is Lucias now?" Alexa inquired.

"That we do not know, which makes him all the more dangerous. He has been lurking in the shadows, waiting patiently for his opportunity. You must understand; Ethan's only desire in leaving was to keep you safe, to let you have a normal life." Elijah looked at his son and Alexa saw so much love in his eyes. "His mother and I realize what a leap of faith it took for him to tell us about you and Chloe. We would have remained silent, but it seems fate has intervened. I was not certain when I met you that you were the girl Ethan described as his soul mate, but I had my suspicions because of Chloe."

At that, Alexa looked up at Ethan, feeling the sting of tears in her eyes yet again. She hadn't imagined their connection. It was real. He was real and he was here with her again.

Elijah stood and walked to the window as he continued. "When I completed your blood work I knew it had to be you. And just a few minutes later, I received word about Dr. James and his practice."

Alexa's gaze shot to Elijah. "Dr. James, Chloe's dentist?

"Yes. He was killed two days ago, along with several members of his staff. His clinic was burned to the ground to cover it up, but not before The Elite intercepted his posts to a dental community website about his findings in Chloe's X-rays. Did he discuss it with you?"

"No, he didn't get the chance. An emergency patient came in before he could view Chloe's X-rays, but he had done an initial exam of her teeth and gums and assured me that whatever was wrong, it did not appear to be related to her teeth. She was screaming the whole time we were there, so I decided to leave. I had already been referred to your practice, so I just thought I would reschedule with him if I didn't get answers."

"Based on what he posted, the X-rays revealed the fangs that you saw earlier tonight. As with all of our kind, they are only visible at certain times, usually when we feed, but they sometimes present themselves in response to intense emotions. Like us, we believe our enemy has been closely monitoring the Internet, looking for any activity that would reveal the coming of the child from the prophecy. We cannot be certain yet, but it is very unlikely that Dr. James' death was an accident. We believe Lucias is getting close."

"Wait, what prophecy?" Alexa questioned.

Ethan ran his hand down his face as he sighed. "I am not sure where to start."

Elijah placed his hand on his son's shoulder to offer reassurance. "Start at the beginning, my son, with your mother."

CHAPTER 13 - *The Prophecy*

He took Alexa's hand in both of his as he began. "My mother is a seer. She has visions of things that have not yet come to pass."

"So, what, you're saying she can see the future?"

"Yes. It is an unpredictable talent that she cannot entirely control. Visions often come to her randomly, but with a great deal of concentration she can focus to see a specific person or event. Her ability is strongest in relation to people close to her, mainly family. Moments after I was born, a very powerful vision completely overcame her before she was even able to hold me in her arms. She saw the end of the war. I was to father a female child with a woman who bore a unique birthmark. This birthmark." He lightly touched the spot behind Alexa's ear where the mark lay hidden beneath her hair. The light touch sent a small tremor through Alexa's body. "That child would grow to become more powerful than any member of our kind to come before and would control the fate of our people."

"And you think Chloe is this child? This is why you left us?" Alexa asked, her voice barely above a whisper as she struggled to wrap her mind around the gravity of what was happening.

Ethan glanced at his father briefly. "Yes, I left because of the prophecy, to protect you and Chloe. We do not know the outcome of the war; only that her coming signals the start of open war that also ends with her. She is what Lucias is after, what he has been searching for for nearly two hundred years. He believes that whoever possesses the child can control her powers. Above all things, he craves power, to rule our people and the humans alike. And, trust me when I say, if he cannot have her, he will stop at nothing to keep her from fighting against him." Ethan stood and began to pace as he proceeded.

"I still don't understand why you left. Why couldn't we have gone away with you?"

"While my mother's talent is rare, she is not the only one of our kind who is able to see the future. Lucias has at least one equally powerful seer in his employ who saw my future, my child, and he has been waiting and watching, trying to find her every day since he first heard the prophecy."

"How can you know that?"

The question prompted Elijah to intervene. "Perhaps it is best if I continue with this part of the story. Ethan was very young when it all happened." As Elijah began to recount that night, it was almost as if he was back in that place, the home he and his beautiful wife had built, well over two hundred years ago.

It was late in the evening in a cozy Spanish villa, where a seven-year-old Ethan lay with his head in his mother's lap as she stroked his overly long wavy hair, softly singing one of his favorite songs in Spanish. Josephine loved to keep his beautiful chestnut locks long, despite his father's feigned disapproval. Elijah had never been very good at denying his beautiful wife anything she desired; the length of their son's hair was no exception. Ethan's eyes began to feel heavy as his mother's words drifted through his mind.

Amor con fortuna
me muestra enemiga.
No sé qué me diga.
No sé lo que quiero,
pues busqué mi daño,
Yo mesmo m'engaño,
me meto do muero.
Y, muerto, no spero
salir de fatiga,
No se que me diga.
Amor me persigue
con muy cruda guerra
Por mar y por tierra
Fortuna me sigue.
¿Quien ay que desligue
amor donde liga?
No sé qué me diga.
Fortuna traidora
me hase mudança
Y amor, esperança
Que siempre enpeora
Jamás no mejora

Mi suerte enemiga
No sé que me diga..."

His raven-haired little sister, Camille, was just a few feet away playing with a new toy their father had brought home the night before, clapping and giggling as the wooden top spun and bobbled before eventually falling on its side. Her giggling was quickly replaced by whining as she toddled over to her mother and brother, her perfect ringlets bouncing with each step. She held the little top out in front of her, demanding one of them spin it for what must have been the hundredth time.

Josephine gently lifted the head of the now-sleeping Ethan's to lay him down as she attended to her demanding two-year-old. She knelt down beside Camille and looked into her bright green-grey eyes before placing a little kiss on the tip of her button nose. Taking the top and placing it on the floor in front of them, she began a quiet countdown, trying not to disturb Ethan, "Uno, dos...," but before reaching three she was overcome by a vision causing her to fall backward against the end table that housed the oil lamp providing light in the small playroom. The loud crash awakened Ethan with a start and summoned Elijah from the parlor where he was reading.

Camille began to wail, scared and confused as her mother lay still on the ground, her eyes rolled back into her head as the fire from the lamp began to spread across the floor. Elijah dashed around the corner, retrieved a wet rag from the wash basin and tossed it over the growing fire, stamping it out entirely before rushing to his wife's side.

He sat on the ground, lifting her head into his lap as he consoled his terrified children.

"Ethan, Camille, come sit beside your papa. It is all right, your mama is just having a dream. Do you remember what she told you about her dreams?"

Ethan nodded as he slowly approached his parents. Camille was too young to fully understand, but she adored her big brother, so she gripped his hand tightly and followed behind him, her wailing reduced to a slight sniffle as she sucked vigorously on her thumb.

Josephine's eyes returned to normal and she immediately looked up at her husband, her face stricken with panic as she attempted to sound calm, "Mi vida, we must leave now. We have only moments. It is Lucias."

Not one to question his wife's power, Elijah scooped Camille into his arms as he helped Josephine to her feet.

"Ethan, cariño, take my hand. We are going on an adventure." Josephine smiled at her son, trying to comfort his fears as they fled the only home her children had ever known.

They followed Elijah to the study, where he passed Camille to her mother and, using his supernatural strength and speed, he pushed aside an enormous bookcase, revealing a secret tunnel he had built shortly after Ethan's birth and Josephine's accompanying premonition.

Josephine gripped Camille tightly as she jumped down into the darkness. "Ciera los ojos, cariña," she whispered through her daughter's bouncy curls. While Josephine and Elijah could see perfectly in the darkness, both children were many years away from reaching their preternatural potential and would be completely blind in the lightless tunnel.

She hesitated just long enough to see Elijah drop through the opening with Ethan securely in his arms before she sprinted down the long corridor.

Elijah gently placed Ethan on the ground. "Stand right here, my son. Do not move. I must close the entryway."

With only a faint amount of light filtering through the opening above, Ethan could barely see anything and only felt a slight breeze from his father's rapid movements as he jumped back up to the floor of their former home and replaced the bookcase that concealed the tunnel.

Ethan heard the soft thud of his father's feet hitting the ground a few feet in front of him, followed by a loud crash above and a blood-curdling scream.

"God, forgive me." Elijah whispered as he picked up his terrified son and rushed off after his wife and daughter. In all the chaos, he had forgotten their human cook, who had remained in the kitchen. Her eldest son usually came to escort her home by now. The tear that escaped Elijah's eye was immediately whisked away by the force of his speed as he ran. She was gone, and if her son had not already met the danger on the road, he would soon. As much as he cared for the woman and the boy he had delivered nearly fifteen years ago, he could not risk his family. Going back would mean certain death, but still his heart ached with their loss.

A few minutes later, Elijah bounded up through the opening at the end of the tunnel, finding himself in the field several miles from their home where Josephine and Camille waited.

Josephine immediately recognized the pain in her husband's expression and reached for his hand in silence. She already knew. She saw the fate of the cook and her young son, but could do nothing to prevent it without damning her own children. She had hoped Elijah would not know, at least for a while, but it was done. Her own heart ached with the loss of the humans who had helped to care for her children all these years, but now was not the time for grief.

"Mi vida, we must keep going. It will not be long before Lucias discovers how we escaped. Lucias has already called for his seer, Asana, to join him and she is less than two days journey from here. Asana is very powerful and is no doubt focused on Ethan. He was ignorant to my ability before, but once she is in our home, near my things, she will know I have sight and he will not be so careless in his future pursuits of our family. He will keep Asana by his side at all times."

Elijah gently squeezed Josephine's hand. "My love, I will always follow you."

She smiled and stood up on her toes, shifting Camille slightly to the side, as she pressed a light kiss on his lips.

"There is a ship leaving for the Americas in a few hours. It is the last one for several weeks. We must make for the coast and barter passage. Lucias will be forced to wait to pursue us, giving us time to reach the settlement of our people in the new land and contact The Elite. They are our only hope."

"We boarded the ship that night and headed off to the Americas. Once we reached the settlement and contacted The Elite, we were immediately moved to their compound near Boston and guaranteed their protection. That was around the time we first met Barb," Elijah chuckled as he recounted the memory.

"Barb, the nurse I met this morning?" Alexa inquired.

"Yes, the one and only. I do not know what we would have done without her."

"And I don't know what I would have done without all of you pestering me all these years," Barb said, chuckling in the doorway.

Alexa had been so engrossed she hadn't noticed the woman's entrance, but the sight of her was comforting. Ethan stood and rushed over to the plump woman, scooping her up into a big bear hug as she kissed his cheek.

"Well, it's good to see you, too, boy. You've stayed away far too long," she said swatting his bottom as he set her back on her feet.

"But that is impossible." Alexa shook her head, feeling thoroughly confused. "She's human, and that was like, two hundred years ago, right?"

"Exactly how do you know I'm just a human, child?" Barb asked, obviously enjoying herself.

"Well, it's kind of hard to describe. I didn't actually listen to your thoughts, but I'm sure that I could have." She blushed slightly at how cocky she sounded. "Your mind doesn't feel like theirs do, it feels, human, I guess. I didn't realize it at first. I suppose because I was laboring under the delusion that everyone was human, but after being around the three of you," she gestured to Ethan, Elijah, and Chloe, "the difference has become quite obvious. I'm pretty sure I could identify any vampire that got close enough now."

"Interesting. You are partially correct. Barb is human, though I doubt you would be able to read her mind," Elijah said smiling at the nurse.

"You might be strong, child, but I can guarantee you can't crack into this hard head of mine," Barb stated surely, tapping her temple.

"She is an extremely powerful witch, probably the most powerful in the world, though she would never own up to it. She protects her mind with magic," Ethan said, still smiling at his old friend.

"You're right, I am far older than I look, though I look plenty old. It goes against the code of my people to use magic to extend one's life beyond their natural potential, but all those years ago I bound myself to this family," she said, pointing at Elijah and Ethan, "and I swore to protect them until this damn war is finally ended."

"Yes, she is a stubborn old woman and, though she could have passed on the responsibility and her knowledge to the younger generations, she says she could not trust anyone else to see it done right. Not to mention, most of her kind are not nearly as tolerant of our race as Barb." Elijah smiled as he spoke of the sassy old witch. It was obvious that he was very fond of her.

"We had been living with The Elite as protected guests on their compound for a few weeks, but were forced to remain indoors at all times for fear of Lucias' seer catching a glimpse. You see, the compound is protected by a blocking spell that keeps anyone on the outside from seeing inside in any way, including through visions of the future. Unfortunately, that spell requires physical barriers as well, which is why we could not venture outside. Trying to keep a rambunctious little boy like Ethan contained for so long proved most challenging." Elijah looked at his son, all of the love and affection he felt evident in his warm green eyes.

"Ethan, being the resourceful young man that he was, had managed to slip away from his mother one day while she was playing with Camille. He was mere moments from stepping outside and into potential disaster, when he found himself frozen in place with his hand on the door."

"Imagine my surprise. My heart pounding with the anticipation of freedom, to see the sun and play outside in the yard and suddenly I was completely immobilized. I could not even move my eyes. I began to panic, thinking the enemy had found me as my parents had warned me about time and again."

"Foolish boy. I ripped into him like hounds on fox about disobeying his folks. I had half a mind to pull down his trousers and give him the spanking of a lifetime for being so stupid. I left him stuck there for a good long while to teach him a lesson while I took my sweet time fetching his parents." she recalled, moving to take a seat on the floor next to Chloe, who smiled broadly at her new companion. Barb groaned with the effort of squatting down.

"Yes, unfortunately we received a fairly sound tongue-lashing, as well, for letting Ethan out of our sight with everything that was at stake. She had not even bothered to tell us who she was before she started with the lecture, but by the time we reached Ethan we had been properly introduced and, once her initial irritation with our carelessness wore off, she was quite pleasant company. Of course, we were less than pleased with Ethan running off as he did."

"Father, let us not forget that my little stunt gave Barb the idea for the charm that gave us back our freedom."

"Don't go gettin' cocky, boy. I would have thought of it on my own eventually," she chided. "Go on, show it to her."

Elijah rolled up his sleeve, revealing an intricate tattoo, identical to the one on Ethan's chest. The sight of it took her mind back to the last time she had seen it and her faced flushed at the thought. "She placed a blocking spell that is represented by these markings on each member of our family. So, long as she lives, no seer can track our paths."

"Yes, quite an ingenious idea, if I do say so myself, but it has its limitations since it also blocks your pretty wife from seeing you."

"A small price to pay, and I think it has given my love some unexpected and overdue peace over all these years. It has been nice living in the present for a change, not constantly being obsessed with the future."

Just then, a faint ringing sound echoed from across the room. Elijah moved to his desk, his movements only a blur to Alexa's still-human eyes, and retrieved his phone from the drawer.

"Well, speak of the devil," he said, smiling wide, but that smile immediately faded when he placed the phone to his ear.

"Slow down, my love. Yes, we are all here," he said, his expression worried. "How long? I understand. I will call Camille from the car," he said, slipping the phone into his pocket and rushing over to help Barb up from the floor. "We have to leave immediately," he stated, his tone urgent.

✧

Ethan grabbed Chloe and Alexa, each in one arm, and whisked them out to the back parking lot. Elijah was on his heels with Barb in tow, holding the large woman in his arms as if she weighed nothing at all.

"What's happening?" Alexa questioned, her voice cracking with panic. She could feel the anxiety pouring off of Ethan and Elijah.

"My wife, Josephine, had a vision. Lucias' men have found my facility. She only saw them outside; the spell keeps her from knowing what happens after that. We have some time, maybe a few hours as it was almost light out when they were here, but it is best not to linger. I will not risk a fight with you and my granddaughter near," he declared protectively.

"Amor, I must go move your car away from here. We do not want to leave any clues to your identity for them to discover," Ethan said passing Chloe to her. "Stay here with my father. I'll drive it to the parking garage around the corner; it will only take a few minutes."

"Then where are we going?" she asked of no one in particular.

"To my home; to Josephine," Elijah said.

"No, we have to go back to my house first," Alexa said defiantly, her voice cracking. "We have to get Tilly; I can't leave her there locked up alone all night."

"It may not be safe. If they have found my father's office and Chloe's dentist, it is possible they already know where you live."

Tears began to well up in Alexa's eyes. "Ethan, I can't just leave her there. Elijah said we have a few hours. If I leave her there and they come, she'll try to protect the house, and they'll kill her. Please, she's my only friend. She's been there when no one else has."

Ethan squeezed his eyes shut as the guilt her pointed words evoked washed over him. It would take more than a night for her to forgive his terrible mistake in leaving her. He knew that and so he had to do whatever it took to earn her forgiveness.

He wrapped his arms around her and Chloe, pulling them close. "Then we will go and get her."

"Father, take Barb and go to Mother; we will meet you there shortly."

"Be careful, my son, and be quick. Your mother will not like us separating. You know how she worries."

CHAPTER 14 - *Tilly's Rescue*

Alexa was silent as they started their drive back to her house in Fishers. Every couple of minutes she glanced over at Ethan in the driver's seat of her Lexus 570 SUV to assure herself that all of this was real. Ethan was really back in her life and she was in love with him; even if he wasn't technically human. Who was she to judge? If she believed everything she had learned over the past few hours, neither was she. As much as it should scare her, she accepted that this was her life now.

"Tell me more about your, um, our people," Alexa said, breaking the silence and trying to ease some of the tension. She knew she was asking a lot of Ethan to go back to her house for Tilly and she felt guilty about how she had gone about it. "Where do they live?"

"All over the world, anywhere humans live. Our people can exist among them completely undetected, but many choose to live in large communities, or colonies. The war sent many away from that way of life, but over the last few decades they have started to rebuild. Unlike what is suggested by the myths, we eat human food, go out in the sun, go to church, have children, and mostly live fairly ordinary lives whenever possible."

She tilted her head back and asked, "So I could have met others? How many are there?"

"I do not know an exact number, but the last I knew, our population was nearly one million, spread all over the world. We have a government, my father mentioned it, The Agency that administers our laws and keeps all of our records."

Though she already knew the answer, there was another question that was burning into Alexa's brain. "You said you eat food, but you need blood, too. How often do you have to feed?"

Ethan sighed. "Yes, all of our kind requires human blood to sustain us. As a result of the mutation, it is nearly impossible for our bodies to generate new blood cells. We feed on humans as a means of transfusion, and because we crave it," he said glancing at her hungrily.

She nodded, looking down as she whispered, "Do you, um, kill people?"

Ethan placed his hand on her shoulder, keeping the other on the steering wheel. "No, Amor, I have never killed an innocent human. We only need to feed once a month, sometimes less, unless we are injured or allow another to feed on us. When we do feed, we only take what is needed, usually what one would give if they donated blood."

"And the people you feed on don't remember it because you can erase their memories," she stated recalling the information from earlier.

"Yes, but if a human did happen to leave with their memory of a feeding, or some other interaction, intact, there are those of my kind who are able to intercept reports of the information. The Agency constantly monitors the Internet and other news outlets. We have people in human government, police, and the military to help protect the secret of our kind."

"Wow, that's impressive, and a little scary," Alexa said shifting nervously in her seat.

"Are you alright, Amor?"

"I'm sorry, I just need a minute." She waved around pointing at Ethan and Chloe. "All of this, you, everything is a bit overwhelming and beyond disconcerting to think that you have lived among us, among humans, that is, for so long without being discovered. It makes me wonder about all of the ridiculous conspiracy theories I've ever heard. Maybe all of it is true."

"It is possible that many of those things are true. That is something I have learned over many years. Myths, legends, rumors, whatever you want to call them, often have some basis in fact."

She sat there for a moment, processing everything, and then asked, "Exactly how old are you, Ethan?" Not certain that it mattered at this point, she nevertheless wanted to know. She wanted to know everything about him.

He looked a little nervous as he replied, "Two- hundred and four."

"Well, shit," Alexa sat there for another moment.

"Ok, so what about your accent? Your dad said you lived in a Spanish villa. Is that where you're from?"

"Yes, España, Spain. My mother was born there and my father traveled there for work. They met, fell in love, and were married within a few months. That was well over two- hundred and fifty years ago. They waited quite a while to have children. My father wanted to keep my mother all to himself, for a while, at least."

"You know, that day at the diner, you told me before you hardly spoke to your parents anymore. I actually thought they were the big secret you were so concerned about telling me. I figured they were really old-fashioned and wouldn't approve of me because I was American or something."

"That was true. As I told you, we had not spoken in many years until I went to see my mother that night after we swam with the dolphins."

The reference caused Alexa to grab her necklace. "Why did you make me promise to wear this?"

He glanced at her hand briefly before returning his eyes to the road. "For protection. After I saw my mother, I went to Barb and asked her to make a charm to shield you. There is a spell on it, much like the one in my tattoo. As long as you wear it, your future is blocked from those with the ability to view it. I had to know you were protected."

Alexa couldn't help the smile that spread across her face at his declaration. "So what about the other vampire stuff? Is it only the infected that the common myths apply to?"

Ethan chuckled slightly. "Yes, only the infected suffer from such strange afflictions. I suppose you would expect our kind to be allergic to the sun, silver, garlic, crucifixes and holy water. These are the things you have learned from, how do you say, popular culture about vampires."

"Actually, right now the popular vampires sparkle in the sun and drink the blood of animals, but I learned the other things when I was younger. It's kind of ironic; I've always loved movies and books about vampires. I even fantasized about being one."

"And now how do you feel about them?"

She pondered for a moment before answering. "I love them, at least some of them," she said, reaching over and placing her hand on Ethan's thigh. "I know how I feel about you; despite everything, that has never changed. I tried to hate you. I wanted to hate you for leaving me. Perhaps it's foolish, but no matter how hard I tried, I couldn't erase the love I felt for you. Maybe I'm just a hopeless romantic, but I believe that true love can conquer all things, even a broken heart."

Ethan placed his hand over hers and laced their fingers together. "I believe this, too, Amor. I will forever regret losing sight of that belief when I left all those months ago. I thought I was doing what was best for you. I was a fool. I hope that one day you can forgive my mistake."

He pulled her hand up to his face and gently kissed her knuckles.

Alexa looked up and saw they had entered her neighborhood. Ethan killed the headlights and eased the car into her driveway as he turned to her.

"Wait here for a moment, Amor. I want to get out and look around before you go inside."

Alexa opened her mouth to protest, concerned for Tilly, considering how long it had been since she was last let out to relieve herself, but Ethan was gone before the first word escaped her lips.

Tilly hadn't had an accident in the house since she was a puppy, but Alexa wasn't keen on the idea of cleaning up a Great Dane-sized mess, so she hopped out of the car, opened the back door, and started unbuckling the straps to Chloe's car seat.

Ethan was just being paranoid. He had been gone for months and nothing had happened. His mother's vision showed the men at the clinic at first light, so they still had several hours.

With a very drowsy Chloe on her hip, she moved around to the driver's side and reached through the window to hit the button to open the garage door. Feeling a little on edge, she was thankful that she had purchased a new garage door and opener a couple weeks ago. It was practically silent as the beige door slid upwards, revealing her compulsively organized garage. The prior set up would have alerted everyone within five miles that she was home.

Shit. It occurred to her that, with their supercharged hearing, any member of the race within five miles would probably still be able to hear it.

She stood there in the driveway just outside the garage, listening. She didn't hear anything, not even the crickets that were normally singing on such a clear July night. Even Tilly remained silent, evidence that the garage door was as quiet as she thought. One of the only things that could get the big couch potato excited was the sound of her family coming home.

Ethan must have startled the crickets while checking out the yard.

Alexa quietly moved through the garage over to the door that led into the house. Holding her breath, she reached out with her talent, searching for that now-familiar feeling of a vampire's presence. Not finding anything unusual, she grabbed for the handle, her hand sliding off from all of the sweat on her palm. She held her hand up in the moonlight to see it shaking with anxiety. Letting out a half-hearted laugh, she thought to herself,

I really have to get a grip. Everything is fine, I'm just freaking out because of all the insane shit I found out in the last few hours. All of it existed before I knew about it, so what's really changed? I'm just being paranoid, but God, they weren't kidding when they said 'ignorance is bliss'.

She leaned her head back trying to peek around at Chloe who was fast asleep. Steeling her nerves, she quickly twisted the knob and stepped inside her home while she reached out and flipped the light switch.

As the light chased away the darkness, she glanced around, seeing everything in its place. Everything seemed perfectly fine, except that Tilly hadn't come sliding across the hardwood floor to greet them as was her custom.

"Come on, Tilly! Let's go outside, girl!" Alexa called. Still nothing. Her heart started pounding as she rushed down the hallway towards her room, more specifically, her bed where Tilly loved to snooze. Maybe she was sick, or worse. Great Danes didn't have a very long life expectancy, six to ten years being the norm, and Tilly was rapidly approaching that range. Just a couple of years ago they had a major scare when Tilly developed a case of bloat, something typical of large, deep-chested dogs. Her stomach had twisted in her abdominal cavity, cutting the blood supply off completely which would have killed her if Alexa hadn't noticed something was off as she was getting ready for bed. Having fully educated herself on the potential problems of owning such a large dog, Alexa immediately recognized what was going on and rushed Tilly to the emergency veterinary clinic. After several hours, an emergency surgery, and several thousand dollars in vet bills, Alexa was gratefully driving home with a rather groggy and confused Tilly. That night had taught Alexa just how precious life is and had further cemented the bond with her canine companion.

Just as Alexa reached the doorway to her bedroom, she slowed, thinking she had heard something off to her left in the living room. Realizing her mistake too late, she felt the strange presence of the vampire's mind just as he spoke.

"Ah, finally. I've been waiting a dreadful long time for you, love."

Alexa froze as the stranger's strongly-accented voice sent a chill up her spine that went as deep as the marrow.

Slowly turning to face the intruder, while simultaneously moving

Chloe as far away as she could in the moment, Alexa straightened her spine and asked, "Who are you? What do you want? I don't have much cash or jewelry in the house. Take anything you want and just leave. I won't call the police if you leave now." She knew he didn't want money or any other material possession, but she needed to buy some time.

The responding laugh that echoed around the room was nothing short of sinister.

"Sorry, poppet, but what I'm after is right there in your pretty little arms."

Instinctively, Alexa took a step back, her mind racing, trying to find a way to escape.

In a flash, the stranger was standing directly in front of her, covering the distance across the living room in an instant.

Alexa's heart kicked into overdrive as the truth barreled down on her. This was a member of the race, too fast and strong for her to defend herself against on her best day. But this vampire was vastly different from Ethan and Elijah. The irises of his eyes were the color of blood, and his skin was as pale as if he had never stepped into the sunlight.

"Why do you want my daughter?" she inquired, hoping to stall and give Ethan a chance to come rescue them. Unfortunately, she then considered the possibility that the resulting altercation could cause her to lose Ethan and Chloe in one fell swoop.

"Listen 'ere love, I just have orders to bring back the lil' one, but I wouldn't mind having a bit of fun with you first. You choose, hand 'er over now, or I'll take my time enjoyin' myself and tearin' you to bits before I take 'er anyway."

The fear was washing over her as she closed her eyes, silently praying for courage. Alexa felt her legs start to shake and she was powerless to control it, but no matter how afraid she was, no matter what would happen to her, she would never give up her child. She would die first.

Her thoughts turned to Chloe, to her first day of kindergarten, her graduation, her wedding, all the future moments that Alexa would miss if she gave up hope now. With those images strengthening her resolve, she straightened her spine and looked the enemy in the eye as she spat, "Fuck you! You'll have to pry her from my cold, dead hands, and even then, I'll haunt you for eternity."

The viciousness in Alexa's tone surprised her.

The unnaturally handsome stranger's mouth turned up into a devious and excited smile. "Have it your way, love. I'm going to enjoy this."

In a blur, the intruder had his hand firmly clasped around Alexa's throat as he groaned into her ear, "Best set the lil' one down for this part, love." He ran his tongue up the side of her face as a tear slipped from her eye.

Her mind was racing, trying desperately to find a way to spare her daughter as she moved to lay her down on the couch a couple of feet away. It was difficult to form any thought over the panic she felt with the monster's hand confidently gripping her neck. She would die, but she would provide the distraction that would allow Ethan to save their daughter. Ethan would protect Chloe.

Once Chloe was safely laid down on the couch, the stranger yanked Alexa up and pulled her tightly against him and used his free hand to grab her ass. Panic washed over her once again as she felt his apparent arousal through his pants.

He started dragging her towards the bedroom. Alexa didn't fight; she didn't want Chloe to wake up and experience any of this horror. All she could think about was keeping him occupied for as long as possible to give Ethan and Chloe a chance.

As they approached the closed door to her bedroom, he moved his hand up her neck, wrenching her head back to expose the vulnerable arteries. He opened his mouth wide as the razor-sharp fangs dropped from hunger-swollen gums. He leaned around, making sure she could clearly see him. He wanted to shock her; he wanted to see her fear as she realized what he was. Knowing about vampires and seeing one in the violent throes of bloodlust were two totally different things. Despite her best efforts, Alexa couldn't contain the whimper that passed her lips and the look of terror that flashed across her face.

Satisfied and desperate to taste her fear, the intruder wrenched her head back again as he kicked the door open, preparing to sink his fangs in, not to kill her, just to feed. He had great plans for how he would pass the evening with Alexa before he finally killed her and took Chloe. His master needn't know that he had a bit of fun carrying out his mission.

Alexa heard her bedroom door slam against the wall, followed by a vicious growl unlike any she had ever heard. She squeezed her eyes shut as she waited for the pain that didn't come. She felt her assailant fall back from her as the grip on her throat loosened, though she could feel the sting left by his nails as they slid away.

Opening her eyes, she saw a flash of fawn-colored fur as Tilly landed on top of the intruder, giving Alexa a precious few moments to attempt an escape. She ran for the door, feeling a cavern open up in her heart at leaving Tilly alone with this monster. He was a vampire; there was only one way it would end, but she had to think of Chloe first.

Using the surge of adrenaline, Alexa dashed into the living room to scoop up Chloe, who was now sitting up awake on the soft leather couch. Once Chloe was safely in her arms, she sprinted towards the garage door, screaming for Ethan and silently praying for Tilly. The door was open and Alexa felt a strong gush of air as she approached, followed by an ear-piercing roar behind her that stopped her in her tracks.

She turned toward the source of the noise as she started backing out the door, expecting to see her attacker barreling down on her once again. Instead, she was met with an image that was both terrifying and comforting.

Ethan stood just outside her bedroom, his body shaking with anger, his arm outstretched and covered in blood as he gripped the still-beating heart of the intruder whose body slumped to the ground and grew still. In the doorway, all she could see of Tilly was her giant paws scratching aimlessly at the air. Holding Chloe tightly against her, she rushed back to her dear friend's side. Her hand shot up to her mouth and she felt the sting of tears in her eyes as she looked down. She knelt down beside her long-time companion, covering her worn blue jeans with blood that was rapidly pouring from the gaping wound in Tilly's neck. Alexa could see the panic in her dog's normally calm and gentle eyes.

Lightly stroking Tilly's head Alexa whispered, "Shh, shh, it's okay. You are such a good girl, Tilly. Momma loves you so much."

She felt Ethan's strong hand on her shoulder as she let loose the sob that was rising in her throat. She knew Tilly's injuries would take her soon. There would be no saving her brave companion from this tragedy. The grief washed over her as she saw the light in Tilly's eyes dimming more and more with each labored breath she took.

Chloe struggled in her arms, trying to get down to her best buddy as Alexa always called her, making her sob even harder. She could only hope Chloe was too young to remember any of this. Alexa moved her arm, attempting to adjust her grip on Chloe and prevent her from sliding down into the mess of blood. In that moment, Chloe went entirely limp and slipped down Alexa's side, landing on her bottom right next to Tilly's head. Before Alexa or Ethan could react, Chloe reached out and laid her tiny hand over Tilly's heart.

The gesture was so sweet; neither Alexa or Ethan had the heart to move her away despite all of the gore that surrounded them.

Alexa turned towards Ethan, leaning against his leg as she waited and cried, unable to make herself face this terrible loss.

"Mira, Amor. Something is happening."

Wiping the tears from her face, she opened her eyes and hesitantly turned to look over at Tilly. Her heart leapt as she saw Tilly struggling to stand as Chloe giggled, the wound on her neck miraculously closing before her eyes.

"I, I don't understand. Ethan, what happened? How is this possible?" At that point, a fresh round of tears began to flow, but this time they were tears of joy.

"I do not know, Amor. I have never witnessed anything like this in all my long life."

Tilly ducked down and licked Chloe on the cheek, evoking even more giggles before she turned on her wobbly legs and nuzzled Alexa.

"We must leave soon. I encountered three others outside and I imagine more will follow when they do not report back to their master. The rumors are true; these vampires are not like the rest of our kind. They are much more powerful."

Ethan stepped into the bathroom to wash the blood from his hands before continuing, "I would guess that we have a few hours at most."

"How could you possible fight three others like him at once?" she asked, gesturing toward the body lying on the wood floor.

"I am blessed with strength, unlike any other of our kind. I'm told even the infected from so many years ago could not match me. I suppose that must be true, since these vampires bear all of the signs of the infected, but they remain in control; they are not the beasts of the past I have heard described. Those vampires would not have been able to enter a human neighborhood and wait patiently with so many beating hearts nearby without giving in to their bloodlust and killing everyone within range of their senses."

Alexa cringed, thinking of all of the people who lived around her who were so close to danger.

Jill and Jesse. What if they had come to check on me like they have on so many nights before? She couldn't bear the thought, so she turned her mind to more practical matters.

"What are we going to do?" Alexa asked, looking around at the mess that was now her house. There was blood everywhere, but she was beyond caring with everything that had happened. She was just so happy to still be alive and that her family was intact. Not that she was one-hundred percent sure how that was possible. Tilly should have died.

"Take Chloe and go get cleaned up, change your clothes and throw everything you are wearing into a trash bag. Then pack one bag for you and Chloe. The bare essentials, just enough clothes for one night and anything you feel you cannot leave behind. You will not be able to come back here to retrieve anything once we leave."

"Never? But all of my clothes, our pictures, Chloe's toys?"

"Most of that can be replaced. Choose some photos to keep, but it must not look like you left. That will lead to too many questions that cannot be answered. More of Lucias' minions will come when these do not report back to their master. It may buy us some time if they believe you may still return. When we are safely away, you must call anyone who might come looking for you and make some excuse to keep them away. Perhaps that you went on vacation or had to tend to a family emergency out of town. Please understand, Amor. You cannot go back to your old life; it will never be safe for you now that the enemy has found you."

Alexa nodded slowly as the gravity of everything started to push down on her, making her body feel anchored to the floor with its weight. Through sheer force of will, she pushed it back and started thinking logically, making a mental checklist of everything she needed to grab as she scooped Chloe up into her arms.

The lockbox under my bed has all of our important documents. There's a box in the basement with all of the duplicate pictures and the spare diaper bag already has enough stuff for Chloe for the night. I think it's in the back of my car. I'll have to call Jesse and Jill right away; they'll be worried about me.

"Here," Ethan said as he entered the passcode and handed his phone to Alexa. "Put any contacts that you will need into my phone. Your phone could be used to track you, so it stays here as well."

"Wait, my car has GPS. If we leave in it, will they be able to track us?" Alexa asked with concern

"It is a possibility, but do not worry, I will take care of that." He stepped towards them, putting his arm around Alexa and placing his forehead against hers as he exhaled heavily. He moved back slightly, looking Alexa directly in the eye as he continued, "I know that I have hurt you, Amor. I will spend the rest of my life making it up to you and to Chloe. I swear to you that I will do whatever it takes to protect you both from anyone or anything that threatens to harm you ever again. Whatever it takes."

Alexa saw so much emotion, so much pain in his eyes, that it nearly broke her heart. And there was something more. As always, she could not clearly hear his thoughts, but she could sense an intense conflict within him as he spoke these words.

But it was not the time for questions, so she moved to do as Ethan requested, preparing to leave her old life behind forever.

CHAPTER 15 - *The Name's Cami*

Ethan made a couple of brief phone calls, and a black SUV with heavily tinted windows pulled into Alexa's driveway about thirty minutes later. Ethan opened the back passenger door and, much to her surprise, there was already a car seat in place for Chloe; though, given everything she had learned, she wasn't exactly certain it was even necessary for her somewhat-immortal child.

As she leaned in to secure Chloe in the seat, she looked towards the front, preparing to say hello and thank the driver for their help. However, due to what she assumed was vampire speed, the driver had already stepped out and was apparently behind her speaking in Spanish to Ethan as he loaded Tilly into the back.

She finished putting Chloe in the seat and reached back to give Tilly a reassuring pat before she turned to see the ravened-haired beauty standing on her lawn talking heatedly with Ethan, her face only inches away from his as she spoke, her long curly hair swaying as she seemingly gave him a piece of her mind. Alexa struggled to remember some Spanish from high school, but the words were passing too fast for her to decipher.

She felt jealously flare up and take over her mind, making her want to jump on the woman's back and beat her to a pulp for being so close to Ethan, though she knew she was no match for her preternatural strength, not to mention the variety of weapons that were strapped to her body. From this angle, Alexa could clearly see what appeared to be two short swords crossing her back, along with a gun on her hip and a dagger handle coming up from her black combat boot. She stood there watching, different scenarios playing through her mind. The interaction seemed intimate. Was this woman an ex-girlfriend, or, God, someone he was still involved with?

Alexa closed the door forcefully, drawing their attention. Seeing the irritation etched on her face, even in the darkness, Ethan swiftly moved to her side and gestured towards the stranger.

"Alexa, this is Camille, my baby sister."

A small sense of relief washed over her at hearing who this woman was, but she was still leery as she extended her hand to the obviously lethal woman. "It is so nice to meet you, Camille."

"The name's Cami, and I'm no one's baby," she stated flatly, completely ignoring Alexa and her offered hand.

Her tone was like a slap in the face to Alexa. She could feel the animosity towards her pouring off of the woman who seemed so unlike her brother. Ethan was kind and gentle, at least when he wasn't defending Alexa. This woman seemed hard, on edge, like she was always looking for her next fight. Based on her attire, Alexa assumed she must be some sort of soldier.

She didn't know what she had done that was so offensive to Ethan's sister, but she knew she was going to keep her mouth shut and stay out of the clearly dangerous woman's way.

As they stood there in awkward silence, Cami pulled a vibrating phone from her pocket and placed it to her ear. "Yes, sir. There are three bodies outside. I have not entered the house to check. No, no humans appear to have noticed anything yet. I understand."

Alexa looked at Ethan, who was watching his sister intently.

She slipped the phone back into the pocket of her black fatigues. "The team will be here in ten minutes. I suggest you be gone before they arrive. I have remained silent for you, brother, but I will not lie to my commander if asked a direct question, which their presence will surely raise," she said, flicking her hand towards Alexa and Chloe.

"You would betray me, your family?" Ethan asked, his anger evident.

Cami narrowed her green-grey eyes at Alexa as she responded to her brother's question. Her eyes were identical to Ethan's but they contained none of the warmth and affection that Alexa was accustomed to seeing in those eyes. These were full of anger and resentment. "I am already betraying my family by letting you take them from here. You are the one who turned your back on your own people, on your family, on me. And for what, because you are afraid of your destiny, of your duty to our kind. You have squandered your gifts all these years and Mother will always go along with you, so proud of her precious pacifist son," she spat as she returned her gaze to Ethan. "The Elite are my family now. I only help you because our father has commanded it. So take them and leave; I have work to do."

Ethan opened the passenger door and placed his hand on the small of Alexa's back, guiding her into the seat.

Closing the door, he turned to face his sister with a deep sadness in his eyes. "I am sorry that I am such a disappointment to you, sister. There are things that you do not know; they are not your burden to carry, but I hope someday you will understand and forgive me for my choices."

Faster than Alexa's eyes could follow, Ethan sped around the vehicle and was in the driver's seat. With one last glance at his sister standing in front of the garage door, her arms crossed over her chest, he shifted the car into reverse and backed out of the driveway.

Alexa turned around and watched as her home shrank into the distance before they turned out of the neighborhood and it was forever gone from her sight.

Ethan looked over at Alexa briefly and reached for her hand. "I am very sorry about my sister. That is not how I hoped for you to meet, but it could not be helped. We have to be certain the evidence of the attack at your home is removed, and only The Elite have the capability to discreetly contain such incidences with so little notice."

"Your sister is one of The Elite?"

"Yes, she was the first female ever invited to join. There have been others since, but she opened the door," Ethan said, obviously very proud of her.

"Why is she so angry with me? I could sense it coming off of her in waves."

"It is not you she is angry with, not really, but I think it is easier for her to direct it at you. She believes that you are the reason I left so many years ago."

"It seems like you have a bit of a pattern doing that," Alexa said, trying to be funny. She immediately regretted the comment when she felt the shift in Ethan's mood.

"She was right to call me a coward. I have lived in fear for so long, always running from my destiny, from you."

"But you came back to me, that's all that matters now," she said, squeezing his hand.

They sat in silence for a few moments before Ethan began speaking, his voice sounding as if he was off in another place.

"When I went through the change, when my abilities surfaced, I was so arrogant. Like so many other young vampires, I left, wanting to break free from my parents and their rules. It was different for my parents; it was far more dangerous for me to be on my own, but I was too selfish and stupid to care. They had warned me that Lucias would be looking for me ever since that night we escaped from Spain. But even with my powers only newly emerged, it was obvious that my strength and speed were extraordinary. And I had Barb's spell protecting me, so I thought I was invincible. I traveled all over the country, using my ability to control minds to get whatever I needed, or wanted. I stayed away, torturing my parents for over seven months."

"A few months after I left, my mother started having visions. She could not see my future because of the spell, but she could see my presence in the futures of those I was around. Then there were the reports of the attacks on the colonies. It took some time to piece it together, but eventually she saw the pattern. Lucias was using his seer to track me through similar visions and his men were attacking the colonies I had visited, torturing and killing anyone he thought had knowledge of me."

He took a deep breath. "Dozens perished because of my arrogance, while I was having the time of my life. When they realized what was happening, my parents used the blood bond to find me out West. It was then that my mother revealed the details of the prophecy to me. She told me of the woman I would love," he reached up and stroked the side of Alexa's neck, "and the extraordinary child she would give me. How the future of our people was tied to my fate."

"That is a lot of pressure for a young man," Alexa said, trying to imagine what it must have been like for him to carry such a heavy burden.

"Yes, Amor. I was so riddled with guilt over the deaths I had caused, that I could not bear the thought of anyone's life depending on me again. I refused to accept that my future was not my own to choose. So I went home and secluded myself, avoiding anyone who was not protected by Barb's magic, for fear of showing up in their future's streams."

"My mother had seen that Lucias would no longer pursue me once I was fully matured, instead turning his focus towards the child I would father. The year that I reached that milestone, Camille was recruited by The Elite, despite our mother's protests, having shown great promise in the training program of a nearby colony. She was young and so eager to please her new comrades. She told them of my abilities, causing them to pursue me endlessly, hoping to persuade me to join their ranks."

"Her ambition clouded her judgment; she wanted so desperately to prove herself. She revealed the prophecy to them, which is something my mother has yet to forgive her for. I think she believed they could use it to convince me that it was my duty to join them, to fulfill my destiny and give our people the weapon to defeat Lucias."

Alexa cringed, and Ethan gave voice to her thought. "I would not think of my own child as a weapon, thinking it better to never have a child than to see them used so callously. So I left. I spent many years alone, traveling around the world, never staying in any one place for long, and over that time I built a wall around my heart, thinking if I never fell in love, the prophecy could never come to pass. I eventually found my way home, and made what I now know was only a shell of a life for myself here."

"I was so very foolish, so focused on not letting the prophecy control my future, that I did not realize that was what it was already doing. When I tasted your blood that night, I panicked. I was afraid for you. I am still afraid for you, and for Chloe. Lucias will not give up the hunt for our daughter, and it is only a matter of time before The Elite learn of her."

His fear and his words lay heavily on Alexa; she was afraid, too.

"I do not know what will happen, but with you here next to me, I cannot imagine a life without you, Amor. You are my destiny and I refuse to let go of you ever again." He pulled her hand up to his chest and placed it over his heart. "This belongs to you, it has always been yours. I love you, Alexa."

Alexa smiled and closed her eyes as tears of joy ran down her cheek. "I love you, Ethan. So much. Whatever happens, we will face it together." She pulled his hand to her heart, mimicking his gesture and his beautiful words. "This belongs to you, it has always been yours."

CHAPTER 16 - *Girl Time*

They passed the rest of the drive in contented silence, reveling in being together again. Alexa looked up as the car started to slow on the seemingly never-ending country road they were on. Chloe and Tilly had been silent for the majority of the drive, only the sound of their slow, even, breathing floating up and occasionally falling upon Alexa's ears in the quiet. Ethan, of course, could hear every breath, every heartbeat, every small shift in movement. All of it warmed his slowly beating heart.

Alexa looked to her right and then up trying to see the top of the massive wrought- iron fence that encircled Ethan's parents' property. It was the only structure she had seen for miles. Ethan turned right and eased the car in to the short drive before the gate. He opened the window and leaned out, rapidly entering a long series of characters on the keypad, which caused the giant gate to part.

They continued down the long driveway and around a barrier of trees before Alexa caught her first glimpse of the massive house, and gasped.

"Oh, my God, Ethan, it's so beautiful!" she exclaimed, her eyes drinking in the beautiful architecture and intricate landscaping that surrounded them.

"Yes, it is," he said, never taking his eyes off of Alexa's face. "My mother has excellent taste; it runs in the family."

The sexy tone in his voice pulled Alexa's attention back to Ethan. Her cheeks flushed slightly when she realized his meaning.

Ethan maneuvered the car into a space in front of the open door of a multiple-car garage to the right of the house. She could see Elijah's BMW inside and something cherry-red parked next to it, but she couldn't make out what it was in the darkness. She imagined there were a variety of beautiful vehicles in the large structure. She unbuckled her seatbelt and reached to open the door, but it was already open before her hand touched the handle, Ethan offering her his hand as she stepped down from the SUV.

She inhaled deeply, the smell of lilacs and a variety of other fragrant flowers tickling her senses. The sound of running water drew her eyes towards the house to a beautiful waterfall flowing into a lily pond, the reflection of the full moon dancing brightly on its rippling surface. It made her koi pond look like a little mud puddle.

Chloe giggled as Ethan lifted her from the car, which was rocking with Tilly's excited movements in the back. She squeezed Ethan's neck with her little arms, causing a full-dimple smile to spread across his face. The impulsive display of affection between Chloe and her father made Alexa's heart light.

After releasing Tilly from the back, and still holding Chloe in one arm, Ethan slung the bag Alexa had packed over his shoulder and grabbed her hand, gently pulling her towards the house while Tilly ran around exploring excitedly.

"Come, Amor, it is time I introduce you to my mother. She is rather excited to meet you and her granddaughter."

She was suddenly nervous and her heart began to pound as a result.

Hearing the change in the steady beat, Ethan stopped and turned to face Alexa. He released her hand and placed his on the side of her neck, drawing her closer as he looked into her grey eyes.

"Do not be nervous. She will love you, as I do." He placed a soft kiss against her lips and stroked the side of her neck with his thumb.

His words and his kiss gave her the reassurance she needed. She took a small step back and gave Chloe a quick peck on the cheek before taking Ethan's hand again. "Okay, let's go."

They quickly made their way across the driveway and took the stone path past the pond and up to the house. Alexa looked around in awe of the beauty that surrounded them, catching the occasional glimpse of Tilly as she made her way through the wide variety of flowers, shrubbery, and trees.

Just as they ascended the stairs and passed through the tall white pillars that framed the entrance, the double front doors flew open.

Ethan's mother stepped out from the dim light inside into the bright light that flooded the porch, and stood for a moment, looking first at Chloe, then Alexa, then Ethan.

Seeing Ethan's mother for the first time, Alexa's anxiety ratcheted into high gear. The similarity between the woman before her and Cami, who had been less than warm towards her, was absolutely uncanny. Josephine could have more easily passed for Cami's twin than her mother, the only noticeable differences being their eyes and hair. While Cami's eyes were green-grey, identical to Ethan's, Josephine's were a deep rich brown, and where Cami's hair was wildly curly, her mother's was perfectly straight.

When those brown eyes returned to Alexa, her nerves receded as she saw the genuine warmth in them and felt the wave of affection and excitement radiating from Josephine. She considered lowering her shields to test her ability on Josephine, but as the thought registered, she realized her shields were almost completely down already.

Before she could give it another moment's consideration, a bright smile spread across Josephine's face and she flung her arms open as she moved towards Alexa. She pulled her into a tight embrace, holding on to her for far longer than what Alexa would have normally been comfortable with, but this felt natural, not at all forced or awkward as she would have expected.

When Josephine finally released Alexa, she stepped back slightly and gave her a light peck on each cheek before saying, "Alexa, I am overjoyed to finally meet you. I, we," she corrected glancing at Ethan with a smile, "have been waiting a very long time for you. I am

Josephine, but you can call me Jo, or Mama, if you are comfortable with that."

Ethan cleared his throat and glared at his mother as Alexa coughed and stuttered trying to respond. "I, I, um, it's very nice to meet you, too," she finally managed.

"I am sorry if I have made you uncomfortable, you must forgive me. My sight sometimes gets me into trouble when I forget that others have not yet traveled the paths I have seen."

Alexa's cheeks flushed slightly at the implication of Josephine's words.

"Oh my, look at me, being so rude and pouncing on you before you have even gotten through the door! Please come inside." Jo closed the doors and turned to her son. "Mi hijo, you know that I am happy to see you as always, and I know we have much to discuss, but you will have to wait; so kindly hand over my beautiful granddaughter."

Ethan chuckled as he passed Chloe to his mother. Chloe practically jumped from his arms to get to her. Ethan watched his mother carefully; concerned that she might have a vision when she touched Chloe, since she didn't have a charm to block her yet. But several minutes passed, the two just staring, assessing, and absorbing one another.

Elijah stepped up behind his wife, surprising Alexa with his sudden appearance. She still hadn't adjusted to the supernatural speed. "Dearest, how do you feel?" he queried, the concern in his voice evident.

"I am filled with a joy that is beyond words, but that is not what you are asking. There is no vision; I do not see anything of Chloe's future now, even when I try to focus on it. Perhaps her future is still too uncertain to form in a vision. Or, it could be…" her voice trailed off as if she was suddenly lost in thought.

"What is it, my love?" Elijah inquired.

"She is very strong; I can feel it in her. It is possible that she shields her own future, though that should be impossible without the aid of magic."

"There is no way for us to know the bounds of her power yet, but we cannot take any chances," he said as he pulled something from his pocket. He moved around behind Chloe and lifted the delicate silver chain up over her head and brought it together behind her neck to clasp it.

Ethan looked at his father, a question in his eyes. Elijah responded aloud, "Barb made it right after they left my office. Said there was no point in waiting for the blood, she already knew Chloe was the one."

Alexa leaned around to get a better look at the necklace. She gently picked up the little four-point star that rested against Chloe's chest. "What does it mean?"

"It is the mark, your mark. The birthmark that identified my soul mate," Ethan said, smiling; no hint of the resentment that he once felt about the prophecy remained as he placed his hand against the small of her back.

"This is what my birthmark looks like?" Alexa asked, having never actually seen it because of its placement and the thickness of her hair.

"Well, I see everyone is acquainted now," Barb said stepping out from a door a little way down the long hallway that led into the house. "Jo, I think it is high time you had a little chat with, Alexa, alone," she said, pointedly looking at Ethan.

"I do not see why I should not stay with her. There is nothing Mother need say that I should not hear," Ethan responded through gritted teeth.

"That's not for you to decide, boy. You can take your things to your room and join me and your father in the kitchen and let these two have a little girl-time or, if you prefer, I can stick you right where you stand for the rest of the night, and it will happen anyway," Barb said, standing up as tall as her short frame would allow.

Alexa couldn't help but admire the old woman's strength. Witch or not, she was still human and she was thoroughly putting one of the most powerful vampires in existence in his place.

"My son, just allow us a few moments," Jo said softly, resting her hand against Ethan's forearm. "Chloe needs to eat, and you should spend a little time with her and your father. Do not worry, you will have Alexa all to yourself soon enough. Elijah and I have a great deal of grandparent time to catch up on," she whispered, winking at him playfully.

"Mama, please," Ethan huffed, trying to sound exasperated. The truth was that, while he was eager to spend some time getting to know his daughter, he needed to be alone with Alexa. Since the moment she walked into his father's office, his body had been practically vibrating with need for her. The draw to her was like a call from his soul, and now that he had her back in his life, the thought of letting her out of his sight, even for a few moments, ached all the way down to his marrow.

Alexa was just as reluctant to leave his side, but when Josephine held out her manicured hand, she took it without protest and followed her down the long hallway, away from the two loves of her life.

Ethan watched Alexa's back longingly, as she followed his mother down the hallway to her private parlor which he already knew to be soundproof. There would be no listening in, even with preternatural vampire hearing. He was suddenly gripped by fear as he worried about what might be revealed when the two were alone. Would his mother tell Alexa the entire prophecy? While he had been honest with her, there was one particular detail that he had omitted. How could Alexa love him once she knew?

He nodded and smiled as Barb and Elijah talked and fawned over Chloe, who seemed to be eating up all of the attention, but his focus was trained directly on Alexa and his mother as he strained to hear anything that passed between them before they entered the parlor.

Nothing was spoken by the two women until they reached the door, when Josephine turned to Alexa holding out her hand. "Please remove your necklace, Alexa," she requested softly.

Alexa instinctively grabbed the large diamond, as she often did when she was nervous or anxious. "I can't. I promised Ethan I would never take it off." she declared, determined not to break her promise.

"It is to block your future from the enemy, but this home is protected by one of Barb's spells. You will be safe without it while you are within these walls. I wish to look at your future and I cannot so long as you wear it. I am sure Ethan will consent to its removal for this, and since he is listening intently, you need only look at him for confirmation," she explained, smiling slightly. She knew her son well.

Alexa turned back to see Ethan, whose eyes were fixed on her hand over the necklace he had given her. He quickly looked up at her eyes and nodded, reluctantly giving his consent.

She reached back to unclasp the chain, but before her hands reached it, Ethan's were there. He quickly undid the necklace and tucked it into his pocket while he kissed her neck in the same way he had done when he gave it to her.

"I will keep this for you, and I will put it back on when you are finished with your discussion," he breathed against her neck, ignoring the fact that his mother was watching the exchange.

He just hoped she would want it, that she would want him, by the time they were done.

Alexa thought to turn and wrap her arms around Ethan, feeling his anxiety and wanting to comfort him. But before she had the chance, she felt the swift breeze that signaled his departure back to the company of those who were now in the kitchen. So she took a clarifying breath and passed through the door that Josephine was holding open.

CHAPTER 17 - *AB Negative*

Ethan waited for what seemed like ten lifetimes while his mother spoke privately with Alexa. Barb and Elijah chatted lightly while she made some eggs and grits for Chloe. After Chloe scarfed those down, Barb let her take some blood from her wrist, while Ethan stepped outside. It had been far too long since he had blood and he feared his response to the smell of fresh blood in the air.

Elijah joined him. "My son, how long since you last fed?" He had eaten some human food just that afternoon, a grilled cheese sandwich and tomato soup, but he knew that wasn't what his father was asking. "I can see it has been too long by the color of your face. You have grown pale."

Ethan looked at his father. "It has been quite a while. I have only fed a handful of times since I first met Alexa. It just feels so wrong. I do not understand how you can do it, loving mother, but feeding on another with all the feelings it evokes. I never thought about it before, since my heart was free and I could do as I pleased. But now, the thought of drinking from another woman turns my stomach far more than my hunger."

Elijah clasped his shoulder firmly as he chuckled. "There are ways around that feeling. Have you never thought of feeding from a man?"

Ethan considered for a moment. No, honestly, it had never crossed his mind; the instinct of the hunt always focused him on females.

"No, I suppose not," he admitted.

"Well, never mind that now. You will be able to feed from your love tonight, and I have a large supply of stored blood available. While it does not offer the same thrill from the bag as it does from the vein, it will sustain you. Perhaps you should have some now, before you are alone with Alexa. You do not want your hunger to override your judgment and cause you to take too much from her."

While the thought of cold blood from a bag was not at all appealing, the thought of hurting Alexa in any way was unbearable.

Ethan followed his father to the basement and into the walk-in refrigeration unit.

They entered the cold room and Ethan looked around, seeing a variety of bags lining the shelves of the cold room.

"We have all blood types. I would recommend the AB negative; it is the least bitter in the cold state. It is also the rarest type and was quite difficult to come by, but I believe there is enough to temper your thirst for now, my son," Elijah said.

He plucked a bag from a nearby shelf and handed it to Ethan. "I will give you a moment alone and go enjoy some time with my granddaughter," he stated before ducking out of the room and pulling the door just short of closing to give Ethan some privacy, but not wanting to trap him in the air-tight room.

Ethan sniffed the thick liquid through the plastic; even with the barrier, the smell was quite pungent and caused his fangs to erupt from his gums. He considered trying to procure a pair of scissors to pierce the thick bag, but instinct overrode conscious thought, and he bit down on it roughly, his sharp teeth easily penetrating the barrier.

The taste was cold and bitter, evoking no emotion or excitement like fresh blood. Still, as the thick coppery liquid slid down his parched throat, Ethan felt his hunger begin to dissipate. The stored blood satisfied his physical need for blood, but it did nothing to quench the burning desire in his heart, the deep need to feel the pulse of his love as her warm essence coated and soothed him from the inside out.

As he removed a second bag from the shelf, he said a silent prayer hoping that, no matter what his mother revealed, Alexa would return to him. That she would still love and accept him as he was. That he would again feel her skin against his, taste the sweet liquid that pulsed in her veins, and make her his in every way possible.

He had suffered greatly these many months, struggling with the truths of the prophecy that had already come to pass, and hoping beyond all things that he could still change what he knew in his heart was beyond his control. While he had accepted part of his role in the prophecy, that he would love Alexa, that he would father the child who would lead his people into the future, not knowing what that future would be, he refused to believe it in its entirety. He would never hurt Alexa; he would die first.

Having finished two bags of the AB negative, Ethan felt full. However, wanting to be certain he was in control when and if Alexa returned to him, he grabbed the nearest bag, not paying attention to the type, and gulped it down.

Ethan emerged from the basement, feeling far more in control than when he'd first entered, and rejoined Elijah, Barb, and Chloe in the kitchen.

Alexa and Josephine remained in the soundproof study down the hall and Ethan tried to keep his focus on the conversation around him.

"I'll return to the clinic, explain the sale to the other staff, and gather up Chloe's records," Barb stated. "Now, you know you'll need to come back and say goodbye to everyone soon if you expect them to believe you've decided to retire. It won't do for you to just disappear into thin air all of a sudden."

"Yes, I know, but we need to close down for a few days first. If Lucias has discovered our location, we cannot risk the employees being there when his men come looking. I need you to call everyone before we are scheduled to open, tell them that I am ill, that they can take the next few days off until I am well again. That will give us some time to come up with a reason for my sudden retirement."

"We could say it's cancer; that is a common affliction among humans these days and they will understand your need to focus on your own health for a while."

"What would I do without you, Barb?" Elijah asked, his eyes full of affection and admiration.

She chuckled before responding, "I surely don't know. Let's not find out just yet, but you know the time is coming soon, don't ya? I have been clinging on to this life for far too long, my old friend. My soul is weary and I am ready to move on."

An expression of pure sadness covered Elijah's face, and Barb's last words even pulled Ethan's attention from the door he had been singularly focused on for the last few minutes.

"Now, now, don't you boys fret," she said gently, patting each of them on the sides of their faces. "I have lingered in this world with you far too long and you know it. I'll stay until the job is done, but you've gotten spoiled having me around to fuss over you all these years. Humans aren't meant to stay here like this and you know I'm so very tired. I feel like one of those rubber bands that's been stretched a little too far for just a little too long so it can't bounce back again. Of course, I'll miss ya'll, too, but we'll see each other again someday. You know you boys have plenty left to do on this side first."

She looked at both of them sternly. "I expect you both to see this thing through, ya hear? You be strong for these three girls here, understand?" she insisted, gesturing to Chloe and then down the hall to where Josephine and Alexa were still shut away.

Both men nodded and Ethan felt a chill spread over him. So much was still uncertain. Alexa could come out of that room hating him. He didn't know if he was strong enough to face everything that lay ahead without her. But he would try; he would do everything he could to fulfill his promise and to protect Alexa and his daughter, even if that meant forfeiting his own life.

CHAPTER 18 - *A Proposal*

When Alexa finally emerged, with Josephine following closely behind, Ethan kept his eyes down, taking a deep breath to prepare himself for the fear and rejection he expected to see in her eyes.

Steeling his nerve, he looked up and met her gaze. Instead of fear and rejection, all he saw was love and understanding. His glance immediately moved to his mother, whose face revealed nothing.

Ethan breathed a sigh of relief.

She didn't tell her. I still have time.

In an instant, he was down the hall sweeping Alexa into his arms and wrapping her in a warm embrace. "Te amo, Alexa," he whispered in her ear, casting a grateful glance at his mother who looked back at him with a knowing smile.

He placed Alexa back down on her feet and pulled her necklace from his pocket, quickly placing it back around her neck with a kiss. He then took her hand as they walked back to the kitchen to where

Elijah, Barb, and Chloe were waiting.

"I take it it was a good discussion," Elijah said, a broad smile covering his handsome face as he approached his wife and wrapped his arms around her waist.

"Yes, an excellent discussion, mi vida," she stated, casting a quick glance at Alexa. "Hold on to this one, my son. She is a remarkable woman."

"Mother, Father, I think you two should spend some time with your granddaughter tonight," Ethan said, his eyes on Alexa. She blushed slightly under his gaze, which was already darkening with desire at the thought of being alone with her.

"An excellent notion, my son," Elijah added as Josephine scooped Chloe up into her arms. "My dear wife has been dying to get to know our sweet Chloe for quite some time."

Alexa looked uncertain. "I'm not sure if that's such a good idea just yet. Chloe still needs to eat, and she's never slept away from me before."

"We already fed her, child," Barb chimed in, "and she looks mighty happy in her grandma's arms, don't you think?"

As if to ease her mother's mind, Chloe giggled and wrapped her arms around Josephine's neck.

"So, it is settled then. Chloe will sleep with us tonight," Josephine stated, as she turned to walk towards the bedroom she shared with Elijah. "We even have a crib ready for her in our room, Alexa. Every mother needs a night off," she tossed over her shoulder, as she disappeared around the corner, brooking no refusal of the arrangement.

Seeing that she had no choice in the matter, Alexa conceded and turned to Ethan for direction as Elijah followed Josephine and Barb chuckled, heading away from them down another hallway.

✧

Ethan led her down yet another hallway, to a separate wing of the large home where his bedroom was located.

As they stepped through the doorway to Ethan's room, Alexa felt like her body was buzzing with emotion and anticipation. There was the fear and confusion of the prophecy and what was happening with Chloe, the excitement and hesitancy about Ethan being back in her life, the fear of losing him again, and the love for him that was once again consuming her heart and soul. But now that they were alone, something far more urgent began to take over. Pure, unadulterated lust.

Alexa contemplated simply attacking Ethan and ripping all of his clothes off but, before she could fully form the thought, he had sped across the room faster than her eyes could register. As her mind processed his action, the room filled with a beautiful sexy beat that was all too familiar. Alexa's eyes widened in surprise.

"I searched everywhere for this song. I can't believe you remembered. How did you find it?"

Ethan looked at her from across the room, his eyes smoldering. Even from such a distance his intense stare took her breath away. In a flash, he was beside her, his arms around her waist pulling her against his body.

He whispered in her ear, "How could I possibly forget the first song we ever danced to, Amor? I found it the day that I-," he closed his eyes and sighed heavily, "the day that I left. I am sorry; you must know how truly sorry I am."

Alexa's heart ached with the pain and regret evident in his voice. She placed her hand on his cheek, pulling his face towards her and forcing him to look into her eyes. "Ethan, I'm not going to pretend that I fully understand why you decided to go, and I won't deny that it was a very dark time for me. At first, I drove myself crazy trying to find you. I was convinced if I could just see you, I could make you see that we needed to be together. After a few days I-"

Ethan placed his finger against her lips.

"I know, Amor. I was always there; I saw it all. Please do not speak of it. Every day, watching you in so much pain, it broke my heart into a million pieces. So many times I wanted to rush to you, to hold and comfort you." He gently stroked her cheek as he spoke.

Her eyes widened in surprise. "You were watching me?"

"Yes, Amor. I wanted to do what was right, to keep you safe, but I could not stay away. I had to see you even if I could never have you."

He leaned down and gently placed a chaste kiss on her lips. "As hard as those first weeks were, it became so much worse as I watched your belly swell with my child. You looked so beautiful, so alive. I would have given anything to touch you, to feel our child moving inside you. Then there was the day downtown that you tripped and fell on the curb. It took every ounce of willpower I possessed not to run to you. Then that man appeared to help you. When he reached out and grabbed your hand, I was at once grateful to him and filled with rage that he dared to touch you."

Alexa looked confused as she tried to recall the day he was referring to. As recognition lit her expression she spoke, "I thought I saw you then, like so many other times. He asked if I was all right and when I said I was, he asked to touch my belly. He wanted to know how far along I was."

"Yes," Ethan husked through his clenched teeth, "you were eight months pregnant, and then he rubbed the ring finger on your left hand and asked if you were married and if he could buy you lunch when you told him you were single. I wanted to kill him as I watched him put his hand on the small of your back and lead you across the street to that cafe where you ate."

Alexa could feel the rage radiating from Ethan at the memory. "He was kind and I was so lonely. He asked for my number before we left, if he could see me again. I refused him." She looked into his smoldering eyes. "I don't even remember his name. There is only you, Ethan. It has always been you."

With that, Ethan crushed his mouth onto hers; kissing her with all of the longing and emotion that had built up over the past year and a half. Alexa returned the kiss with just as much fervor and desperation. When she parted her full lips slightly it was more than enough of an invitation. Ethan invaded her eager mouth with his skilled tongue, exploring every surface, kissing her with more passion and desire than she had ever known was possible.

He reached down under her thighs, gripping her ass he lifted her up and she wrapped her legs around his waist. He moved them up against the wall, pressing into her forcefully and letting her know without a doubt how much he had missed her. She moaned into his mouth as she felt his unbelievable hardness press through her jeans along her sensitive core and into the flesh of her abdomen.

With his incredible speed, Ethan moved them the short distance across his bedroom. So engrossed in their kiss, Alexa hardly registered the movement until her back connected with the silky sheets of his bed and he broke their kiss to remove his shirt and take in the sight of the woman he loved in his bed at long last.

As she lay there, Alexa lifted her head and looked around the room, taking in the masculine decor that was purely Ethan. Her breath caught when she glanced over his shoulder at a large portrait hanging on the wall directly across from the bed. She blinked several times before asking, "Is, is that, me?"

"Yes, you are the only woman who has ever been in my bedroom, this one or the one in my own home. I brought the portrait with me when my father called," he growled, as he once again covered her body with his and began kissing along her collarbone, up her neck and jawline. When he slowly dipped his tongue into her ear, Alexa nearly came apart from the inside out. It had been so long. In all these months, she couldn't even muster the desire to touch herself, the only sexual release coming from the intense dreams that she would sometimes have about her time with Ethan. Now with him here, touching her with all of his masculine perfection, there was essentially eighteen months of unreleased sexual arousal thrumming through her body, demanding to get out.

Completely overcome with the intensity of her feelings, both physical and emotional, Alexa clutched at Ethan's hard body, straining to get as close as possible. Without even thinking, she opened her mouth wide and bit down on his muscled shoulder with her blunt human teeth so hard she drew blood. When the potent essence of it touched her tongue and descended back to her throat, she jerked her head back and cried out his name as a life-altering orgasm ripped through her body, forcing her back to arch up off of the bed as she writhed with pleasure.

The entire display was the single most erotic thing Ethan had ever witnessed in his life. His erection so hard it was threatening to shred through the denim that remained between him and his love, but he just sat back on his knees and watched intently, not wanting to miss a single second of Alexa's pleasure.

Several moments passed before her body stilled and she jerked up, an apology on her lips as she looked to the shoulder she had just ravaged, only to find that there was no evidence of the terrible wound she'd anticipated.

Ethan followed her eyes to his shoulder and grinned, his sexy dimples evident in the dim light, "No te preocupes, Amor. I heal very quickly."

She touched two fingers to her mouth and pulled them back to reveal the dark liquid that stained her lips, her tongue reflexively shooting out and around to gather the remaining blood. She closed her eyes and savored the strangely delicious flavor for a moment before she opened them again and stared directly at Ethan as she stuck her fingers in her mouth and sucked the last remnants of his blood from them.

Under any other circumstances, the primal growl that escaped his throat would have been terrifying but, in that moment, it was the sexiest sound she had ever heard.

In a couple of quick flashes, Ethan tore Alexa's jeans and blouse from her body so efficiently she would have sworn she had been naked the entire time. He jumped back off the bed, his body shaking with restraint as he gazed down at her exposed flesh. He would hurt her like this; he had to get control, to calm down before he could claim her. The blood he had consumed earlier should have reduced his hunger, but in this moment he felt as though he had gone without her sweet blood for a hundred years.

As he stood there, his hot gaze burning into Alexa's skin and making her squirm with anticipation, he began to recognize how much her figure had changed since he last saw her like this. He probably should have felt it earlier, but he was so preoccupied with having her in his arms again that he hadn't realized. She was still the most beautiful woman he had ever laid eyes on, yet gone were most of the soft sexy curves he loved. She had lost weight, a lot of weight, despite having a baby, and his heart squeezed a little, knowing it was because of the pain he had put her through.

Seeing a touch of sadness cross Ethan's face, Alexa felt bold. She was done with sadness and regret, so she did something that just the thought of would normally have sent her running off blushing and giggling. Staring directly into Ethan's eyes, she trailed her right hand slowly down the side of her neck, between her breasts and down to her navel. Feeling encouraged by the heat that was reentering his eyes and how good her own hand felt against her skin, she continued lower, teasing along the inside of her thigh before moving between the soft folds of her tender flesh. As she lightly touched the sensitive ball of nerves at the apex of her thighs, she couldn't resist closing her eyes and enjoying the sensation.

When she opened them, Ethan was hovering over her, his intense eyes boring into her so deeply she thought he could see her soul.

Neither of them spoke, they just stayed there, staring at one another, their eyes saying all the things their hearts needed to hear in that moment. The engorged tip of Ethan's hardness was pressing insistently at Alexa's soft, wet opening as he continued to forcibly restrain himself, just trying to take in the moment, reveling in the delight of having Alexa back in his arms.

"Ethan, please; I need to feel you inside me," Alexa husked breathily.

That was it; he couldn't take it any longer. In one fluid movement he pushed inside her soft warm center, squeezing his eyes shut and gasping at the sensation of her body gripping him like a tight wet fist.

Her body shuddered, already on the brink of another glorious climax. He stayed there, remaining still inside her, praying for restraint as his primal self threatened to take over.

Sensing his struggle, Alexa gripped his face with both hands, "Ethan, look at me. I love you. I trust you, I'm not made of glass, you're not going to hurt me; so please, just fuck me, baby. Make me come again."

Ethan's cock grew impossibly harder at her words. Unable to stop himself, he began to move with long deep strokes inside her as she moaned in satisfaction and encouragement. It wasn't long before he felt her body beginning to tense beneath him, her arms pulling him closer with each stroke. His fangs descended, filling his mouth as lust coursed through his veins. Sensing his need, Alexa tilted her head back, exposing the irresistible flesh of her neck and setting Ethan's throat on fire with thirst.

"Amor, I need to taste you," the words came out as a growled question, his accent thick and his speech slightly obstructed by the sharp points.

"Do it, Ethan. I'm yours, every part of me is yours. I want it. Please," she managed to whisper through the haze of pleasure that was clouding her mind.

With that he struck, his eyes widening and the pace of his strokes quickening as her sweet taste filled his mouth.

She cried out, the sensations emanating from both points that Ethan was penetrating sweeping through her and colliding within her core before exploding outward all over her body.

Ethan could taste it in her blood, feel it in the rush of liquid that coated his throbbing cock, and he was lost, spiraling down into his own delicious climax as he pulled his mouth from her neck and groaned her name over and over again in her ear as he pulsed inside her.

They laid there, tangled in each other's arms for several minutes as their breathing evened out again. Ethan held himself up on his elbows and swept his tongue over the puncture wounds in Alexa's neck, sending a shiver down her spine. He stayed there for a moment, watching as the small holes immediately began to heal, before he moved to lie beside her and pull her into his arms.

She moaned lowly, a lazy smile spreading across her face as she started to slip into a deep and much needed sleep, wrapped up in the comfort of Ethan's strong arms.

As Alexa's breathing grew deep and even, Ethan pressed his lips to her hair and breathed in her sweet scent. "Te amo, Alexa."

He closed his eyes tightly, making a silent promise to her and to himself. The prophecy would not rule them; he could stop it and he *would* stop it. He would die if he had to.

As they lay there, tangled in each other's arms, Alexa spoke through her sleepy haze.

"Ethan, I can feel that you're still holding something back. I won't push you; I know you must have your reasons. I hope someday you will trust me enough to share with me, but I am here with you now and you must promise me that no matter what happens you won't do that to me again. You have to promise you won't leave, no matter what happens or how hard it gets."

He pulled her tighter and whispered into her hair as a lone tear ran down his cheek, "I promise, Amor. I will never leave you again."

Feeling overcome with the need to show Alexa how he felt, to prove to her that he meant to keep his promise, Ethan felt the words trying to burst from his heart. He had thought to ask it the first night he met her, but he knew it would have been too sudden for her then. Now, with her knowing what he was and still accepting him, he could not contain his desire to make her his, and only his, any longer.

He sat up in bed next to her, stroking her hair as her breathing evened into the pattern of sleep. He quietly got up from the bed and retrieved his pants from the floor, removing the ring he had been carrying all these months from his pocket.

Quietly slipping back into bed, Ethan wrapped his body around Alexa's, gently slipping the ring on her left hand and taking a moment to admire how good the large diamond looked on her finger.

He was suddenly gripped with fear. What if she refused him? He swallowed his nerves. She loved him. She was his soul mate. They were made for each other, and he needed to do this as much as he needed to take his next breath.

Pulling her with him to the edge of the bed, he slid off onto one knee with her lying on her side, beautifully naked as he stroked her cheek trying to wake her gently.

"Amor, Amor; wake up, sweet Alexa."

Her eyes fluttered quickly and then stilled, before he spoke again, slightly louder this time.

"Alexa, Amor; you must wake."

With that, her eyes snapped open and she sat up in a panic. "Is everything okay? Is Chloe okay?" she asked, her mind still clouded by sleep.

"Yes, my love, everything is perfect; but I must ask you a question."

As the haze started to lift, she focused on Ethan, a question in her eyes until they fell upon the hand he was holding and the large diamond ring that encircled her finger.

Her other hand shot up to her mouth as she realized what was happening, and she gasped.

"I loved you from the first moment I saw you, Alexa. There were none before you, and there will be none after. You possess me, body, mind, and soul. So I ask you, I beg you; please grant me the great honor of becoming my wife."

Alexa couldn't speak as tears of joy streamed down her face. Her first thought was to pinch herself. This had to be a dream, but as she felt Ethan's warm fingers stroking her hand, felt the cold metal and weight of the platinum band on her finger, she knew this was real.

Like Ethan, she had known that first night. Even then, his soul called out to hers so, just like that night, she gave the response that was in her heart as she smiled down at him lovingly.

"Sure."

CHAPTER 19 - *Big Announcement*

They made love again, slowly reveling in each other's bodies, in each detail and sensation. As she started to drift off to sleep, Alexa couldn't help but feel like this was the quiet before the storm. But she pushed the thought from her mind and let herself enjoy the feel of being wrapped in Ethan's strong arms. She would savor these quiet moments, even though she already knew they would be fleeting.

Alexa woke the next morning, scared to open her eyes for fear that everything that had passed the night before had been a dream. But as she regained consciousness, she could feel Ethan's warmth enveloping her, feel the hardness of his muscular body against hers, and the fear floated away. He was hers, even if for just a short time.

Sensing the change in her breathing, Ethan smiled. "Good morning, Amor."

She turned in his arms to face him and pressed a kiss on his full lips. "Good morning, my fiancé," she declared, a bright smile spreading across her face.

He returned the smile as he pulled her closer, letting her feel his growing arousal at having her so close to him in his bed.

Tempted by the feel of his hardness against her abdomen, Alexa moved away. "I should go check on Chloe."

"She is still asleep. I can hear her heartbeat and her breathing. They are steady with sleep."

Alexa's cheeks immediately flushed. "Oh, my God, if you can hear that, oh no, your parents!" she exclaimed as he chuckled at her embarrassment.

"Do not concern yourself. We are adults and they understand. I spent far too many nights listening to them over the years, or rather trying to block them out. My mother is quite vocal," he said, shaking his head as if trying to rid his mind of the thought.

Alexa buried her face in her hands in humiliation. "This vampire hearing of yours clearly has its disadvantages," she whispered, peeking at him through her fingers.

"You learn to block things out over time," he said, pulling her hands away from her face. "Their focus last night was on Chloe, and I am sure they are not paying any attention to us now. I only hear her so clearly because I am trying to and I can assure you they are both still asleep, as well, Amor." He smiled, flashing his adorable dimples at her, clearly amused by her discomfort.

She smacked his shoulder playfully. "This is not funny!" she exclaimed as he rolled her on to her back, swiftly grabbing her hands and pinning them above her head with one of his as the other freely roamed her still-naked body.

"Perhaps you should learn to be quieter," he said softly, before claiming her mouth with his own. After thoroughly kissing her, he pulled back slightly, a mischievous grin lighting his face as he slid his hand down between her breasts, and then lightly circled each already-hardened nipple, eliciting a low moan from deep in her throat. "I think this is a good time for you to practice."

"How can I be expected to be quiet with you touching me like that?" she implored huskily, as she closed her eyes, thoroughly enjoying this playful side of him.

As he moved his hand lower and dipped his fingers between her soft folds, he groaned at how wet she already was, before whispering against her ear, "Like I said, practice."

Before she could respond, he slid two fingers deep inside her and covered her mouth with a passionate kiss, swallowing the moan his ministrations elicited.

"You must try harder, Amor," he said looking down at her, relishing the way she squirmed under his touch.

Before she lost herself to the climax that was threatening to overtake her, Alexa snapped her eyes open and pulled her hands from the light grip Ethan had on them. She hooked her leg over his trim hip and rolled him over to his back, fully appreciating the fact that he could easily overpower her, but he was letting her take control.

"Let's see how you like it, Mr. Kellar," she murmured, grinning wickedly as she straddled his hips and began kissing the side of his neck.

"Do your worst, Mrs. Kellar," he challenged, a megawatt smile spreading across his face at the sound of what would soon be her new name.

"Mmm, I really like the sound of that," she whispered, as she lifted her head, returning his smile, "but you won't distract me so easily."

With that she returned to her task, planting soft kisses over his shoulders and down to his chest. She paused to look up at him as she lightly flicked her tongue over one of his hard nipples, causing his breathing to increase slightly. He remained silent, his eyes fixed on her, watching the delicious torture intently.

She slid her tongue across his smooth, hard chest, over to the other nipple, gently pulling it into her mouth and nibbling lightly.

Ethan sucked in a breath through gritted teeth at the sensation, causing her to grin at the small triumph, but she was far from finished.

Releasing his nipple, she continued her slow journey, kissing all the way down over his stomach, then moving to run her tongue slowly up the inside of each thigh, carefully avoiding any contact with his impressive erection.

She could feel how difficult it was for him to remain still, his body practically vibrating from the effort. Knowing that he was so much stronger than she, that at any moment he could overpower her and do whatever he wanted, yet remained still and let her take the reins, turned her on more than she thought possible. She might not have the strength to conquer him physically, but in that moment she knew with certainty that she possessed something far more powerful. She had his heart.

When she finally moved so that he could feel her soft breath on his cock, he lifted up on his elbows, "Alexa, Amor, I," he paused, swallowing hard, "You do not need to do, that. It is not something I have ever done before."

Alexa's eyes, which had been fixed on the magnificent sight of his engorged manhood, snapped to his face in surprise. "Really? Never?" she asked, genuinely shocked, having assumed that women fell all over themselves to do any and every thing this man could ever want.

"No, never. No woman has ever…Madre de Dios!" he moaned loudly as she sucked the head into her soft, warm mouth without warning, gently swirling her tongue around the rim.

She wrapped her hand around the thick base and pulled back. "Mr. Kellar, that was not quiet. If you can't behave, I'm afraid I'll have to stop," she chastised jokingly.

Ethan squeezed his eyes shut and dropped his head back against the bed, willing to do anything to get Alexa to put her mouth on him like that again.

After a moment, Alexa began again, gently licking the drop of his arousal that had emerged before pulling the entire head of his throbbing cock into her eager mouth.

Feeling a desperate urge to move, Ethan fisted the satiny sheets in both hands, fighting with everything he had to remain still as Alexa began to take him into her mouth with steadily deepening strokes, her hand tightly gripping his stalk and following the motion of her mouth.

It wasn't long before her steady rhythm started to draw the intense waves of sensation that would push Ethan over the edge into a mind-blowing orgasm.

When he could hold it back no longer, he pushed his hands into her hair and held her head as he tensed and growled loudly, spilling his seed into her mouth with powerful throbbing pulses.

Ethan closed his eyes and relaxed back into the bed while Alexa greedily lapped up every drop of his essence before lightly kissing the tip of his still-engorged cock. She climbed up to straddle his hips, watching his face intently while his eyes remained closed. After a moment he smiled and opened his eyes, looking at her with wonder. "Alexa, my God, that was magnificent."

She frowned at him slightly. "I don't know, Mr. Kellar." His smile faltered slightly, a look of concern in his eyes. Had he hurt her somehow? "You were supposed to remain quiet, remember?" She grinned wickedly, almost drunk on the power of bending this strong, beautiful man to her will.

"Hmm, you are right, but it is not as easy as you might think." In a blur of movement, he flipped her on her back and covered her body with his, pausing just to say, "Let us see how you do," before he pushed his hardness deep inside her in one fluid motion.

The sound that escaped her throat, something between a moan and a growl, was far from quiet, but at that point they were both far from caring about the noise.

✧

Several orgasms later, Alexa gathered the sheet around her body and climbed out of bed on rather wobbly legs. She turned and leaned down to place a soft kiss on Ethan's cheek while he slept, but as she started to move away he swiftly wrapped his arms around her and pulled her back into bed.

She let out a surprised squeak. "I thought you were asleep!"

He drew her closer, his body spooning hers, and kissed her hair. "I was, but it is difficult to sleep when my heart is moving away from me."

"Well, I have to leave your side sometime. I need to use the bathroom or I'm going to burst," she said, as she wiggled out of his arms again and stood. "And I really need a shower."

"We can shower together," he said as got up off the bed, completely naked, and began stalking towards her as she backed towards the bathroom, like a big cat tracking its prey.

She held her hand up to halt him, knowing that if he touched her she would be lost. "No way," she said half-heartedly, as her eyes greedily drank him in. She bit her lip as her gaze fell onto his tattoo and followed the fascinating pattern down. With her eyes already so low, it was impossible to ignore his steadily growing erection.

She quickly closed her eyes and took a deep breath. "You know as well as I do, if you get in that shower with me we might never get out, and as tempting as that sounds, we need to check on Chloe."

Ethan stuck his bottom lip out slightly with his disappointment, but conceded. "You are right, Amor. She is beginning to stir."

Seeing her opportunity, Alexa turned quickly, grabbed the bag she had packed from the floor, and walked through the door of the bathroom, closing and locking it behind her. Once she was inside, she leaned back against the door, fighting the urge to change her mind and tell Ethan to join her.

"You know, there is no need for you to lock the door, Amor. If I wish to enter, this door will not stop me," he stated, sounding somewhat amused.

Alexa couldn't help imagining Ethan pushing down the door and bending her over the marble vanity top. Her pulse quickened with the thought.

"Do not worry, I will not interrupt you. While I would thoroughly enjoy coming in there and having my way with you, I am eager to share the news with everyone. My mother will be thrilled. She has been waiting many years to plan this wedding." Alexa could hear the smile in his voice through the door.

Her eyes drifted to the large diamond perched on her finger. She hadn't even thought about the actual wedding. Most girls started planning their weddings when they were little, but Alexa had given up the hope of ever having one shortly after she started dating when she realized her talent made it impossible to get close to anyone.

She was suddenly giddy thinking of the possibilities.

"I will go shower in the guest bath. You would be wise to hurry and be finished by the time I return or I cannot be held responsible for what I do, knowing you're still in there naked and wet," Ethan said through the door, before grabbing a change of clothes from the large chest of drawers next to his bed and exiting the large bedroom his mother always kept ready in the event of his return.

Ten minutes later, after a nice hot shower, Alexa exited the expansive bathroom, refreshed and dressed for the day, fully expecting to find Ethan waiting impatiently for her. Instead, she found the large room empty.

She opened the door leading to the hallway and was met with the scent of food cooking, which caused her stomach to growl. She wasn't certain of the time, but based on the light and how refreshed she felt after such a late night, she knew it must be well into the afternoon, meaning she hadn't eaten in well over twenty-four hours. As she stepped out and pulled the door closed behind her, she heard the beautiful sound of Chloe's laughter coming from the kitchen.

She slowly walked down the long corridor, taking in all of the breathtaking artwork and photographs that lined the walls along the way. One item in particular caught her eye; a family portrait including Ethan and Cami as children. Alexa smiled as she viewed Ethan as a child. He couldn't have been more than five or six years old at the time it was painted, and she thought how much she would like to have a son who looked just like him someday. Of course, she already knew that that wasn't in the cards for them and her heart ached with the loss of all the things that she longed for, which simply couldn't be.

Ethan wrapped his arms around her, startling her with his sudden appearance, and whispered next to her ear. "You took far too long, Amor. I missed you."

Shaking the maudlin thoughts from her mind, she giggled and turned in his arms to face him, placing her arms around his neck and placing a chaste kiss on his lips. "I was only in there for ten minutes, my impatient love."

"Come, I waited for you to make the announcement," he said, as he took her hand and pulled her towards the kitchen.

When they entered the surprisingly modern room, Alexa looked down, a look of complete shock on her face as Chloe ran across the room and jumped into her arms.

"Mama!" she exclaimed, as she hugged her mother tightly. Alexa stared at Chloe, unable to find any words as she took in her daughter who was much changed since the previous night.

She was so much bigger and appeared older; if Alexa didn't know better she would have guessed her to be nearly two years old, instead of her true age of nine months.

Alexa looked around at everyone in the room, wondering if any of them were as thrown as she was by the change.

Elijah stepped towards her. "I see the surprise in your eyes and trust me; we were just as shocked when we woke up this morning. Chloe's growth is unprecedented. I have never seen anything like it. My assumption is that the introduction of fresh blood to her diet has sped up the process. If I had to guess, I would say that she will be fully grown by the time she reaches three years, perhaps even sooner, depending on her diet."

Alexa pulled Chloe close and inhaled the scent of her hair. She even smelled different, no longer like a baby, and her heart clenched. No mother liked to see her child grow up, especially *this* quickly.

Chloe began to squirm, trying to free herself from her mother's embrace. "I wanna eat," she said as Alexa set her down on the floor, once again surprised, this time by the obvious improvement of her vocabulary.

She dashed across the room and around to Barb, who was standing at the stove frying up some eggs, sausage, and bacon. "This child has quite the appetite," Barb stated as she gave her hand to Chloe ,who immediately bit down on her wrist.

Alexa cringed at the display. "Don't fret, child. I'm a strong old bird and she has a small stomach. She's not taking too much blood, but with her growing like she is we're going to need to find another source to feed her." Chloe released Barb's wrist and swiped her tongue over the puncture marks.

Ethan grabbed Alexa's hand again. "Our daughter is a fast learner," he stated proudly. "And I think she will make an excellent flower girl for the ceremony."

His statement caused everyone to turn and stare at him and Alexa. Josephine's eyes shot to Alexa's left hand and the magnificent ring that adorned it.

"Even with the benefit of foresight, I had not expected this happy news so soon," she said, looking warmly at her son whose eyes were proudly fixed on his bride-to- be.

"How do you feel about this weekend?" he questioned Alexa, brightly.

She looked up at his face, "For the wedding? Are you serious? That's only a few days from now!"

He took both of her hands and placed his forehead against hers as he whispered, "Amor, I have wasted so much time being afraid, not truly living my life. I do not want to waste a single moment of my time with you. I wish to be bound to you in every way possible, starting with making you my wife. And then my mate, if you will consent to it."

Alexa pulled back to look into his eyes, slightly confused by his words. "Aren't they the same thing, wife and mate? I've already agreed to become your wife, Mr. Kellar."

"Not exactly, no. Mating creates a more tangible bond, a blood bond. The process..."

"Ethan, perhaps it is best you explain the process to Alexa when you are alone," his mother interrupted, knowing Alexa would feel uncomfortable learning about the intimate ceremony with so many eyes and ears nearby.

"I suppose you are right, but she looks so very beautiful when she blushes, maybe it would be worth it just to see her face flush," he said, grinning mischievously.

As if on cue, Alexa felt her cheeks begin to heat up as she smacked Ethan's arm. "No! You can tell me later. And don't worry; I'm sure you'll have ample opportunities to embarrass me over the years."

Everyone chuckled but, even though she was smiling, Alexa couldn't help wondering if what she said was true. Would they have years together?

CHAPTER 20 - *Wedding Plans*

"Come, Alexa," Josephine said, taking her hand. "It looks like we have a wedding to plan. Barb, would you mind keeping Chloe occupied for a few hours?"

"Of course not, she'll be just fine with me. Don't you worry, Alexa," she said when she saw her opening her mouth to protest. Alexa snapped her mouth shut and frowned slightly, knowing it was pointless to argue with the stubborn woman and, though she was eager to spend some time with Chloe, she was already feeling anxiously excited about her pending nuptials and wanted to get started with the planning. "Miss Chloe and I will head on off outside, that big ol' dog of yours has been nosing around the windows and could probably use some attention. Practically scared me to death peeking in at me this morning," she chuckled, scooping Chloe up and heading out of the room.

Alexa immediately felt guilty; she hadn't even remembered to feed Tilly last night and she was not accustomed to sleeping outdoors. After everything that had happened, after what Tilly had done for her, she couldn't believe her own thoughtlessness.

Ethan rushed over and gave each of the two remaining woman a quick peck on the cheek. "I will leave my lovely women to it then. Amor, I will get Tilly fed. I am sorry I kept you so, distracted, last night," he said, seeing the distress on Alexa's face.

"Thank you." She loved that he was so considerate of Tilly. The truth was that, after what happened the night before, with Tilly saving Alexa, Ethan probably loved the giant dog as much as Alexa did.

"Mi vida," Josephine turned to Elijah, who was leaning against the counter quietly observing. "We will need for you to arrange for someone to perform the ceremony, and the witnesses we discussed." She gave him a pointed look and he nodded his understanding with a smile. Alexa wondered when they could have possibly had any discussion about the wedding, since they had just learned about it a few moments before.

"Consider it done, my love," he replied before turning to Ethan. He pulled him into a tight hug. "Congratulations, son." He then moved in front of Alexa and took her free hand. "Alexa, I cannot imagine a better match for my son. I am proud to have you join my family," he said warmly, causing tears to well up in her eyes. At a loss for the right words, she did what felt right and pulled him into a warm embrace.

After a moment, the two men went off to get to work on their appointed tasks.

"Well, then, Alexa let us get started. Given the circumstances, I am afraid we must have the wedding here. I am sure you understand that it would just be too dangerous anywhere else, but you have yet to see the back gardens; they are quite lovely this time of year. Come, I will give you a tour, then we can discuss the dress," Josephine said, rather excitedly.

They walked out of the kitchen through a side door and on to a stone path that wound around to the back of the house, to a large patio and salt water pool with a waterfall and high back wall made of stone. As they rounded the back of the pool to the gardens, Alexa gasped as she took in the beauty of her surroundings. "I can't imagine a more perfect place to get married. It's absolutely breathtaking."

"I thought the gazebo would be a good place for you and Ethan to stand for the ceremony," she said, pointing down the path through the fragrant wildflowers that stretched some distance across the yard to the structure that was in a small open area of grass. "We can place a few chairs in the grass there in front for the guests. You understand it will just be family?" she asked concerned.

"Yes, don't worry; there's not really anyone I would invite anyway, except maybe my old neighbors. There's no way I could explain my getting married so suddenly when they have never even seen me date, not to mention the change in Chloe since they last saw her. I understand that I cannot go back to my old life." While she had already accepted it, Alexa couldn't help but feel a little sad about never seeing Jill and Jesse again. She had felt terrible when she used Ethan's phone that morning to email them with a fake story about taking an impulsive vacation. She told them she would be gone for three weeks, buying her some time to come up with a more permanent story.

"Now that it's settled, let us talk about your dress. I may have something suitable but, if not, we could order something from the city and have it sent overnight."

✧

After a little more than an hour poring through Josephine's expansive closet, it became apparent that nothing she owned would work for Alexa to wear on the big day. While several gowns were absolutely stunning and Alexa loved them, Josephine was more than one size smaller and neither woman was very skilled at sewing.

Just as they agreed it was time to start exploring other options, Ethan poked his head in to check on them with Chloe in his arms. He kept his eyes squeezed shut as he said, "I am not peeking, but I wanted to check if you needed anything, and Chloe has been asking for you, Amor."

He set Chloe down on her feet and she took off for Alexa. Ethan couldn't resist and opened one eye to take a quick look at Alexa, but that peek forced him to open both eyes to blatantly stare at her.

The beige dress fit Alexa's figure tightly, its V-neck and lace inlay showing off her cleavage and causing Ethan's pulse to quicken. All he could think about was peeling it off of her.

His mother's voice snapped him out of the trance, "None of my dresses are going to work. I am afraid your bride is far more blessed in certain areas than I," she said, smiling.

"I rather like that dress," Ethan said, swallowing hard.

With Chloe now in her arms, Alexa laughed and turned to show Ethan her back. "Yes, it's great from the front. Too bad I can only get it zipped up half-way."

Seeing her from that angle, with her soft curves wrapped tightly and on display, Ethan felt his blood rush.

Trying to snap out of it before he grabbed Alexa and rushed her off to his bed, he shook his head and turned to his mother. "What can I do?"

Josephine laughed, "First, you can attempt to stop drooling; you will have plenty of time to admire your bride after the wedding. Go and fetch your father's laptop from his study; we will just have to order something. Alexa, I assume you can use a computer? I never really learned. It has been exhausting trying to keep up with the technology all these years. Each time I master one thing, something new comes along. I only learned to drive an automobile ten years ago."

Ethan looked at her surprised. "I did not know you had finally learned."

"Yes, well you have stayed away far too long, mi hijo."

Ethan shifted uneasily, feeling the guilt pressing down on him before his mother continued. "No te preocupes, mi amor. Everything has happened as it must."

Ethan nodded and headed off to his father's study, trying to choke down the emotion that had gathered in a tight knot in his throat. He had wasted so many years hiding himself away from his life. Then the meaning of his mother's words began to sink in. Alexa was very young. If he had lived differently, he could have married someone else before she was ever born.

Yes, everything has happened as it must. He thought as he entered the room lined on all sides with full bookshelves and took the laptop from the large desk in the back. He paused for a moment, looking at the photos that lined the desk. The one that drew his gaze was black and white. It was of him and his sister, taken when he had first returned home in the nineteen-fifties. It was the only photo of them together as adults. He couldn't recall the exact year, but he remembered that the reunion had been brief; his sister still hell-bent on his joining The Elite. Since then, he had only seen her a handful of times, and each meeting had been tense.

She would not accept his choices, seeing the prophecy as a gift; a duty to their kind that he had selfishly abandoned.

He turned from the picture to return to his love. He would not dwell on sad things from the past. Someday, perhaps Cami would understand, but for now he was going to focus on the present, on the happiness in his heart at being with Alexa again. In a few days, he would make her his, and he would be hers in every way. He was convinced that the bond would save them from the only thing he still feared; the one detail that he had kept hidden from Alexa, but would reveal to her before they wed. He just needed to find the right way to explain, to let her know he would never let it happen.

Ethan returned to his parents' bedroom and delivered the laptop to Alexa with a quick peck on the cheek and a whispered declaration of love before he left to find his father. There were some things he needed to discuss with him.

Alexa opened the computer and got online, immediately browsing some of her favorite shopping sites for the right gown for her wedding, while Chloe played happily with her grandmother. It wasn't long before she had narrowed it down to what she felt was the perfect dress, a slim-line summer gown with gossamer chiffon, which was pleated toward a beaded, deep V-neckline with silver encrusted halter straps and a silver ribbon at the waist. It was elegant, yet sexy, and she was certain Ethan would love it.

"Oh, my!" Josephine exclaimed, drawing Alexa's attention. Chloe sat on the bed and giggled heartily at the pillow that was floating mid-air several inches above the comforter.

Alexa looked to Josephine, who was smiling as she watched the display. "What's happening?"

"Well, my dear, it looks like our girl has more talents than we realized. I have never seen it first hand, as it is a very rare ability, but it appears that Chloe is telekinetic."

235

"Mama, pillow," Chloe said, pointing at her trick, struggling slightly to pronounce the L-sound that came out sounding like a W.

Alexa just stood there in awe of her daughter. "That makes three," she stated as she watched the pillow float gently back to the bed while Chloe clapped, clearly amused with herself.

"Three?" Josephine said in a questioning tone, not understanding what Alexa was referring to.

"Three talents, abilities, or whatever. She's telepathic, which I assumed she inherited from me. She started communicating with me when I was five months pregnant, but I stopped being able to hear her mind a couple of weeks ago. And she can heal with her touch; at least I think that's what it was. Last night she was able to heal Tilly when I was certain she would die after she saved me from one of Lucias' men. Now telekinesis.

"Remarkable," Josephine whispered. "In all my life, I have never seen one with so many gifts. Even in my visions, I did not see this. So much about her remains a mystery."

"I wanna see dress," Chloe stated, interrupting the two older women.

Alexa laughed, "I almost forgot. Here," she said, spinning the laptop to show the dress she had settled on. It seemed strange to talk about such normal, everyday things, like a wedding dress, amidst a life full of vampires and supernatural powers.

"It is perfect, Alexa. You will look bellísima," Josephine said, warmly.

CHAPTER 21 - *The Night Before*

Alexa lay awake in bed, too anxious and excited to sleep. She was getting married in the morning. With her eyes moving between her ring and the elegant gown that hung on the closet door, she kept feeling the urge to pinch herself just to be sure.

Chloe, who had become quite attached to Barb, was sleeping in another part of the house with her as she had done the previous two nights. The arrangement was convenient for Chloe's feeding, since Elijah had recommended that she stop nursing and increase her blood intake. Though, as she continued to grow so rapidly, it was clear that she needed more blood than Barb could safely donate each day.

Elijah had suggested supplementing her with some stored blood from the basement. As was expected, she was not overly happy with the cold substitute but, with some encouragement and an explanation about how taking too much blood would hurt Barb, she learned to tolerate it.

At supper the night before, Alexa had suggested Chloe feed from her; she was her daughter, after all.

"It is best she only feed from human sources, for now," Elijah said, gently. "While our kind does take blood from one another, it is a practice that is typically limited to mature adults, mostly mated pairs. Without getting too scientific, after the transformation, our blood lacks certain proteins that carry hormones which are essential to growth. That is why, other than in emergency situations, young vampires are taught to only take blood from humans."

"Why does she need so much blood?" Alexa asked. "Ethan told me your, um, our kind only needs to feed, like, once a month."

"Again, that is when we are mature. New vampires require blood more frequently, once or twice a week; but with Chloe's accelerated growth, she should feed at least daily," Elijah explained.

Alexa nodded and returned to pushing the food around on her plate. While the few bites that she had taken of grilled chicken and creamed asparagus were delicious, she just didn't have much of an appetite.

"Elijah, why don't I need blood? Why haven't I changed yet?" The question had been burning in Alexa's mind since the night she first learned of her true origins.

It was Barb who replied. "You've got a repression spell on you, child. It took me a while to figure it out, but I been thinkin' on it, and readin' through some spell books these past days. It would take a powerful witch to cast it; there are only a handful in this world who could manage it, but that's what it is. That birthmark of yours is not just a birthmark. It's been filled with magic, like the blocking spell in the tattoos I put on this family, here. The magic keeps the mark dark, almost vibrant with color. If I were to lift the spell it would fade."

"But who would do that?" Alexa asked, looking around.

"Your parents," Josephine interjected. "It was an ingenious idea. Our kind cannot breed with humans, and you were made to look like a human and so could not be the woman from the prophecy Lucias would be looking for."

They really were just trying to protect me, Alexa thought of her parents.

"So how do we take it off? If I change, I can help to protect Chloe. I could fight."

"There're only two ways for a spell this powerful to be lifted, child." Barb announced. "The witch who put it on you has to willingly reverse it, or if she was to die, so would her magic."

"Then we have to find her and persuade her to take it off," Alexa said, forcefully.

Ethan took her hand under the table. "Yes, Amor. We will find this witch, but it can wait a few days. We are getting married tomorrow," he said, as he nuzzled her neck.

"Of course," she breathed, leaning into his touch. "I'm sorry, I just feel so weak being surrounded by all of you who are so strong."

Ethan gripped her chin and turned her to look into her eyes. "Alexa, you are perhaps the strongest person I have ever met. Physical ability is not a true measure of strength. Your strength lies here," he said, placing his hand over her heart, "and here," he gently stroked her temple, "and now, here," he finished, placing her hand over his own heart.

"Someone is here," Elijah announced, pulling Ethan and Alexa from their private little moment. Ethan had been so consumed with Alexa that his senses had not picked up on the sounds of approach. Seeing his parents, who had remained focused and alert to what was going on outside, respond calmly and without alarm put him at ease as he trained his senses on the visitor.

It was a vampire, the steady heartbeat far too slow to be human. When he heard the beeping of the keypad and creak of the side door to the south wing, he knew who it was, and if that hadn't been enough, his acute sense of smell immediately picked up the barely-there fragrance of the perfume his sister pretended not to wear.

From a very young age, Cami had been a tomboy, showing no interest in the typical pastimes of the other girls. She had idolized her brother and begged him and her father to train with her since she was too young to enter the program at the colony. When they were not training with her, she was practicing on her own, mastering the sword and bow long before her preternatural senses had developed.

The light dusting of fragrance that she applied daily was the only evidence that she gave any consideration at all to her femininity. Of course, the family all noticed with their acute senses of smell, but they also knew better than to mention it.

Alexa was gripping Ethan's forearm tightly. "What's happening?" she whispered, as quietly as possible.

"It's just my sister," he said, looking pointedly at Elijah. "My father must have demanded her attendance tomorrow. That should make things interesting."

Alexa tensed at the announcement. *Wonderful; I'll really be able to enjoy the day feeling her hatred battering against me all day,* she thought, sarcastically.

"Not at all, son; I did not speak to her about it," Elijah replied, glancing sideways at his wife, who was avoiding eye contact with Ethan.

"Mother, you know how she feels. Tomorrow is one of the most important days of my life, of our life," he said, squeezing Alexa's hand. "We do not need a dark cloud hanging over our heads."

"Ethan, she is your sister. This has gone on far too long. I know that much of the divide between us has been of my own making." Tears began to well up in her eyes as she spoke. "I have been stubborn with Camille, with you, thinking I could force you to make different choices. I have missed you both so greatly and I no longer wish to let the years speed by without the joy of my children, and grandchildren, all of them, in my life. What better time to reunite our family than on such a happy occasion, my son?"

He was at a loss for words. While he had wanted to make things right with Cami for years, he did not want anything to take away from the happiness he felt in making Alexa his wife.

"She understands how important tomorrow is for you, Ethan. She will not impose upon your day," his mother continued, gently. "And I will speak to her again tonight; we have much to discuss, but I will be certain to impress upon her the..." she glanced almost imperceptibly at Alexa, "...delicacy of the situation."

Ethan sighed and nodded.

Ethan paced the floor of his large bedroom, regretting the decision for him and Alexa to sleep separately in the days leading up to their union. It had seemed like a romantic notion when he suggested it; a way to make their wedding night and honeymoon all the more special, but after two nights without her next to him, unable to lose himself in her warmth, he was starting to feel nervous and uncertain.

Each night as he listened intently to the steady beat of her heart through the walls, he considered going to her in the guest room, but he was held back by more than their agreement to stay apart. When left alone with his thoughts, he began to doubt his strength, his ability to protect her. How could he protect her from himself? That thought brought his mother's words to the front of his mind,

He had gone to his mother while Alexa slept the night they arrived.

He took a breath and raised his hand to knock on his parents' door, when it slowly swung open to reveal Josephine, who had been expecting the visit.

She smiled knowingly up at her son who was nearly a foot taller, then quietly slipped out and padded silently down the long hallway to her parlor while he followed.

When the door closed behind him, he turned to her, "I must know what you told her tonight. Please, what did you see, Mama?"

Josephine reached up and took his face in her hands, seeing so much desperation in his eyes that it nearly broke her heart.

"Mi hijo, you worry too much," she said, softly. "Sharing my vision with you all those years ago is one of my deepest regrets in this life. Knowing your future kept you from living your life for so many years. It is a mistake I will not repeat."

"As you have said before, things have happened as they must, but I need to know now, did you share the rest of your vision with Alexa? Has it changed or am I doomed to destroy her?"

She sighed deeply, "Ethan, what I told Alexa was for her, and her alone. She will make her choice as you must make yours."

"What choice? I cannot stay away from her any more than I can stop breathing! I made a promise to her to never leave again, but how can I bind myself to her only to lose her to my own weakness? So tell me now, is there any hope that I can change it? Can I save her?" he pleaded, with tears streaming down his chiseled cheeks.

She pulled him to her, wrapping her arms around him as he crumpled to the floor, clinging to her for comfort. "There is always hope, mi amor. Alexa is very strong, perhaps stronger than you realize; you must trust in her choice. The question is not whether you can save her, rather can she save you. So have faith; she will not fail you."

Was it true that he would be the one who needed saving? Though she refused to tell him anything further about her vision, his mother's words had given him comfort that night and allowed him to return to Alexa with hope in his heart.

But on this night, only hours before their wedding and mating, the seeds of doubt were growing like an infection in his mind. He had to go to her, needed to tell her of his fear before she bound herself to him, before it was too late for her to change her mind.

As he reached for the handle to his door, there was a soft knock. He had been so lost in his thoughts he had not heard her approach, but his heart leapt as he turned the knob, expecting to see Alexa standing on the other side. He couldn't hide his surprise when he opened it and found himself looking down at Cami. His normally stoic sister stood there with tears staining her face before wrapping her arms around his neck.

He remained still at first, confused by the sudden display of affection and contrition after so many years of distance and disapproval.

Finally, Ethan hugged her close, his forearms lying against the holster that crisscrossed over her back. Even in this seemingly fragile state, she was well-armed, though she had at least removed her swords.

Ethan backed them into the room and gently closed the door as Cami clung to him. "I am so sorry, my brother," she whispered, "I did not know."

They stood there in a warm embrace for several moments before Cami pulled away and sat down on the bed with her elbows on her knees.

"Why did you not tell me, brother? she asked, as she wiped the tears from her eyes, angry with herself for appearing so weak. "All of these years I have been so angry with you; if only I had known, I could have helped you."

"It was my cross to bear. There is nothing you could have done to change it. It took me all of these years to realize there was nothing I could do to change it either." He sat down next to her on the edge of the bed and put his arm around her shoulders. "So Mother told you everything, then?"

"No; not everything. She made it very clear that she told me what I needed to know, and nothing more. But I feel like I understand her so much more now. I never considered what a burden her gift has been. To see the future, but be essentially powerless to change it. I have been very selfish. I was so focused on my place with The Elite, on impressing the commander; I lost sight of the importance of family." She swallowed the knot that was building in her throat. "I hope someday you can forgive me, brother."

"There is nothing to forgive; we have all made mistakes. I no longer want to live in the past, or let the prophecy guide my actions." As he said the words, Ethan knew it was not entirely true. There was still a piece of the past, of the prophecy, that he couldn't let go of, not until he talked to Alexa.

Alexa had just started to doze off when she felt the soft touch of Ethan's fingers stroking her face. She forced her heavy eyelids open and strained to see his face. The only light in the room was filtering in from the moon outside, so she could only make out his outline.

"Hey, there," she whispered softly, her voice a little scratchy with exhaustion. She moved to sit up, simultaneously reaching for the lamp on the nightstand.

"No, Amor. Do not get up, I will not keep you long," he said as he continued stroking her cheek. "I must speak to you, though I do intend to keep our agreement to wait to be together until after we are married," he took a shaky breath, "if you will still have me when I am finished."

"Ethan," she started, but he interrupted.

"Please, just let me speak before I lose my nerve. It is about the prophecy. I do not know what she told you, but I can only assume my mother did not tell you the entire story since you are still here. I need for you to know; I need to give you a chance to leave while you still can."

He sat down on the bed and took her hand. "The vision, the prophecy, foretold your death." Ethan paused, expecting a reaction from Alexa at hearing the tragic truth, but she remained still, listening intently.

"And it is to be by my hand, but I cannot..." he pulled her hand to his mouth and gently kissed her knuckles. She felt the moisture from his tears on her fingers. "I will not believe it to be true. I love you more than my own life. I could never hurt you, you must know that, but my mother's visions have never been wrong. You can take Chloe, go into hiding far away from here. I will give you everything I possess; you could be safe without me."

Alexa waited for him to continue, but he stayed quiet, softly crying, waiting for her to respond, and expecting her to demand that he let her leave.

She took his hand and shifted over on the bed. "Lay with me, Ethan." He obliged hesitantly and lay down in the space she had made and she wrapped herself around him, pulling him close as she continued. "I have accepted my fate, whatever it may be," she whispered and gently kissed the tears on his cheek. "Before I met you, my life was empty. I was just going through the motions, existing. In such a short time, you have given me more than I ever hoped for in this life. I will take whatever time I have left, however long or short it may be, with you, and with Chloe. I have made my choice, and I choose you."

Ethan released the breath he had been holding, at once relieved and terrified by her words. He could not bear the thought of losing her.

Alexa sat up and moved to straddle him, taking his face in her hands as she looked down into his eyes. "It will be okay, my love. No matter what happens, we will face it together. You, as my husband, and I, as your wife. I will never lose faith in you," she said, before leaning down and kissing his full lips.

He wrapped his arms around her, hugging her to him tightly as he returned her kiss. She deepened the kiss, delving her soft tongue into his mouth, sending his blood rushing and eliciting a low growl from the back of his throat. He swiftly moved and slid her body beneath him and kissed her with all of the passion and emotion that had been threatening to burst free for the last two days.

Mustering every ounce of willpower that he had, Ethan broke the kiss and pulled back, quickly moving to sit on the edge of the bed. Alexa whimpered at the loss of his weight and warmth.

"Thank you, Amor," he whispered, as he quickly stood to leave. Though every fiber in his body was protesting, he was determined to wait until she was completely his before he took her again.

He rushed to the door, needing to put as much distance as possible between them if he was to have any hope of resisting the delicious call of her body.

Without words, Alexa understood his intentions and couldn't help but smile, sensing how difficult it was for him to walk away. She was glad to know that he was just as affected as she was.

"Goodnight, Mr. Kellar. I'll see you at the altar," she said softly.

Hearing the joy in her voice lifted the burden from his heart, yet did nothing to temper the lust that was coursing through his body. He desperately wanted to go back to her, to kiss her again and hold her in his arms, but he knew if he so much as looked at her again, let alone touched her, he would have no prayer of getting out of her room before the morning.

"Goodnight, sweet Alexa," he said as he turned the handle and stepped into the hallway. "You better get some sleep; come tomorrow night, you are going to need your strength," he tossed over his shoulder, playfully, before he disappeared from view.

"As will you," she challenged, even though he was gone, knowing that he would still be able to hear her with his superhuman senses.

She sat up for a few moments, silently hoping he would change his mind and come back, before finally rolling over, her body tingling with unquenched need.

Great, how on earth am I supposed to sleep now? she thought, as she snuggled into the soft down pillow and smiled. It was a delicious torture, wanting Ethan so badly, but choosing to wait until after the wedding.

Mrs. Ethan Kellar.

Her new name was the last conscious thought she had before the heavy tug of exhaustion finally pulled her into a deep and peaceful sleep.

Ethan chuckled as he closed his door, Alexa's words nearly making him turn around and go back to her room to show her exactly who was going to be needing their rest when he got his hands on her again.

He looked down and groaned at the massive erection that was tenting his black cotton pants. He considered hopping in the shower to relieve the tension, worried that if his need built up any further he wouldn't be able to control himself with Alexa after their wedding.

Tomorrow she will become my wife. A full-dimple smile spread across his face at the thought.

He had told her everything and she had not run. Just considering the possibility that she could have left him that night brought his arousal down several notches. He didn't know what he would do without her. She and Chloe were his life.

Their future was still uncertain but, there in the darkness, only hours before he and Alexa were going to say their vows, he finally realized why his mother refused to tell him anymore about her visions. Uncertain is exactly what a future should be.

CHAPTER 22 - *Family Reunion*

Alexa turned to see her reflection in the full-length mirror that stood in Josephine's dressing area and she couldn't believe her eyes.

She had never looked or felt more beautiful in her entire life. She could hardly believe she was the elegant woman in the mirror.

"You are a masterpiece, Alexa," Ethan's mother said proudly from behind her. She had spent the last two hours helping Alexa dress, doing both her hair and makeup. The front of her hair was pulled up into an elegant twist with a beautiful butterfly comb encrusted with blue sapphires, the rest cascading down her back in loose curls. The comb, Josephine explained, was a family heirloom that she had worn on her own wedding day. Her makeup was light, except on her eyes which were smoky and dramatic, making the extraordinary color of her irises stand out perfectly.

Alexa spun around to face Josephine, who was dressed in a lovely, yet simple, mid-length emerald-green gown. "Thank you so much; you are a miracle worker!" she exclaimed, as tears of joy started to well up in her eyes.

"I am no such thing; you are an incredibly beautiful woman. All I did was showcase that. Please, no tears. We cannot have you ruining all of my hard work."

Josephine walked over to Alexa and pulled her into a warm embrace. "Thank you, for this, dear girl. You have made my son so very happy." She moved her hands to Alexa's shoulders and looked into her eyes. "You have given me back my family. I can never thank you enough for that."

A lone tear slipped down Josephine's cheek. "If I can't cry, neither can you, Mama," Alexa said, trying out the new title. The word was strange on her lips, never having anyone to call that before, but it felt right. After just a few short days, the graceful woman before her had become family.

Hearing Alexa use the term drew another wave of emotion from Josephine and she grabbed her again, squeezing her tightly as tears flowed freely down her face.

Alexa struggled to keep her own tears at bay as she returned the hug.

Just then the door swung open, causing both women to turn. Josephine quickly retrieved a delicate handkerchief from a nearby table and started dabbing her eyes, as Cami strode into the room. She looked amazing, but rather uncomfortable, in the floor-length plum dress that was pulled tight at the waist by a black leather belt adorned with a large silver buckle. It had a deep V-neckline that Alexa could have never pulled off, but the look was still modest on Cami's athletic frame.

"I just wanted to check and see if I could help with anything," Cami said, as she approached the two women, stopping short in front of Alexa.

"You look lovely, Cami," Alexa said, uncertainly, not having spoken to her since the awkward meeting in front of her old home.

"I hate dresses; they are so inefficient," she said, grabbing the skirt of hers and pulling it up slightly to reveal her black combat boots, complete with her dagger handle coming up from the right one. "But this is a special occasion, so I'll deal."

She lowered the skirt and shifted uncomfortably, "You look great, too, Alexa. Listen, I'm sorry for the way I acted the other night. I just didn't understand everything then, but that's no excuse; either way, it's not like any of the crap I was mad about was your fault."

Alexa was surprised by Cami's manner of speech; it was vastly different from the rest of her family who all spoke so formally. She supposed it was the product of a life spent around a bunch of badass vampire soldiers.

"It's really not necessary, but thank you," Alexa said, as she approached her tentatively. "I'm really glad you decided to come. I really love your brother and I would love for us to be friends, sisters even." Overcome with the happiness of the day, Alexa shocked even herself when she pulled Cami into a hug.

Surprised, Cami remained rigid for a moment before relaxing slightly and patting Alexa's back. The only people she had ever hugged were her parents and brother. All these years with The Elite, the only form of affection between her and her brothers-in-arms was the occasional slap on the ass or pat on the back after a good battle or training session. She was so focused on her duty, that there was no time for anything else, like friends or romance.

Josephine stood by quietly, smiling as she watched the somewhat awkward exchange. It was such a relief to have all of her family under the same roof, even though she knew it wouldn't last long.

As Alexa pulled away, there was a knock on the door. "Ladies, are you all decent?" Elijah called from the hallway.

"Yes, mi vida, you can come in, so long as Ethan is not with you. He is not allowed to see his bride before the ceremony."

The door opened and Elijah filled the doorway with his tall frame draped in a perfectly tailored tuxedo, but Alexa could see there were people behind him that she didn't know.

As he entered the room, he gestured behind him, "Alexa, I would like to introduce you to our guests." He moved aside to reveal a man, also dressed in a tux, looking at Alexa rather strangely. He was a couple of inches shorter than Elijah, but no less handsome. Next to him was a woman who was close to Alexa's height and another man who appeared slightly younger with a crooked grin and longer, somewhat spiky, hairstyle. Alexa hadn't needed to keep her shields up since arriving in the home, so she already knew the guests were vampires.

255

She could sense their presence, but their thoughts were silent.

She glanced over to Josephine and Cami, who were both crouched down slightly facing the guests with their heads bowed. She looked back at the newcomers with confusion as Josephine spoke. "My lord, it is such an honor to have you in our home."

"Ladies, there is no need for such formality," the man said, his voice a rich, pleasant baritone. "After today, we are all family," he continued, with his eyes fixed on Alexa.

Alexa's confusion deepened and she looked at Elijah, who was smiling broadly. "Alexa, may I present William II, High Commander of The Agency and leader of our people; his lovely wife Rebecca; and his son Jared. The Commander has graciously agreed to perform the ceremony today."

She smiled and extended her hand to the gentleman as he approached her, but instead of taking it, he completely shocked her by scooping her up into his arms and hugging her almost too tightly.

He set her back down on her feet and clutched her shoulders as he looked at her intently, almost as if he was trying to memorize her face. "How could I refuse to marry my only daughter?" he stated, with a bit of sadness in his grey eyes.

Alexa suddenly felt dizzy and everything became fuzzy. She couldn't have heard him right. She looked at Elijah, and then at Josephine, who both were looking back at her with concern as they took in her suddenly ashen complexion.

Her knees began to buckle, and William quickly moved behind her and placed his hands under her elbows to steady her.

She leaned back into him as she tried to get her bearings; his wife standing in front of her, looking distressed. She reached out cautiously and took Alexa's hand. "Are you all right, dear?"

As things came back into focus, Alexa looked at the woman who was watching her carefully with tears starting to fill her brown eyes. Taking in the details of her face, she didn't need to be told that the woman now holding her hand was her mother.

Again able to stand on her own, she took a small step away from William's grasp and turned to face him, as Rebecca, still holding Alexa's hand, moved to his side.

Everyone remained silent while Alexa stared at her parents for several moments. She didn't even blink, afraid that if she looked away they would somehow disappear from her life again. A lifetime of questions and emotions were racing through her mind, making it impossible for her to find her voice, so she just kept staring. Her mother lightly squeezed her hand, causing Alexa to look down briefly before Rebecca pulled her into her arms.

"Oh, Alexa. You are so beautiful," she said, her voice shaky with emotion. "I have missed you so much, baby girl."

Any hope Alexa had of keeping her own tears at bay was lost with her mother's sweet words. She wrapped her arms tightly around the woman, whose embrace she had longed for her entire life, and began to sob.

William wrapped his strong arms around both women and they all clung to each other for several minutes, while everyone else looked on.

✧

Still standing near the door, Jared felt like he was glued to the floor, his eyes locked on one of the beautiful woman whom he had yet to meet. He should have been focused on his sister; he had been waiting his whole life for this day, yet his attention was utterly and completely captured by someone else. She was the most beautiful creature he had ever seen.

Cami could feel his gaze boring into her while she struggled to keep her eyes on anything but him. When he first entered the room, their eyes met and it was as if she was lost in the deep pools of his amazing grey eyes, completely overcome by the jolt that went through her at the sight of him. So much so that it took her a moment to recognize the presence of the High Commander and drop her head in deference, as was customary.

Her mother had taken her hand as they watched the emotional reunion of Alexa and her parents and all she could think about was what the warmth of his hand would be like. She silently cursed herself for her weakness. No man had ever affected her like that before.

It's just all this emotional shit going on around here. He's just another man and I'm not interested, Cami thought, trying desperately to convince herself of the lie.

"Son, what are you doing? Come, meet your sister," William summoned, as he reluctantly broke away from Alexa and Rebecca.

At the authoritative sound of his father's voice, Jared finally tore his gaze away from Cami and approached his family.

As she and Rebecca let go of one another, Alexa gratefully took the handkerchief that her father silently offered and dabbed at her face, as she looked up at the young man crossing the room. She had never even dreamed that she might have a sibling.

Jared ran a hand through his tousled hair, grinning sheepishly as he approached Alexa.

"Hey, sis," he said before he flashed the rest of the distance and pulled her into what could only be described as a big bear hug, making her giggle with surprise and lightening the intense emotional atmosphere that had taken over the room.

"Hey, kid," she joked, as he put her down, amazed by how natural their interaction already felt.

"So, I hear you're getting married today. That's heavy. We just met your future husband, he's a little old for you don't you think?" he joked, causing everyone to laugh, except Cami.

She was still battling with herself over how this stranger was making her feel. When Jared had finally looked away from her, she took the opportunity to really look at him as he crossed the room. Delicious was the word that entered her mind when she took in his sexy, confident swagger and boyish good looks. He was dressed as the other men were, in a well-tailored tuxedo, but there was something defiant in the way he wore it, like he didn't like being confined. Much like how she felt wearing a dress.

With the highly emotional climate starting to settle, Alexa finally spoke, "How is this possible? How did you all get here?"

"For that, we owe thanks to Dr. Kline and his beautiful wife," William said, clasping Elijah's shoulder.

Elijah shook his head, "The credit belongs to Josephine. She was clever enough to look into Alexa's past. I only made the phone call."

"My lord, it was merely luck on my part. Had you not been so famous amongst our people, my vision would not have proved very useful," Josephine said, humbly.

"No matter, we are forever indebted to your family and, please, from now on, you all must address me as William," he said and took Alexa's hand and kissed it, "except you, my darling. I realize we have only just met, but I would be greatly honored if you would call me Father, or something close to that."

"Of course," she replied, without hesitation.

He stroked the side of her face gently and said, "You truly have grown into a beautiful woman, but you will always be our baby girl. Now," he said, stepping back, "I'm sure you have many questions for your mother and me; however, I believe we have a wedding to get to, and there will be some time for that after, yes?" he said in question, looking toward Elijah.

"Yes, I believe they will have a few hours before their flight is scheduled to leave," Elijah responded.

"Who's flying somewhere?" Alexa asked confused.

"I am sorry, dear," Josephine started, as she glared at Elijah for his slip, "Ethan meant for it to be a surprise. He has chartered a plane to take you on your honeymoon tonight and, before you ask, the destination is also a surprise."

Alexa's heart started to beat a little faster; she had never been on a plane and had always thought that the prospect sounded slightly terrifying. Her time in solitary confinement had left her a little claustrophobic, never mind being thousands of feet above the ground.

"One other thing," William began, "if you all don't mind, Rebecca and I would really like to meet our granddaughter before the ceremony. I understand she will be the flower girl today." He already sounded like a proud grandpa.

As if on cue, the sound of Chloe's new dress shoes clicking on the wood floors echoed in the hall, before she came barreling into the room giggling with delight, clutching a gold-colored mid-heel shoe, and looking over her shoulder. As Alexa took in her frilly white dress and white patent leather shoes, she was thankful that Josephine had taken into account her rapid growth when they ordered her clothes only two nights before. She was at least one full size larger than she had been on that night.

"Mama, Barbie get me!" she squealed, as she ran over to Alexa and ducked behind her skirt.

Moments later, Barb came around the corner, dressed in a purple skirt-suit hobbling with only one shoe on. "Now, where did that girl get off to with my other shoe?" she pretended to ask with a big smile, since Chloe was doing a poor job of hiding with all of her giggling.

Unable to contain her excitement, Chloe jumped out, "Found me!" she yelled, still giggling, as she ran back over to Barb, handing over the missing shoe.

"Thank you kindly, honey," Barb said, as she slipped the shoe on and stood upright.

"Pardon me for my rudeness," she said, addressing Alexa's family. "I'm Barb Wilson, and you all must be Alexa's people. How wonderful you could get here in time!"

Chloe had been so engrossed in the little game that she had run right by without noticing William and Rebecca, but now she stood quietly, as she looked at each of them carefully. They both appeared frozen, watching Chloe with expressions of complete awe. She turned to look at Alexa, then back to them before a bright smile lit her face and she took off running into William's arms.

"Hi, Gampa," she said into his ear as she hugged his neck, and then turned to Rebecca and reached out for her.

As William released her, he addressed Elijah. "I know you said that her growth was accelerated, but somehow I was still not prepared. She is remarkable!"

"Yes, she is very special," Elijah agreed, proudly.

"Mi vida, perhaps you should escort our guests to one of the sitting rooms and give them the remainder of the time before the ceremony to spend with Chloe. Alexa and I need a few moments to freshen up her makeup and put on the final touches before she sees Ethan."

"Speaking of the groom; I better run and check on him, too. Lord knows he's probably losing his mind trying to stay away with all this commotion in the house," Barb said, as she headed for the door.

Cami, who had been silent since the arrival of Alexa's family, jumped at the opportunity to escape the confinement of that room. While it was more than large enough to easily accommodate five times the number of people, Jared's presence made her feel anxious, confined, and had her heart beating much faster than normal. She only hoped that the presence of Alexa's, and now Barb's, faster human heartbeats were enough to keep anyone from noticing.

"I'll come with you, Barb," she said, as she sped to the door while Barb walked through. Before she could follow, Jared flashed to her side, his hand gripping her forearm. She felt as if she couldn't breathe with him touching her bare skin, or maybe she was just holding her breath; she wasn't certain.

"Excuse me, but we were never properly introduced. I'm Jared, Jared Ryan," he said, releasing her arm and holding out his hand. Cami looked down at the proffered appendage, afraid to touch him again, but his father was the High Commander, and she couldn't be rude to him, so she reluctantly took his hand.

"Um, hello, I'm Cami Kline. It's nice to meet you. I'm sorry, I must go check on my brother," she said quickly, as she tried to pull her hand away, but Jared held on and began stroking her knuckles softly with his thumb, sending shivers down her spine.

He stepped a little closer and looked into her eyes. "The pleasure is mine, Cami. That's a beautiful name. I look forward to seeing more of you later," he said, as he gave her a devilish grin, his tone implying more than a friendly chat in the parlor.

Not knowing how to respond, she simply nodded, pulled her hand from his grip, and turned to follow Barb who had stopped only a couple of feet down the hallway to wait for her and watch the little exchange. She smiled wide at Cami and chuckled, but didn't say anything.

Jared leaned against the doorway and watched, as Cami retreated down the hallway, breathing deeply to take in her lingering scent and wondering if she had felt everything that he had. Her face and demeanor had remained impassive, yet her heartbeat told a different story.

He stepped out of the way as Elijah led his parents out of the room, with Chloe perched comfortably on Rebecca's hip and, despite his desire to go after Cami, he followed them in the opposite direction.

CHAPTER 23 - *I Do*

Thirty minutes later, Alexa picked up her bouquet of white calla lilies and stepped out of the dressing room on rather shaky legs. Josephine had reapplied her makeup and given her a simple diamond tennis bracelet and matching studs, before she left Alexa alone for a few minutes to gather her thoughts.

She placed her hand against her stomach and took a deep breath, trying to ease some of the butterflies she was feeling. Of course, she had expected this day to be one of the most memorable of her life; she just hadn't anticipated that so many of the memories would be made before she walked down the aisle.

She made her way through the house to the back door that led out to the garden, where everyone was waiting. As she approached the stone wall that still kept her hidden from the views of Ethan and the other guests, Josephine, who was waiting at the edge, sent Chloe down the aisle with her basket of flowers and signaled the musicians to begin playing the song that Alexa had chosen for her walk down the aisle, and then moved away to take her seat.

The first notes of Pachelbel's Canon in D being plucked on the harp floated through the air, causing the butterflies in Alexa's stomach to move to her chest. Her hand instinctively moved up to her neck in search of her dolphin pendant, which she often gripped for comfort.

A wave of panic washed over her briefly at its absence, before she remembered that it was wound securely around her ankle since the cut of her gown didn't really allow for a necklace.

She paused a moment longer, smoothed the front of her dress carefully, then grasped the bouquet with both hands and rounded the corner, coming in to view of the guests right as the violinist began to play.

Her eyes scanned the small gathering in search of Ethan, but he was still obscured from her view by the others in attendance. She walked slowly, using brides she'd seen on television and in movies as her example, having never attended a wedding herself. She was too nervous to look at anyone as she continued down the long aisle carpeted with a white runner that ended at the stairs of the gazebo where she would become Ethan's wife.

Instead she took in scenery, admiring Josephine's handiwork in all of the white lights and flowers that decorated the gazebo and breathing in the scent of the beautiful wildflowers on either side of her. When she finally reached the clearing where the guests were standing, she was shocked to hear a familiar voice in her head.

Oh, my goodness! Look at our girl; she is so lovely!

Having been surrounded by vampires the last few days, there had been no need for Alexa to keep her shields up. She should have considered that there would be two humans in attendance playing the harp and violin, but the voice did not belong to either of them.

She looked up immediately and saw the owner of that voice, Jill, with Jesse holding her hand, both smiling proudly, standing near her mother and brother. It was all she could do not to drop her flowers and run over to them, as she had been certain that she would never see their friendly faces again.

With great effort, she kept moving with a giant smile on her face, wondering how on earth they came to be there, but too happy to see them to care.

In the last few feet of her walk, she glanced around at everyone; her heart feeling completely full as she realized how far she had come in the last two years. As she looked at each of their faces, smiling at her with love, she was home. She finally had what she had longed for her entire life; a family.

Then she saw him and, the moment their eyes locked, everything else faded into the background. In his eyes, she saw every hope, every dream, every possibility. Again she felt the urge to run, wanting to throw herself into his arms but, with great effort and concentration, she took the last few steps at the same pace she had taken the others before she joined hands with Ethan and finally breathed a sigh of relief, knowing that the next time she took a step, it would be as Mrs. Ethan Kellar.

✧

The entire morning had been torture for Ethan. After he left Alexa, he had fallen asleep for a couple of hours, only to be awakened suddenly by his father, who was practically vibrating with excitement.

"Son, I have the most wonderful news!" he said, far too cheerfully for five o'clock in the morning. "Your mother, brilliant woman that she is, and I decided not to mention anything until we had more information, but now it is certain."

"What is it, Father?" Ethan asked, his voice scratchy from sleep.

"We have found Alexa's family," he paused to give Ethan a moment to absorb the information.

"Really?! How?!"

"Your mother,. When she spoke with Alexa and looked at her future, she also looked at her past. She saw her parents."

"I did not realize her vision worked in both directions of time. Why has she never mentioned that before?" Ethan wondered aloud.

"She did not realize that she could. She had never even tried, but something that Alexa said gave her the idea to try and, when she focused on her past, she caught a glimpse of her mother and father," Elijah stated proudly.

Ethan stood and paced beside his bed, "But even if she saw them in a past vision, how could you possibly find them so quickly amongst all of our people, unless…?"

"Unless we happened to already know them," Elijah filled in. "In a manner of speaking, at least. Her father is William II, High Commander of The Agency."

Ethan froze mid-step. "How is that possible? Why would someone with so much power send his child away?" He could feel his anger building at the thought of Alexa feeling abandoned her whole life. "He could have easily protected her!"

"Do not be so quick to pass judgment, my son. Consider his position. As High Commander, he knew of the prophecy. His daughter was born with the mark. How long do you think they could have kept that hidden with her in the public's eye? Even with extensive protection, we know that Lucias is remarkably resourceful. The Commander did what he thought was best to protect her. Surely, you can understand his decision," Elijah said, looking at his son pointedly.

Of course he understood; he had done the exact same thing, and he was ashamed of his judgment and his weakness.

"You must forgive him, and yourself, Ethan. And you must do it quickly," Elijah said, as he moved to leave."The High Commander, along with his wife and his son, will be here in a few hours. I am sorry to have woken you, but you need to be prepared. As you well know, without his blessing, there can be no official mating between you and Alexa."

Ethan practically fell back on to the bed as his father pulled the door closed on his way out. The law stated that every non-genetic blood bond be registered and approved by the High Commander. It was just a formality, and it was well known that requests were typically approved immediately, but this was his own daughter, one he hadn't seen in over two decades. He may not be so amenable to the idea of instantly having his bond superseded.

Ethan waited nervously in the parlor for the arrival of Alexa's family. One of the disadvantages of being a vampire is that everything is heightened, including emotions, making experiences more intense and sometimes more stressful. His mother had suggested they use the soundproof room, given the delicate nature of the topics that were likely to be discussed. William's armed guard would be accompanying him and, though he trusted the men with his life, Alexa was his most closely held secret.

Elijah escorted them into the parlor and quickly took leave. Ethan was nervously pacing the room, so lost in thought that he was surprised by their entry.

"So, this is the fortunate young man who is marrying my only daughter today," William said, as he approached him and extended his hand. He looked Ethan over thoroughly. "It would have been preferable for this introduction to occur sometime before the wedding, but I suppose that could not be helped, given the circumstances."

"Now, William, I am sure poor Ethan is nervous enough without you giving him a hard time," Rebecca chided, as she stepped up to introduce herself.

Ethan couldn't help but feel a little more at ease in her presence. While there were some distinct differences, Alexa looked a lot like her mother, especially her sweet smile.

When Jared approached, he stood up tall and shook Ethan's hand rather roughly, gripping just a little too tight as he glared at him seriously. If that wasn't a clear enough signal, his words made his intentions quite transparent. "I've been waiting twenty-five years to get my sister back. I know you're supposed to be the biggest, baddest vamp out there, but so help me, if you screw around with her, I'll find a way to make you pay."

"Understood," Ethan replied coolly, though he was pleased to see the protective streak in Alexa's brother. He would take all the help he could get keeping her safe.

With that, Jared flashed him a bright smile. "Well, then congratulations, man!" he said, clapping Ethan on the shoulder.

After a minimal amount of small talk, Rebecca and Jared took their leave to go join Elijah and give William and Ethan some privacy to have a more in-depth discussion.

When the door clicked shut, William turned and walked across the room to a small table that housed a silver tray with a bottle of well-aged scotch and a set of tulip-shaped whisky glasses. He poured two generous glasses full and took a seat in one of the two wingback chairs in the room.

"I am not much of a drinker, but I think the occasion calls for it," he said, holding a glass out to Ethan as he took his first sip.

Ethan took the proffered drink and sat down in the opposite chair.

"This is excellent scotch," William complimented.

"Yes; my mother is quite the aficionado, though I could not tell you how she ever developed a taste for it. It is a strange drink for a woman; in my experience they tend to prefer wine or mixed drinks."

"And is your experience with women particularly extensive?" William questioned, his tone casual, but Ethan knew the time had come for the real discussion.

"No, my lord. For a man of over two-hundred years, I would consider my experience unusually limited." He took a sizable swallow of scotch and placed the glass on the coffee table between them. "Forgive me, as High Commander, I assume you are privy to the details of the prophecy and are no doubt aware of my part in it."

"Are you referring to the part where you impregnated my unmarried daughter or the part where you take her life?" William questioned, showing no emotion. He could have still been talking about the quality of the scotch, based on his tone and demeanor.

Ethan felt his heart sink to the floor. He had never considered that anyone beyond his parents knew the complete and horrible truth. He sank back into the chair, completely defeated. It was settled then. The High Commander would forbid the union and take Alexa and Chloe away under his protection.

"Do not despair, young man. I have no intention of taking your bride or denying you the privilege of bonding with her. I only needed for you to consider the possibility of what the prophecy foretold," he said, smiling.

Ethan could only stare at the High Commander, a look of utter confusion on his face.

"Come now, Ethan. Had you never wondered where my daughter came by her gift?" he questioned, one eyebrow raised with amusement. "Apparently not, which pleases me greatly. Had you been aware you may not have been so open with your thoughts."

Utterly speechless, Ethan could only sit there in stunned amazement.

"I believe I know all that I need to; you love my daughter completely and you will do everything in your power to protect her. That is all any father can ask," he said, standing. He stepped over to Ethan and laid his hand on his shoulder, "She is strong, son; that was evident from the moment she was born. Trust in that. Now if you will excuse me, I would very much like to meet her," and in a flash he was gone, leaving Ethan to his thoughts and what was now an irresistible glass of scotch.

For the next hour, Ethan remained there alone, fighting his need to be with Alexa. He did himself the small favor of closing the door after the High Commander left, knowing that if he heard any sign of distress from Alexa in what was sure to be an extremely emotional reunion, he would have no prayer of staying away.

After what felt like an eternity, the door slowly opened as Barb and Cami entered the room.

"Well, now, aren't you looking handsome this fine morning," Barb greeted, as she looked him over with a smile.

"How is Alexa?" he questioned urgently, looking first at Barb and then his sister.

"She's just as right as rain," Barb answered, " I can't imagine anything making this day more complete than having her folks show up after all these years."

He looked back toward his sister, who was oddly silent standing in the doorway, looking towards the window.

"Cami, is something wrong?" he questioned, looking at her intently and with concern.

The sound of her name got her attention, "What did you say?" she asked, having not heard anything Ethan said other than her name.

"I asked how Alexa was," he repeated, a puzzled look on his face as he took in his sister's demeanor. He had never seen her so frazzled. She was typically the picture of discipline and duty in her manner and stance, and this was more than just the change in her attire. She was distracted, unfocused.

"Oh, she's great," she replied though, to be honest, she had no idea how Alexa was doing since her attention had been so inexplicably trained on Jared.

"And how are you feeling? You seem off somehow," he said, looking at her quizzically.

Cami stood up straighter, trying to snap herself out of whatever it was that had her feeling so out of sorts. "I'm perfectly fine, Ethan," she replied. "I just hate being in these silly clothes and without all of my weapons."

That was a reasonable excuse which seemed to satisfy Ethan, who had too many other things on his mind to question her further. "Members of the High Commander's personal guard are posted all around the property. I can assure you there will be no need for your weapons today."

"Your brother is absolutely right," Josephine said, appearing in the doorway. "This is a day for celebrating, not fighting." She walked over to Ethan and took his hand. "It is time, cariño."

Ethan stood next to the beautifully decorated gazebo, his heart pounding almost as fast as a human's as the harpist began to play the music that signaled Alexa's walk down the aisle.

He was painfully aware of Alexa's father standing above him to the right at the top of the gazebo stairs, able to hear his every thought. That was a rather inconvenient ability for a father-in-law to possess, but an invaluable one for a leader.

Chloe came into view, moving a little too quickly and throwing the white rose petals from her basket around haphazardly, with a wide grin on her face. When she saw Ethan, she ran over and hugged his legs, the top of her head already reaching mid- way up his thigh.

Her sweet presence helped to ease some of Ethan's anxiety and he scooped her up into his arms, planting a quick kiss on her cheek before he set her down and shooed her over to Barb, who was standing at the front of the other guests.

There were more attendants than he had anticipated. Along with the surprise of Alexa's family had come the addition of her former neighbors, Jesse and Jill. Before everyone took their places, William had introduced them to Ethan, informing him that they were actually long-time friends of the Ryan family and had been sent to help keep an eye on Alexa. They were not the only humans that the High Commander had employed for that purpose. Apparently, he had been keeping a fairly close eye on Alexa over the years, at least as close as he could without raising suspicion.

Then she stepped into view, smiling shyly as her eyes met his, and he felt as if his heart had stopped. Every worry, every fear, every doubt melted away in that moment and a broad smile spread across his handsome face as he looked at her with reverence. Involuntarily, his gazed slid lower to take in the cut of her gown that fell perfectly over her curves.

When he looked into her eyes again, he saw a spark of arousal as she took in his appearance. He was dressed as the other men, in a well-tailored tuxedo, except his colors were opposite of the others, his jacket a beautiful ivory, the vest below onyx. The look on her face enflamed the passion which had been simmering since he left her bed in the night and he'd had to fight to keep the beast inside him leashed.

William discreetly cleared his throat, drawing Ethan's attention back the matter at hand. He chanced a brief glance back at him to see him fighting a smile.

Alexa took the final steps to stand before Ethan and reached out with a visibly shaking hand to take his. His touch soothed her nerves and they turned together to take the three steps to stand before her father.

Everyone behind them sat in the chairs draped in white fabric that had been set up with intricately-tied silver bows on the backs that matched the detailing on Alexa's gown.

William nodded to the musicians, who stood and exited down a path that ran perpendicular to the gazebo to wait until they were summoned once the ceremony was complete. Since this was a vampire wedding, certain traditions would be difficult to explain to the humans, but they could not risk inviting other vampires to play, for fear of exposing Alexa and Chloe.

Alexa and Ethan stood facing one another, both sets of hands firmly clasped together as they looked into each other's eyes.

Ethan mouthed, "I love you," silently, to which Alexa replied equally as silently, "I love you. I am so happy."

William began to speak to them in a tongue that few present could understand. Josephine had informed her earlier that the first part of the ceremony required the use of the old tongue, one only spoken by the eldest of vampires. She herself only remembered some of the words which Elijah had taught her so many years ago when they were bonded.

After speaking for several minutes, the High Commander looked to the small crowd, who all bowed their heads in response before he turned to the small table to his left and retrieved a small silver dagger and red satin ribbon. He turned first to Ethan and spoke the sacred words in English for Ethan to repeat.

"I bind myself to you, Alexa; blood, mind, body, and soul. I give myself to you freely and without reservation, to serve you, by my life or my death, from this day into eternity," Ethan recited, with love and adoration in his eyes as he took the offered dagger and made a small cut on the inside of his wrist.

He passed the dagger to Alexa as William instructed her to recite the same words to Ethan. Then she, too, cut her wrist, fighting not to wince at the pain, before passing the knife back to her father.

William took their two hands and placed their wrists one on top of the other so that the blood from each incision was united between them. He then bound them together with the red ribbon, while again speaking words in the old language.

Then he said to the crowd first in the old tongue, then in English, "Let all those present witness and rejoice in this most sacred union."

They repeated in unison, "By the blood, we bear witness."

Though it was not typical of vampire unions, Ethan could not resist the temptation and pulled Alexa to him with his free arm, kissing her fiercely in front of everyone present, eliciting a couple of whoops and hollers from the crowd, mainly Jill and Jesse, but Jared joined in with a low whistle.

When Ethan finally released her, Alexa wobbled for a moment from the force of his kiss as she turned to face the crowd with a guilty smile and flushed cheeks. The music started up again and Ethan, with a megawatt smile on his face, turned his wrist within the binding of the ribbon to take Alexa's hand. He leaned down and whispered in her ear, "Time to take our leave, Mrs. Kellar," and led her back up the aisle through the cheering guests.

CHAPTER 24 - *Family Time*

Back inside the house, Ethan and Alexa made their way to his bedroom where he undid the binding and pulled her wrist to his mouth, sliding his tongue over the small laceration to seal it before repeating the action on his own.

He then pulled her body to him, sliding his hands up her waist along the silky fabric of her gown before crushing his mouth to hers hungrily. She melted willingly into his kiss, sliding her arms up around his neck and pushing her hands through his soft hair.

He pulled back slightly, leaving her breathless as he looked lovingly into her eyes and said, "Te amo, Alexa. You are mine and I am yours."

She looked back at him, slightly confused, a question burning in her mind.

"What is it, Amor?" he inquired.

"I just thought, I don't know, that once we were bonded I would feel different. Your mother mentioned the physical connection that the bond creates, but I don't feel anything more than what I did before."

Ethan chuckled slightly at her obvious disappointment. "That is because we have not completed the bond, mi corazón. That part was to make you my wife, as humans do, but it was only the ceremony that unites us before our witnesses. The consummation of our bond is far too intimate to take place in public view," he rasped, leaning in so that his breath slid over the sensitive skin of her neck, sending a shiver down her spine.

"Oh," she whispered lazily as she tilted her head, giving him better access to her neck, "what will that be like?"

"Hmmm," he whispered as he kissed her neck gently, "it will be like heaven."

"Can you be a little more specific, Mr. Kellar?" she challenged, pushing him back slightly.

"Well," he pulled her close again, "first we are going to go on a little trip, where we can truly be alone." He kissed her neck again, "I know how you worry about my parents hearing your screams," he teased.

"And where exactly are we going?" she questioned, fighting not to lose herself in his touch.

"That, Amor, is a surprise." He traced his finger down the side of her neck and down the deep cut of her dress between her breasts, eliciting a low moan. "When we are alone, and I have your beautiful body writhing beneath me," he whispered, "I will bite you here," he kissed her neck again, flicking his tongue over the place he had bitten her before, causing her vein to rise to his call, "and bury myself deep inside you."

Alexa felt the moisture gathering at the apex of her thighs, as she listened to Ethan's hushed words as he continued. "And then you will take my blood from here," he said raising his wrist which had already healed from the earlier ceremony, "to complete the circle."

The thought of taking his blood made her feel thirsty in a way she had never felt before.

He took her face in both hands and slanted his lips over hers, his tongue delving in ever so slightly before he said. "I will be inside you and you will be inside me. Once we have mixed our blood in this way and have marked each other, the bond will be complete. These marks will stay with us, like human scars, letting all others know that you belong to me alone, and I to you."

He kissed her again, deeper this time, before he pulled back leaving them both breathless. "Now I am afraid, Amor, that we must return to our guests. They will want to celebrate with us before we leave, and it would be unforgivably rude for us to stay locked away until our departure."

He took her hand and headed for the door as she used her free hand to smooth her dress and fidget with her hair.

"You look perfect, Amor," Ethan said, smiling back at her as she lagged behind.

Suddenly she froze, "Wait, Ethan; how long will we be gone? What about Chloe? We can't leave!" she said, starting to panic. "At the rate she's growing we won't even recognize her when we get back!"

"Calm yourself, mi corazón. We will be gone for one week and Chloe will be well cared for in our absence. With two sets of greedy grandparents fighting for her attention, she will hardly notice. And we have the benefit of technology. I have already worked out the details so that we will be able to FaceTime with her as often as we like."

While it would not be the same as being with her, Alexa found comfort knowing that she would at least be able to see and talk to Chloe each day.

"Now, let us go and join the celebration; we only have a few hours and I am certain your family would like some time with you before we go," he said, as he opened the door for her.

Once they were back amongst the guests, in one of the large rooms in the west wing of the house that had been expertly decorated for the occasion, Alexa could see that Ethan was right. Chloe seemed quite at home, bouncing around between her doting grandparents soaking up all of the extra attention.

Looking around at all of the food, Alexa thought that Josephine had gone a little overboard. There was enough to feed a small army instead of the twelve who were in attendance. Although, she *had* noted at previous meals that vampires seemed to have exceptionally healthy appetites for human cuisine.

Alexa grabbed a large strawberry from a nearby tray and dipped it into the accompanying chocolate sauce before taking a large bite, sending juice dripping down her chin. She went to wipe it off with the napkin in her hand but, before she could, Ethan was there using his finger to clear it away then he put it in his mouth and sucked in one of the most erotic gestures she had ever seen.

And just as quickly as he appeared, he was gone; back to his conversation with Elijah and Josephine, who simply smiled at her from across the room.

"Anyway, we're really sorry we couldn't tell you, but we made a promise and they only wanted to make sure you were safe without interfering," Jill said, pulling Alexa back to the conversation. "We didn't really do the best job at the not-interfering part. You just seemed so alone, I couldn't help myself," she said, looking at Alexa with compassion. To her own surprise, instead of feeling angry about being spied on, she felt oddly touched that her family had cared enough to go to such lengths as to send humans to keep an eye on her. Apparently, they were not the first humans who had been employed for such a purpose, there having been one or more people watching over her since the moment she left the group home all those years ago. However, the rest had remained completely hands-off; only watching from a distance. Somehow, it made her feel more connected to the family that she had only met that day, though she still had so many questions.

It was then that William and Rebecca appeared at her side. "Darling, would you grant us the pleasure of a private audience?" her father requested, rather formally.

"Of course, Father," she replied, giving Jill a little wave as she turned to follow them. As they passed a tray of full champagne flutes, she grabbed one and downed the contents before they were out of the room.

When they were safely tucked away in the privacy of the parlor, William began to speak. "We wanted to take the opportunity to explain our actions over all these years, before your new husband whisks you away. I understand if you are angry and confused, but you must know that everything thing we did was to protect you."

Tears were already streaming down Rebecca's face. Alexa was silent for a moment, considering how to respond and how to ease some of her parents' guilt because, while her life had been difficult, she now realized that there had been a purpose to all of it.

Before she could speak, William looked at her with surprise. "You are not angry with us? I must say that, while my heart hoped for such understanding, I in no way expected it."

Rebecca looked at William and began to cry even harder, unable to speak as she grabbed Alexa and pulled her into a tight embrace. Now it was Alexa's turn to look surprised, as she returned her mother's hug. She smiled when the truth flooded her mind. "So I inherited my gift from you, Father," she said, with a smile.

"Yes, you are a clever young woman. I want you to know that we are so proud of you. All that you have endured, that you still possess such a pure and compassionate heart; it is remarkable, as are you."

They spent the next hour talking about the past. The anguish that he and her mother felt when they discovered her mark. How they had enlisted the help of a witch to suppress her transformation before they sent her to the group home under the care of Ms. Johnson in order to keep her hidden from the vampire world, which they assured her could be removed as soon as she and Ethan returned from their honeymoon. The told her about the trust fund, the human watchers, how heartbreaking it was to remain separated from her, all of it. By the time they were finished, most of her and her mother's makeup had been washed away by tears and William's eyes were red, but they were all smiling.

"Well, my sweet girl," Rebecca began. "I suppose we should go and get you freshened up and back to your husband. You do not have much time left before your journey.

As they headed for the door, William placed his hand on her shoulder. "He is a good man, Alexa. I have seen his heart. You are both fortunate to have found your mate at so young an age," he looked at his wife adoringly. "I lived many empty centuries before I found your mother. Each year that passed, I felt more and more restless, but I never knew why. It was not until I laid eyes on her that I realized I had been missing a piece of my soul. Cherish and protect that bond."

She threw her arms around his neck and kissed his cheek. "Thank you, Daddy."

Ethan had felt anxious since the moment Alexa left the room. While he didn't want to smother her, and he knew she needed time with her family, it was difficult for him to be separated from her. His body was practically vibrating with the need to complete the blood bond and he knew he would not feel peace until it was done.

He took comfort knowing that he only had to wait a few more hours and, thankfully, observing his sister across the room had provided a much needed distraction while he waited for Alexa's return.

She had changed back into her normal clothes after the ceremony; black, form-fitting fatigues, weapons and all, yet her demeanor was still off. She was fidgety, constantly fingering her sidearm and eating as if she had never seen food before in her life. He focused in and listened to her heart beat, which was erratic and far faster than normal. It wasn't until Jared approached her and her heart rate nearly doubled, that he realized what had her so distracted and he couldn't help but laugh to himself.

Not wanting to be overly intrusive, Ethan did his best not to listen in as he continued to watch. Jared spoke, and Cami appeared irritated, as she responded curtly and moved away to procure a drink; another dead giveaway, since she never partook in alcohol, always wanting to keep her focus sharp. While it took a great deal more alcohol to affect a vampire, it had the same impact on them as it did on humans.

Jared did not appear to be deterred in the slightest, finding a variety of excuses to continue to approach her, whether it was to ask her a question about the house or to offer her more food or drink. Ethan couldn't help but wonder how he'd come to be so confident and resilient. Then he thought perhaps it was because Jared knew something everyone else could not; his father and sister were telepaths, so it wouldn't be unlikely for him to be one as well.

No sooner had Ethan thought the thought, then Jared looked over at him and flashed him a crooked grin, confirming his suspicion.

At that point, he couldn't help the laugh that escaped his lips. Finally, his celibate sister may have met her match.

Jared raised his eyebrows at that tidbit of information and Ethan shook his head in response.

Well, good luck with that one, he sent.

As Jared approached her yet again, much to Cami's relief, Chloe ran over to her and jumped into her arms, offering her a much-needed excuse to avoid the cocky young vampire.

Ethan heard Barb chuckle from a few yards away, drawing his attention. "It's about time," she said, looking at him and then over at Cami and Jared.

That old woman was far too smart for her own good. She had been like his a second mother for most of his life. He couldn't imagine being without her, though he knew someday, when the war finally ended, she would go to the other side. She had mentioned on more than one occasion how ready she was to cross over and be with the rest of her family.

The sound of Alexa's familiar heart beat drew his focus and caused his to speed up, as he turned towards the door in anticipation of her entry.

When she appeared in the doorway, he couldn't stop himself and flashed over to her, pulling her into his arms, eliciting a surprised squeal and leaving her now-bare feet dangling as he kissed her. "I missed you," he whispered against her cheek before setting her back down, but keeping her wrapped in his arms.

"Mr. Kellar, I was only gone for a little while, and you are going to have me all to yourself for the next week," she said, feigning irritation.

"I plan to take full and complete advantage of that time, Mrs. Kellar," he said, with promise in his tone as he kissed the tip of her nose, causing her blood to rush.

Just then, Chloe rushed over, far faster than a human toddler could move and wrapped an arm around each of their legs. "Miss you," she said, looking up at each of them with a smile.

Elijah strolled over, with Josephine following closely behind. "Our little princess is right; it is nearly time for you two to leave for the airport."

Alexa looked at Ethan with panic in her eyes and knelt down to pick up Chloe. "I haven't even packed anything," she said, hugging Chloe tightly.

"That is all taken care of," Josephine said brightly. I sent one of our staff to do some shopping for you, so everything is all packed and loaded into the car.

"Staff?" Alexa said in question.

"Yes, we normally have a staff of five on the grounds," Josephine replied, "but given the nature of everything happening the last few days, we thought it prudent to give them some time off. I just had someone run in to the city to pick up a few items for you and drop them off at the gate. There is enough to give you a variety of options with regard to the occasion and the weather, all in your size, of course."

Ethan and Alexa changed into more casual clothing and, after several tearful and drawn-out goodbyes, they were loaded into the car and on their way to board the private jet.

CHAPTER 25 - *Paradise*

As they neared the end of their fairly short ride to the airport, Ethan could sense Alexa's growing anxiety through her increasing heart rate and bouncing leg. "What is it, Amor?" he asked, with concern.

She pulled her attention away from staring out the window to face him. "I've never been on a plane before and, um, I guess I'm a little claustrophobic," she admitted, feeling slightly embarrassed knowing that thousands of people flew every day.

Ethan smiled at her reassuringly, "Do not worry; the jet will be rather spacious so I do not think you will feel trapped inside. It will be nothing like flying on a commercial plane being packed in with other passengers. We will be free to move around, eat, drink, watch television, and there is even a bedroom," he said, only wanting to offer the option of sleep, but Alexa's mind went in a much naughtier direction and her nerves receded significantly.

With his preternatural senses picking up on her response, he chuckled, knowing exactly what she was thinking. He had to admit, he'd had similar thoughts when he first booked the charter and learned of the bedroom, wondering how on earth he was going to keep his hands off of her until they reached their destination.

There are worse problems to have, he thought to himself, before he picked up her hand and kissed her knuckles. "I like the direction of your thoughts, Amor."

"What; are you a telepath now?" she teased.

"Hardly; however, I am learning to read you, and," he grinned wickedly, "your body betrays your mind. The scent of arousal is all over your skin."

Alexa's cheeks flushed immediately at his words. Something about knowing that she smelled so strongly to Ethan was embarrassing and made her slightly self-conscious.

Guess I better get over that quickly or I'm going to have to shower constantly, she told herself.

Ethan brushed his knuckles over her cheek, "This, I love. Perhaps I should embarrass you more often to see this lovely color light your beautiful face."

"I would think that over a little more, Mr. Kellar, unless you want to spend a lot of time in the dog house," she huffed, glaring at him with false menace.

"Dog house, huh? I surely do not want that; perhaps I must find other ways to keep you flushed then, Mrs. Kellar," he rasped, as he crawled the short distance across the seat to hover over her and look into her eyes before he began kissing the side of her neck.

She tilted her head to the side to give him better access and a soft moan escaped her lips as he ran his tongue in a slow line up to the sensitive skin behind her ear. "I love the little sounds you make when I touch you, Amor," he whispered, and then he dipped his soft tongue into her ear, eliciting a noise somewhere between a giggle and a moan.

He hooked his arm around her waist between her body and the seat and pulled her so that she was almost lying down on the soft leather. She closed her eyes while he returned to his assault on her neck and then trailed kisses down along her collarbone, sliding the straps of her tank top and bra down her shoulder to reveal more of her perfect olive skin. When he tugged the front of the top down further, nearly revealing her left breast, her eyes snapped open and she grabbed his hair in her hand and tugged slightly so that he looked up at her.

She nodded her head toward the front of the car and the driver on the other side of the glass divider, "You are not getting me naked with an audience," she said firmly.

"Amor, I would sooner kill him than let him look upon what is for me alone. Besides, it is one-way glass; he cannot see or hear us," he stated matter-of-factly, before he turned his attention back to her body and kissed the top of the soft mound that he had all but completely exposed.

Instead of pulling her shirt down the rest of the way, he used his fingers to push only her bra down off of her hardened nipple, leaving the thin fabric of her tank top covering it. He grinned at her devilishly and gently gripped the sensitive flesh, shirt and all, with his teeth and tugged lightly, never taking his eyes off her face.

His other hand was sliding ever so lightly up the inside of her thigh, then up over the denim of her shorts where he stopped short of where she needed him and squeezed her leg possessively. At this point, she had begun to pant and squirm, desperate to find release after so many days without Ethan's touch.

Just when she thought she couldn't take anymore, and was ready to start begging, the car slowed and came to a stop.

Ethan skillfully slipped her bra and tank top back into place and kissed the tip of her nose before he sat back up on the seat.

Still in a partially horizontal position, Alexa looked over at him, "You are so mean," she whined in frustration.

Ethan slid his hand down into his lap, drawing her attention there as he tried to adjust his erection to make it less noticeable. "As you can see, touching you affects me just as much as it does you," he said, settling on pulling his hardness up his stomach where it was held down by the waistband of his shorts. "I apologize, but I could not sit here alone with you and not put my hands on your beautiful body, especially with so much of your skin exposed," he stated unabashedly. "Trust me, the anticipation will make the bonding experience so much more intense, but if you prefer, I will do my best to behave until we arrive."

Just the mention of the bond caused Alexa's stomach to flip, as her neck began to tingle. Thinking of Ethan sinking his teeth into her while he was inside her made her impossibly wetter, and did not help at all with the task of calming herself enough to exit the car.

Ethan inhaled deeply. "Amor, if you expect me to resist you, you must try not to think things like whatever just ran through that pretty head of yours. I have a strong will, but a man can only stand so much," he said with a wink, only half kidding.

To Alexa's surprise, they had actually pulled up right next to the large jet that was taking them to whatever mysterious destination Ethan had chosen. Despite numerous pleas from her, he refused to divulge the secret; he wouldn't even give her any hints and she found it extremely frustrating. Being a telepath, she wasn't really accustomed to surprises.

When they approached the stairs to the plane, they were greeted by a cheerful flight attendant whose super short white-blonde hair made her look a lot like a pixie. She smiled at each of them brightly and held out her hand to Alexa, "Hello, Mrs. Kellar. My name is Allie and I will be taking care of you and your husband during your flight today."

"It's very nice to meet you, Allie," Alexa replied. The young woman's gaze hadn't lingered on Ethan at all; there was no batting of her eyelashes, no flirting, just a short professional greeting, which had to be a first. Every other time Alexa had seen women around Ethan, they were practically drooling and giving her the evil eye.

I like her, Alexa thought immediately.

They entered the cabin and Alexa's jaw dropped. Ethan was right; it was far from cramped. The spacious area looked more like a luxurious family room than an airplane, with its plush leather chairs, marble tables, wet bar, and flat screen televisions on opposite walls.

"Please sit wherever you like. Would either of you like for me to make you a drink or perhaps something to eat?" Allie inquired, pointing toward the bar.

"Nothing for now," Ethan replied.

"Very well; please let me know at any time if you need anything," Allie said with a smile, looking at each of them. "I will remain in the front cabin for the duration of the flight to give you some privacy, but there are call buttons on the arms of each chair. I'm just going to go check in with the captain for a moment. We should be in the air in just a few minutes."

"Thank you, Allie," Alexa said. She took a seat in one of the chairs and sank into it with a sigh. "Now this is the life," she said, smiling up at Ethan who was watching her with amusement.

He took the seat opposite her and frowned at her. "What's wrong?" Alexa asked, with concern.

"I do not like this," he said without elaborating.

"What do you mean? This is amazing; what's not to like?" she questioned in astonishment.

A crooked grin tilted his lips, "You are much too far away from me sitting like this."

She snatched up the small pillow that was next to her in the chair and chucked it at Ethan, aiming for his face. He reached out and caught it with one hand before it made contact. "I was actually worried that something was wrong!"

His grin turned into a full smile. "Something *is* wrong; as I said, you are too far away from me. Perhaps you should sit on my lap for the trip," he said, completely serious.

"I don't think we're allowed to do that. Aren't we supposed to be strapped in?" she questioned, her nerves about flying starting to return. Though her claustrophobia didn't seem to be an issue, there was still the small problem of being thousands of feet above the ground and potentially crashing from said height.

"I believe we can do whatever we like, Amor, but I will ask our attendant if it will make you feel better."

"Don't you dare ask her if I can sit on your lap!"

"Then perhaps we should spend the flight in the bedroom," he said lowly, gesturing to the door at the back of the cabin.

Alexa turned her head back to look over the back of her seat, her mouth going dry at the thought of getting in bed with Ethan right then.

"I thought you wanted to wait until we can complete, um," she stopped, thinking it better not to mention anything about blood bonds with humans so close by. "Until we get where we're going," she corrected.

"Hmm, yes, I suppose you are right. While I was suggesting we could just lie together, I should know better than to think I can keep my hands to myself, especially with you seeming so happy and playful. This side of you is very sexy."

She smiled at him, her eyes full of love, "I am happy, Ethan; more so than I've ever been before." She got up and moved around the table that separated them, sitting down on Ethan's lap and wrapping her arms around his neck. She pressed a soft kiss to his lips then leaned her forehead against his. "I love you, Mr. Kellar."

He pushed his fingers through her long, silky hair and grabbed it lightly, pulling her head back so that he could access her full lips. His kiss started out soft, but quickly grew hungry and needy. He let out a little growl and drew back, his breathing heavy.

"I love you, too." he whispered after a moment.

Alexa could sense his internal struggle. She took his face in her hands and looked into his eyes which were darker than normal, like there was a storm raging just beneath the surface. "What is it, Ethan?"

He placed his nose in the crook of her neck and inhaled deeply, letting the breath out slowly. "Your blood is calling to me; my primal need to complete the blood bond continues to grow stronger as the time draws near. It may sound barbaric, but it is in my nature. I need to possess you completely."

"Yes, it did sound a little caveman-like," she said, frowning slightly before her lips turned up into a crooked grin, "but, at the same time, it was irresistibly sexy. Do you need me to go back to my seat?" she asked, not really wanting to leave the comfort of his arms.

"No, I need to be close to you. While your blood draws my desire, your nearness soothes my soul and gives me strength to resist the call, if that makes sense."

She sank down into his lap and snuggled into him. "It does make sense; being close to you calms me as well. I'm not even nervous about the flight anymore," she whispered against his neck, just realizing that the plane had already taxied out to the runway and was about to take off.

Less than three hours later, they were beginning their descent. Alexa had fallen asleep in Ethan's embrace shortly after takeoff.

Ethan lightly stroked her hair and whispered, "Amor, wake up. We are almost there."

She smiled lazily without opening her eyes, "Are you going to tell me where we are now?"

He chuckled as she sat up on his lap and stretched dramatically, letting out a loud yawn.

"Why don't you look for yourself," he suggested, pointing to the nearest window.

She leaned over and frowned. "I can tell we are over water, but I don't have super human night vision like you, so that doesn't really narrow it down for me much," she said, looking at him expectantly.

When he didn't respond, she slapped his shoulder playfully. "Ethan Kellar, if you don't tell me where we are I am going to get off this plane and book the first flight home," she threatened, not at all seriously.

He chuckled then sighed with feigned defeat. "Very well, I have rented a secluded villa on a beach. It is on an island, in the Bahamas. Eleuthera. It is a very good place for swimming with wild dolphins," he said, eliciting a loud squeal from Alexa as she threw her arms around his neck and kissed him fiercely.

When she started to pull away, he gripped her waist tightly and yanked her back, growling possessively as he plundered her mouth with his skilled tongue.

Alexa finally broke away, eliciting another growl from Ethan, and snapped her head up, completely breathless when she heard a small cough from behind Ethan. She looked up to see Allie, her eyes downcast and a slight blush on her cheeks.

"I'm terribly sorry to disturb you, but we've landed and your driver is waiting," she said quickly and turned back to the front cabin.

When they stepped up to the door of their private villa, Alexa was practically humming with excitement and anticipation. She had always wanted to go on a tropical vacation, but not really having anyone to go with and having such a demanding job before she had Chloe, she had never made the time.

The driver had gone in ahead and dropped off their luggage; while Ethan and Alexa looked around outside before returning and passing the keys to Ethan. Alexa was about to walk through the door when Ethan hooked his arm around her waist and yanked her back.

"Not so fast, Mrs. Kellar," he said, as he scooped her up with one arm behind her back and the other under her knees. "Is it not tradition for a husband to carry his new wife over the threshold?" he said, stepping into the large home.

"Oops, sorry; I kind of forgot about that," she said sheepishly, as he set her down and kissed her forehead.

She took a step forward, wanting to explore; but Ethan grabbed her arm lightly, pulling her attention back to him. "Amor, please, do not make me wait any longer; I need you," he pleaded, his hunger for her hitting her with such force that her knees buckled slightly.

And then there was nothing and no one that mattered but him, as her own hunger flared and she went to him, putting her hand on the back of his neck to force him down as she lifted up on her toes and crushed her mouth to his.

He growled in approval of her forcefulness and put his hands on her ass, pulling her up and she wrapped her legs around his hips.

With his vampire speed, he moved them to the bedroom which the owner had decorated in anticipation of newlyweds occupying the space. There were red roses scattered on the floor and on the ivory comforter that covered the large canopied bed. A large portion of the floor was glass, yielding a softly lit view of the ocean floor below through crystal clear blue water.

But they saw none of it in the frenzy of their need to be one; to complete the blood bond and belong to one another forever.

Ethan pinned Alexa to the soft bed, pulling back just long enough to mumble something she couldn't quite understand; the only word that reached her was "naked", and in one swift motion he tore both her tank top and bra open.

Not wanting to be outdone, Alexa reached up and grabbed Ethan's loose-fitting button-down shirt and ripped it apart, sending buttons flying around the room. When she looked up at him she gasped, seeing his eyes, which were glowing in the dim light, and his elongated fangs.

A flicker of concern flashed through the hunger flooding his eyes and he fought to pull back and stand at the foot of the bed breathing heavily. He thought she was afraid of him, her fear the only thing that could temper the beast at that moment.

Sensing his apprehension, she sat up slowly, never taking her eyes from his as she smiled seductively and peeled off the remnants of her shirt and bra before kicking off her sandals. She reached down and unbuttoned her denim shorts, slipped them down over her legs and tossed them onto the floor.

She slid back on the bed to rest on the multitude of soft down pillows in only her lacy thong and crooked her finger at him, beckoning him to join her. He didn't need much encouragement. Immediately, his shorts and shoes were off and flung somewhere across the room, but he remained standing where he was, trying to calm the beast inside him as he looked to her with his eyes full of torment.

"I, I am struggling to stay in control. I am afraid I will be too rough, that I might hurt you," he said, casting his glance downward in shame.

Alexa crawled across the bed and sat up on her knees, stopping just short to avoid actually touching his impressive length which was jutting out just below her ample breasts.

She reached out with one hand and pushed him back, giving herself room to get off of the bed and stand in front of him. She walked into him, forcing his hardness up against her stomach as she grabbed his face and looked into his eyes.

"You will not hurt me; I trust you. I need this as much as you do; your blood also calls to me, my love," she whispered as she leaned her face into his chest to inhale his scent. In that moment, a strange feeling swept over her. She looked up to Ethan again, and then her eyes slid to his neck and the slow pulse that was beating there. Reflexively, she licked her lips and was shocked to feel the sharpened points of her somewhat elongated canines as her tongue moved back into her mouth. Normally it was something that she would have questioned, but basic need and instinct had taken over and before she knew what she was doing she struck, biting down on his pectoral just above his nipple.

Ethan growled with surprise and pleasure as he felt her sharp teeth penetrate his skin. She took several small pulls on his blood before she reared back, exposing her blood-covered fangs to him.

"I, I'm sorry," she stuttered, as she looked down at the wound she had inflicted.

Whatever hope he had of remaining in control was lost when he smelled the scent of his own blood in the air and looked into her eyes that were full of hunger and desire.

In a millisecond, he had her pinned to the bed, the stalk of his hardness pressed firmly between her wet folds as he greedily ran his tongue up the side of her neck, summoning her vein to the surface before he struck hard and deep.

She felt no pain, only intense, mind-blowing pleasure despite his roughness, as he drank up her sweet essence.

Instinctively, she spread her legs wider and wrapped them around his, pulling him towards her with her feet. She moved her hips up trying to move him and his throbbing cock where she needed it. With the beast in control, he didn't need much guidance and pushed his full length inside her in one smooth motion, causing her to scream out his name as an orgasm immediately ripped through her body.

Before the waves of her climax had subsided, she grabbed his arm and pulled his wrist to her mouth, biting down hard as he continued to drink from her neck.

The instant his blood hit her tongue, they were both washed with sensation, every feeling, every movement, every touch, every emotion felt as the other. Alexa could feel how good her soft skin felt to him, how warm and tight she was around his cock, how much he loved and wanted her; while, at the same time, he could feel his weight on her, the fullness she felt with him inside her, the taste of his blood on her tongue.

As they fell over the edge together, there was no way to know whose body the climax originated with, both feeling it as their own and as each other's, making it the most exquisite pleasure of their lives.

Alexa released his wrist, relaxing back on to the bed and he pulled away from her neck, swiping his tongue over the marks from his fangs then repeating the action on his wrist before settling there on top of her, propping himself up on his elbows as he gazed into her eyes.

They remained like that in silence for several minutes, just staring into each other's eyes. There was no need to speak; they could feel everything through the bond they had just consummated.

When Ethan finally rolled off of Alexa, he pulled her into his arms and kissed her hair as she laid her head on his chest, listening to his slow, steady, heartbeat. They stayed there, each feeling complete and whole for the first time in their lives, as they drifted off into a deep, tranquil sleep.

Alexa awoke to the sun shining in through the open blinds of the window off to her right. She didn't need to glance to the left to know that Ethan wasn't in bed next to her. She could feel the cool touch of wood on her feet, the handle of the frying pan he was holding on her hand, and smell the delicious scent of eggs and bacon that he was cooking in the kitchen.

She wrapped the ivory satin sheet around her naked body and hopped out of bed, taking a moment to look down through the glass panel at the school of brightly- colored fish swimming by through the brilliantly blue, crystal-clear water.

She could feel Ethan's smile as he realized she was awake and coming to join him for breakfast.

Wow, this bond is amazing! she thought as she exited the bedroom. Stopping at the doorway to the state-of-the-art kitchen, she leaned against the frame to take in the view of Ethan standing at the counter; gloriously naked as he plated the food he had cooked.

Without turning around, he said, "Good morning, Mrs. Kellar. I was hoping to bring you breakfast in bed, but it appears you are too impatient for that."

"Well, I'm very sorry to have ruined the surprise. In only one night, I have learned to adore surprises. This place is amazing!"

"And you have not even seen the beach, Corazón," he said as he walked to the table and placed two full plates down. "Though, with you looking so fetching, I may not be able to let you out of the house to enjoy it." He rushed to her, wrapped his arms around her waist, and placed a kiss on her forehead. "I missed you."

"You always say that; but how could you miss me when we're in the same house and you can feel everything I do?" she said, smiling brightly at him. "Will it always be like this?"

"I always say it because it is what I feel every moment you are not with me. The bond will be as you desire it; with time you will learn to block some of the sensations. Not that I am saying I will ever let you out of my sight now that I have you," he leaned down and kissed her neck where he had bitten her, making her touch her fingers to her lips as she felt the softness of her own skin beneath them. "But if we are apart, it would be distracting to experience everything so intensely. My parents have been bonded for many years and they have assured me they only feel each other when they wish."

"That's good to know," she said, pulling his wrist up to her mouth and placing a gentle kiss there, as he had done to her neck. The action reminded her of something she wanted to ask. She ran her tongue over her teeth before saying, "Last night, I had fangs. How is that possible with the repression spell still intact?"

"I was wondering that as well, but I was not in any position to have a discussion about it at the time. Seeing you like that, I do not believe I have ever witnessed anything sexier." He leaned down and softly kissed her lips. "It seems that a small part of your true nature was called forward by our bonding."

She smiled up at him. "My father assured me that the witch will lift the spell when we return, so you're going to get to see me like that quite often."

"I cannot wait. Perhaps we should eat before I get too hungry for something else," he said, with a mischievous grin. "You are going to need to keep your strength up for this week."

She flashed him a wicked little smile, stepped back out of his embrace, and dropped the sheet. "What could you be hungry for, other than food?" she challenged playfully, as she stood before him completely naked.

He immediately scooped her up and sat her on the countertop, stepping forward between her thighs and slanting his full lips over hers in a hungry kiss.

"I suppose the food will have to wait," he growled, as he pressed his erection against her already-wet opening. She reached out to wrap her arms around him and pull him towards her, but he stepped back out of her reach causing her lip to come out in a little pout. "I said I was hungry," he dropped to his knees in front of her, lining him up perfectly with what he was craving, "so I am going to eat until I get my fill."

She could feel his warm breath on her most sensitive skin, causing her to close her eyes and lean back on her elbows.

"No, open your eyes; I want you to watch," he whispered, sending a shiver down her spine which he felt down his own back.

When she tilted her head forward and opened her eyes, Ethan pushed her thighs further apart with his hands and swiped his tongue up the length of her sex. She moaned loudly and started to close her eyes again, but caught herself and kept them trained on him as he continued to caress her with his tongue.

It was such an amazing sensation for Ethan, feeling everything that he was doing to her and seeing the sheer pleasure in her eyes. As he felt her orgasm start to build, he knew it was going to take every ounce of self-control he possessed not to fall over the edge himself.

When the first waves of her climax were imminent, Ethan concentrated on blocking some of the sensation while he continued his skillful ministrations, knowing that that was his only hope of holding back. With her eyes still focused on Ethan, Alexa cried out his name loudly as her body trembled with the exquisite orgasm.

Before the last waves of Alexa's pleasure receded, Ethan stood and positioned his hips between her quivering thighs, gripping his thick stalk at the base and rubbing it slowly up and down her wet folds as she moaned in approval. He began to push inside her at an achingly slow pace, wanting to savor every shared sensation. Once he was buried to the hilt, he repeated the delicious torture by pulling out just as slowly. They continued that way for several minutes, making love slowly and reveling in the intense ecstasy of the blood bond before it became too much and they called out each other's names as they found release.

After eating a cold breakfast, they took very quick, separate showers, despite Ethan's protests, because Alexa was eager to get outside and enjoy the island.

They spent the morning on their private beach, sunbathing and swimming, which led to a rather intense splash fight. Ethan's speed gave him an unfair advantage, which Alexa pointed out repeatedly, pretending to be annoyed and demanding that he make it up to her. Naturally, the only way for him to atone for the injustice was to make love to her in the water.

When they were both starting to feel hungry, they dressed and headed into town to try Tippy's, a local restaurant their driver had recommended.

Ethan looked at Alexa across the table as she popped a piece of coconut shrimp into her mouth from the plate they were sharing. "Te amo, Alexa. In my long life, there was not a single moment before I met you in which I felt even a fraction of the happiness you have given me. I wish that I could go back, that I-," Alexa quickly leaned over the table and placed a coconut-flavored kiss on his lips before he could finish.

Sitting back in her chair she said, "I love you, too; but no more regrets, okay? I don't want to waste any more time reliving the past or worrying about the future. I just want to be here with you, to enjoy the moments as they happen." She gestured all around, "I mean, look at where we are; this place is absolute paradise!"

He gave her a bright smile, sexy dimples included. "You are amazing, Alexa."

She smiled back. "Only because that's how you make me feel."

They finished their meals of fresh seared ahi tuna and roasted lobster tail, both of which they split since Alexa couldn't decide which she wanted to order, and spent the next few hours exploring the local communities and shops. They picked up a few souvenirs for Chloe, a shell necklace and bracelet, and a stuffed bear wearing a Bahamas t-shirt. Considering the rate of her growth, they decided against trying to buy her any clothing while they were away.

When they finally returned to the villa, they were just in time to sit out on the sand and watch the glorious sunset on the water. They went inside and immediately set-up the iPad, which Ethan had purchased right before they left, for the FaceTime call they'd planned with Chloe. She was spending the first half of their trip with Alexa's parents, and the second half would be spent with Ethan's.

As the device began to ring, Alexa felt excited, not only to see Chloe, but to see her parents as well. Of course, she was cherishing every moment away with Ethan, but she couldn't help but look forward to spending more time getting to know them. After all, they had over twenty years to catch up on.

It was Rebecca who answered the call, smiling broadly as she greeted them. "I can already see that you two have gotten some sun. Are you having a nice time?"

"It is really amazing here; the weather has been perfect so far and, yes, we're having an amazing time!" Alexa responded. "How has Chloe been? Can we see her? I am missing her like crazy!"

"Of course; just a moment while I go try and steal her away from her doting grandpa," she joked. A few moments later, Chloe popped into view on the screen, her hair already looking thicker and longer and her face slightly thinner, less like a baby and more like a young child.

"Hi Mommy, Daddy!" she squealed excitedly. "I play Grampa!"

"Hi, sweet baby," Alexa and Ethan responded in unison. "You look so big," Alexa continued. "Are you having fun with Grandma and Grandpa?"

"Uh huh. Mommy, I go hide. Bye!" Chloe blurted, as she shot out of view.

"Bye, baby; we love you," Alexa yelled, hoping she could still hear her.

"I believe I'm being summoned to join the game," Rebecca said as she popped back into view. "Don't worry about Chloe; she is amazing and we are enjoying every minute with her. Just enjoy the break and each other and we'll talk to you tomorrow. I love you both."

And with that, the call ended.

"I can't believe how different she already looks," Alexa said with a touch of sadness in her voice. "But she seems to be having a blast."

"Do not worry, Amor. She is being well taken care of and, though I know you fear it, she will not be all grown up by the time we get home," he half teased. "Now I think we should take your mother's advice and get to work enjoying each other," he said huskily as he crawled towards her across the bed, his eyes locked on her full lips.

She pulled the bottom one between her teeth, and her feelings of sadness evaporated as her gorgeous mate covered her body and captured her mouth in slow, tender kiss.

CHAPTER 26 - *A Change of Plans*

The next few days passed in similar fashion, with them relaxing, enjoying the beautiful weather and sampling the local cuisine. Of course, they were newlyweds, so a large chunk of their time was dedicated to exploring their new bond while making love, which had occurred on practically every surface inside the large villa and quite a few outside as well.

On the second day, they went out on jet skis that Ethan had arranged to rent and spent a good amount of time with a pod of curious, wild dolphins. They were even able to touch a couple of brave members of the pod that swam around them when they stopped and hopped into the water. The experience was pure joy for Alexa, who was so fond of the aquatic creatures.

Late one night, after making love in the soft glow of candlelight, Alexa laid with her head on Ethan's chest, listening to his steady heart beat as she traced the intricate pattern of his tattoo with her fingertips, following the same path she had made with her tongue only moments before. Noticing a strange movement in the color, she sat up and turned on the lamp that sat on the table next to the bed.

She looked at the markings on his chest more closely then said to Ethan with confusion, "That's weird, look at your tattoo. It's like the color is fading or something."

Ethan sat up and looked down, seeing that the color was, indeed, fading rapidly from the bottom of the design on his side and working up towards his chest.

He jumped up off the bed and slid on a pair of shorts before grabbing his cell phone from the dresser. "Something is wrong," was all he said as he rapidly tapped the screen, dialing his father. After several rings, the call went to voicemail. He hung up and tried his mother.

"What is it?" Alexa said, her voice laced with panic.

"I cannot be certain, but it is as if the spell is lifting, and there are only two ways that could happen," he stated with difficulty, as he tried to swallow the panic and sadness that were rising in his chest. Alexa's hand shot to her mouth as she gasped.

Just then his mother picked up, her strained voice filling the room through the speakerphone. "Ethan, are you and Alexa all right?"

"Yes, but my tattoo, the color just faded out, as if the spell was lifted."

"Oh, mi hijo, I am so sorry, I thought," she sobbed loudly before continuing, "I thought there would be more time. Your father and Barb returned to the clinic. He thought it would be safe now since he

316

had taken all of Chloe's records before Lucias' men came. They just wanted to talk to the staff, further explain his retirement and sign some papers to transfer the ownership of the practice to the new doctor and nurses. They were both so fond of everyone there, they just wanted to say goodbye," she sobbed again, "but they were watching, waiting. I just had a vision of your father."

"Is he alive?" Ethan cut in.

"Yes, I can still feel him, but he was running, carrying Barb. She was gone." She continued to cry, feeling Elijah's grief along with her own at the loss of such a dear friend and all his loyal employees.

Ethan dropped the phone at hearing his fear confirmed.

Alexa was watching him helplessly, with tears streaming down her face.

Gathering himself, Ethan retrieved the phone. "Where is Cami?" he questioned cautiously, afraid of the answer.

Josephine took a deep breath to calm herself. "She just left to meet with her unit in the city. They are going to take care of the clinic, to make sure there are no questions from the humans."

Just then Ethan's phone beeped, the screen showing his father calling. "Father is calling me now; stay on the line," he said tightly as he answered the call.

Elijah did not wait for a greeting. "Son, you need to get back immediately. We were ambushed at the clinic, everyone is dead," he paused, choking back his grief, "Barb is dead, we are all exposed. I have called the High Commander; they are moving Chloe to The Elite's compound. I must call your mother," he said in one breath.

"I have her on the other line. She had a vision; she already knows, but she needs to hear your voice. We will leave immediately for the compound; just let her know."

"Be safe, son," Elijah said as Ethan ended the call.

Ethan pulled Alexa up off of the bed into his arms, hugging her tightly as she continued to cry. "We will be okay; just sit here, I will take care of everything," he whispered, trying to convince himself as much as her. She nodded, yet remained silent.

Within moments, he had called the rental company to arrange for their car to the airport and flight to the compound. When he'd made the original arrangements, he had paid for the crew from their flight down to remain on the island. At the time, he had only been considering that Alexa might find it too difficult to stay away from Chloe the whole week.

By the time the car arrived, Ethan had packed their bags, and he and Alexa were waiting anxiously on the front patio.

"Sorry to see you go so soon, sir; I hope you enjoyed our little island while you were here," the driver said in his Bahamian accent, as he took their bags and loaded them into the trunk.

"We enjoyed it very much, but there has been a death in the family and we must go home," he stated without emotion. Alexa had not said a word since he hung up with his father, and he was determined to remain strong and in control for her. Saying there was a death in the family provided a reasonable explanation for her red, swollen eyes and, in truth, that is really what had happened. Barb had been a part of his life for as long as he could remember and he knew he would feel her loss deeply. He refused to think about it now; he had to take care of Alexa and Chloe. That was all that mattered. Once they were safe, he could grieve.

Their car pulled up next to the jet and Ethan helped Alexa from the car as the driver loaded their bags onto the plane. A flight attendant came down the ladder as they approached it, but it was not Allie as they had expected.

"Hi there! I'm Molly, and I'm gonna be taking care of ya'll on your flight today," she said cheerfully in a thick southern accent.

"Where is Allie?" Alexa questioned. Ethan smiled just hearing her voice again after such a long silence, but he was curious, too, since he had anticipated the same crew would be flying them home.

"Oh, well, I don't really know, I just got a call from the company a bit ago saying they needed me on a flight back to the States right away, so here I am," she said, completely unfazed.

"Thank you for coming on such short notice," Ethan said as they followed her on to the plane. At this point, he didn't care who got them there; they just needed to get to their daughter.

Within a few minutes they were seated, with Alexa snuggled comfortably on Ethan's lap, his arms wrapped around her as they taxied to the runway.

"Would you like a blanket or some extra pillows?" Molly asked from a few feet behind Ethan.

"I'm actually a little chilly; a blanket would be great," Alexa tossed over her shoulder.

She heard the front cabin door open and close; then a strange clicking sound behind her right ear as Ethan's body tensed, and then his arms fell limply away from her body. Alexa started to turn, but before her mind could even complete the thought she felt a small pinch in the side of her neck, and everything went black.

Ethan had picked up on the increase in the flight attendant's heart beat when Alexa had said she wanted a blanket, but he didn't really give it a second thought. She was human and didn't pose a threat. At least that was what he'd thought until he felt the sharp pinch of the dart in his neck. The tranquilizer was extremely potent, rendering him unconscious before he could react, even with his preternatural reflexes.

Molly had retrieved the gun from the front cabin when she got the blanket for Alexa. She hadn't expected her opportunity to come so quickly and it was all she could do to keep from jumping up and down with excitement. She covered the weapon carefully with the soft beige fabric and walked towards the unsuspecting couple. She was nervous, of course, knowing what he was; she only had one chance at this and if she failed death was the only thing that waited for her, whether it be by his hands or by her master's.

But if she succeeded, he was going to make her an immortal, his queen to rule by his side.

That was what Lucias said when she had impressed him all those days ago. Instead of screaming with fear and fighting, or begging for her life as he tortured and fed on her, she had reacted as if it was pleasurable. There had been only pure fascination in her somewhat empty eyes, as she took in his glowing irises and long inhuman fangs. This human female had intrigued him and might prove quite useful in his plans. Of course he had lied to her, one was either born a vampire or not, there was no way to turn a human. By the time she figured that out she would have served her purpose and could either accept it and stay on as his pet, or be killed.

Everything was falling into place perfectly. Lucias' spy had proved invaluable by not only confirming with absolute certainty that Chloe Ryan was the child from the prophecy, but also providing the location of her father, a much-sought after prize. Unfortunately, he had been unable to track Chloe's current location, the High Commander having moved her after the little incident at the clinic; but no matter, once he had her parents, it would only be a matter of time.

Lucias' phone vibrated on the desk in front of him. "Yes," was all he said in greeting. He listened intently, a satisfied smile spreading across his flawless face. "Excellent. I will meet you there in two hours."

The heavy blackness began to recede and Ethan could feel that he was moving. The last thing he remembered was sitting on the plane with Alexa, but he could no longer feel her warmth in front of him. He attempted to open his eyes, but the lids were so heavy they only fluttered before falling closed again.

Alexa! He tried to call out her name, but had only managed to do so inside his own mind. The panic began to flood over him when he realized he could not feel her at all. Suddenly the motion he was feeling stopped.

"Place him in room two, and bring the woman, Alexa, to me. I would like to have a little chat with her before we begin," instructed a voice that Ethan did not recognize. Relief washed over him at hearing that his wife was alive.

"Yes, Sire," came the response from behind him. When they started to move again, Ethan realized he was lying flat on some sort of gurney or stretcher, which was hard and cold beneath his back. He struggled to remember what had happened. He recalled the new flight attendant and the change in her heart beat, then the click and the small pinch in his neck.

She shot me with a tranquilizer, he realized.

As much as he hoped there was some other explanation, he knew who was behind this.

Lucias, he thought with disdain.

He didn't know what the maniac had planned for them, but he could only pray that the High Commander had gotten Chloe to the safety of The Elite's compound. She would be shielded within those walls, the blocking spell having been reinforced by several witches over the years. Thinking of the spell was a painful reminder of Barb but, instead of letting the sadness weaken him, Ethan used it to fuel his anger. Lucias was responsible for her death.

I will kill him with my bare hands, and if he so much as touches Alexa, I will do so very slowly, he thought, feeling the sedative beginning to wear off.

With great effort, he opened his heavy eyelids and strained to look around as much as possible; still unable to lift his head or move any other part of his body.

From what he could see, it looked like he was in an exam room in some sort of medical facility, which was further confirmed by the antiseptic smell that permeated the air.

Just then, he felt a spike of panic that was not his own.

Alexa jolted up suddenly, feeling completely disoriented as she tried to look around, but her vision was distorted by the contact lenses that were stuck to her eyes. She moved to lift her hands up to her face, but was stopped by the restraints around her wrists that were attached to the metal railings of the hospital gurney on which she sat.

She blinked repeatedly, trying desperately to get her eyes to focus. When she was finally able to see, she looked down at herself, noting that she was wearing a rather thin robe. She felt ill, thinking that some stranger had removed her clothes. Her eyes fell on her left hand and the IV that was taped to the back which gave her a sense of false relief.

I'm in the hospital. Was I in an accident? Where's Ethan? she wondered, trying to remember what had happened. Her eyes followed the tube from her hand up to the hanging bag of fluid and she jumped at seeing the man standing there, completely silent and still.

She already knew he was a vampire and could feel the panic rising in her throat as her eyes filled with tears. Almost immediately she was hit with Ethan's anger and frustration through their bond. She knew he was close, which both comforted and scared her.

I hoped we would have more time, she thought as she closed her eyes and struggled to choke back her fear and sadness.

Opening her eyes, she looked back to the strange man, and then glanced at the tray beside him and the empty syringe laying there.

"What did you give me?" she asked, nodding towards the tray, doing everything in her power to keep the fear from her voice.

The response came from behind her, instead of from the man she was watching.

"Just a small shot of adrenaline to wake you, my dear. A rather potent sedative before that." The sound of the cold, overly-controlled voice sent a chill down her spine.

When the owner of the voice stepped into view, Alexa couldn't deny that he was extremely handsome, with his neatly trimmed sandy blonde hair, high cheek bones and straight, even nose. He appeared sophisticated and polished in what was clearly a several-thousand dollar suit, but there was a darkness surrounding him and bleeding into his green eyes, that she would only ever describe as pure evil.

"So you are the mother of the child, bride to the infamous Ethan Kellar," he stated with certainty. "I must admit, I expected something more."

He placed his hand under her chin and forced her face up. Unwilling to show weakness, she met his gaze defiantly. "I cannot doubt the strength of your will, but everything else about you appears human. But for the small taste of your blood that I took, there would be no way of knowing you were truly vampire. How very odd," he stated as he took a few steps back.

Alexa felt the bile rising in her throat at the thought of him taking her blood.

"Lucias," she spat venomously.

"Ah, my reputation precedes me," he responded with amusement. "Well, I suppose that saves the trouble of an introduction."

"What do you want?" she asked cautiously.

"You already know what I want, my dear; your daughter. So tell me where she is and perhaps we can avoid any further unpleasantness," he stated.

"I don't know where she is, but even if I did, I would sooner die than tell you," she stated with all the conviction she could muster as she stared at him.

"As you wish," he said and then moved across the short distance to her with amazing speed to hover directly above her as Alexa squeezed her eyes shut, preparing for the attack that didn't come.

He leaned down, running his finger down her neck over Ethan's mark and between her breasts as he whispered, "I will have her, make no mistake about that. In fact, you should be proud; I intend to make her my queen. In my long life, I have never taken a bride; she will be the first and once we are bonded, she will help me rule this world," he stated confidently.

Alexa opened her eyes and looked up at him with disgust. "She's just a baby," she said in disbelief, never before considering his vile intentions for her baby girl.

"Not for long," he said as he moved to the door. "I believe it is time you were reunited with your husband," he tossed over his shoulder with a wicked smirk.

✧

A jolt of adrenaline passed through Ethan from the turmoil of Alexa's emotions. He felt fear, disgust, worry, sadness, and then a small glimmer of relief. He used it to push up on his elbows, feeling a small amount of strength returning to his paralyzed body.

He looked down to see the shackles around his wrists and ankles, binding him to the steel table on which he was laying. He didn't have to try to realize he was far from having enough power to break free, since he struggled just to stay up on his arms.

As he prayed for a miracle to release him and get him to Alexa, the door off to his right swung open.

"Wonderful; I see the tranquilizer is starting to wear off. Excellent timing," Lucias said as he stepped into the small room, with one hand behind his back and followed closely by his son, Kaleb.

"I was just speaking with your wife. She truly is lovely, every inch of her," he said as he walked over to Ethan's side, "and her blood, well, it tastes positively divine," he rasped as he licked his lips, hoping to incite Ethan's anger.

It worked, causing Ethan to roar loudly as he struggled against his chains but, even filled with pure rage, he could barely move the heavy metal.

"If you touch her, I will rip your heart out," he promised, glaring at Lucias.

Lucias' wicked laugh filled the room. "I very much doubt that, but rest assured; I have no intention of touching her, again at least," he said with a smirk. "Now your daughter, that is another story entirely.

As I have just shared with your new mate, I intend to touch her in every way possible."

Ethan's eyes filled with red as fury washed over him and he bucked against his restraints, causing the table to bend slightly under the force.

"The rumors of your strength were not exaggerated," Lucias stated with wonder as he moved closer. "You will make an excellent addition to my forces."

With his last statement, Kaleb, who had been silently looking at the ground, looked up with confusion. "But, Father, I thought you-"

"Silence!" Lucias bellowed as he pinned Kaleb with an icy stare. "I have already warned you about questioning me, Kaleb. Do not force me to repeat myself. I have in my possession one of the most powerful vampires in existence. I would be remiss in my duties as a leader to waste such a splendid weapon. He will become a captain in my army and he will lead us to the child."

"My apologies, Sire," Kaleb stated and returned his gaze to the ground. It was then Ethan's turn to laugh. "I will never help you. I would sooner die."

"Is that a family motto?" Lucias mocked. "Your wife said something similar, but only one of you will be keeping your word."

With that, he rushed forward, jammed the needle he had been holding behind his back into Ethan's chest and pushed the plunger down, forcing the contents into his heart as he roared out in pain.

Lucias leaned down. "Very soon, you will be powerless to deny any request I make of you, servant," Lucias whispered into his ear with satisfaction. He pulled the needle back out and took a step away.

"I must warn you, this will be quite unpleasant. But once the transformation is complete, you will be faster and more powerful than ever before, and you will be mine."

With that, Lucias headed for the door. Stopping just short, he turned to Kaleb. "Release him. I will retrieve the girl," he said and left the room.

Kaleb felt his rage bubbling just below the surface as he leaned down next to Ethan and whispered, "It looks like you are someone's prisoner now." He roughly removed the cuffs from around all of Ethan's limbs and tossed them aside, filling the room with loud clanging sounds. His father had promised him revenge; but now, with his vengeance so close he could taste Ethan's blood on his tongue, it was being ripped away.

With all of his chains removed, Kaleb shoved Ethan off of the table and watched him fall to the hard floor beneath. Kaleb stared with hatred as he moaned and writhed in agony while the poison Lucias injected began to take effect. The transformation was excruciating; he had watched it countless times over the years as his father built his army.

Using some of their kind's most talented scientists, Lucias had succeeded in creating a serum from the black plague and his own blood, which not only increased power and speed, but also bound the infected to him inextricably. But there was a price. While not enough to kill them, the infected were sensitive to direct sunlight and silver. They were also overcome with bloodlust immediately after being injected, requiring a large amount of blood to complete the transformation, otherwise they would perish within a matter of hours. After the transition, while the bloodlust would dissipate, they would need to feed far more frequently than a normal vampire to survive.

Kaleb was the only member of Lucias' forces not infected. Because he was his son, he was already bound by blood, but his father had made it very plain that if he ever failed him, he would endure the same fate as the others.

As he walked towards the door, he was overcome with the same rage he had felt all those years ago and couldn't resist the impulse that streaked through his mind. He rushed to Ethan and kicked him in the ribs, relishing in the sound of several of them breaking from the impact.

A moment later, he stepped out of the door and shut it behind him as he leaned back against it closing his eyes. He took several deep breaths, trying to assuage his anger with the knowledge that, instead of dying slowly by his hand, Ethan would live to lose everything he loved.

In that moment, Kaleb saw his brother's face as it had been on that night; the last time he would ever see the only person who ever loved him.

He was a young vampire, not yet fully mature when his father had allowed him to tag along with David and the four other soldiers. They were going on a mission to gather new recruits in a nearby vampire colony. Finding the legendary Ethan had been a happy coincidence, or so David had thought.

"Should we send word to Father?" Kaleb whispered, as the six of them lingered in the alley behind the inn they had watched Ethan enter only a few hours earlier.

"No," David responded harshly. "There is no way to know how long he will be here and it would be difficult to track him from this place on the open road without being discovered. Besides, Father has already been clear that he no longer wants to pursue him and prefers that we focus our efforts on acquiring new soldiers."

"But how can you do this if Father has commanded otherwise?" Kaleb questioned with worry, knowing what happened to vampires that disobeyed the commands of their rulers.

David smirked slightly. "He did not directly command me on this matter. So long as he does not know of our plan, I am free to act as I see fit. In this instance, it is far better to beg for forgiveness than to ask for permission. For two decades, we've searched for him and suddenly we have given up because Father fears the rumors of his strength. It makes us appear weak, but he is blinded by the guidance of that bitch seer." He placed his hand on his little brother's shoulder. "Kaleb, he does not hear the grumblings of our men who have started to question his authority. If we capture this vampire and present him

331

to Father, he will have no choice but to reward us. He will make me his second-in-command, and you will be the youngest captain in the army."

Kaleb couldn't deny that the thought of being a captain, of finally being looked upon with love and respect by the man who barely acknowledged his presence, was what his heart yearned for above all else.

"What should I do?" Kaleb asked as the other five began discussing their strategies for the attack.

"You, little brother, will stay back and, once we have him, you will bring the horses."

"But I want to fight; I have been training my whole life!" Kaleb stated defiantly, tired of always waiting behind.

"Kaleb," he said as he ruffled the younger vampire's hair. "You are not yet mature and do not have full control of your abilities. I cannot look out for you and remain focused on the battle. You will stay behind, but do not worry; all Father will hear is that you aided in the capture. He need not know in what capacity."

Kaleb scowled and crossed his arms over his chest defensively. He hated it when David treated him like a child.

I am a soldier; I can fight. I will not stay back like a woman. Once the battle starts I will join and he will not be able to stop me, he decided as he listened to the rest his brother's plan.

Knowing of Ethan's speed, they could not wait for him to get far from the building before they attacked. Luckily, there were only civilians in this colony so they did not anticipate any interference from the locals if they heard the sounds of battle.

Under the cover of darkness, Kaleb pretended to obey his brother's command as he watched David and the others move to various points around the inn in preparation for the attack. He fingered the grip of his sword nervously as he waited.

No sooner had they reached their posts, but the door to the inn swung open and Ethan stepped out, saying something over his shoulder to someone inside before he closed the door and started walking towards the stable.

Kaleb noted that he did not appear armed; perhaps he would immediately surrender and there would be no battle at all. He found that idea disappointing.

Ethan was only a few paces away from the door when the five vampires surrounded him with their weapons drawn.

Two of them started laughing. "I expected more; he is not even armed!"

"We are taking you prisoner, in the name of my father, the one true ruler of this world," David stated seriously, despite the continued chuckling from two of his companions.

The laughter stopped suddenly when, in a blur that was almost too fast for Kaleb to track despite his preternatural sight, Ethan moved out of the circle only to return to the exact same spot a moment later, just in time to watch the two heads roll to the ground, followed by the bodies of their owners.

The smell of blood reached Kaleb's nose and he was suddenly flooded with fear, realizing that this vampire had just used the soldiers' own swords, which were still in their hands, to decapitate them.

Ethan turned to Kaleb's brother and stated calmly, "I am no one's prisoner. You can let me pass or suffer the same fate as your humorous comrades."

Every urge to fight that Kaleb had felt only minutes before left him as he stood frozen in the shadows, silently praying that David would simply let him go. While his brother's skill with a sword was unmatched by any in his father's army, he knew this was a fight he would not survive.

Several moments passed and all Kaleb could hear was the unusually fast beat of his own heart.

He watched his brother nod almost imperceptibly, and in a flash the three remaining vampires attacked. Ethan jumped up and flipped backwards over them, landing crouched next to one of the bodies. His stood with the newly-acquired sword in his hand and said, "I will give you one last opportunity to walk away from this."

The response came with the two soldiers rushing him again. Ethan met each swing of their swords with one of his own, the loud clang of steel echoing into the night. To anyone watching him, his movements appeared as effortless as if he was merely taking an evening stroll.

When one of the soldiers cried out and stumbled back as his severed arm fell to the ground in front of him, David saw his opportunity. Ethan's back was to him as he continued to battle with the other man. The plan was to take him alive, so he pulled the club from his waist and rushed with it in one hand, his sword in the other. A good blow to the head would knock him out for hours, perhaps even days. David leapt into the air, coming down hard with the club aimed at the back of Ethan's head; but before he found his mark, Ethan turned and raised the sword.

Kaleb sunk to his knees as he saw his brother suspended in the air, impaled through the heart on the sword Ethan was still holding up high in the air.

He dropped David's lifeless body to the ground and quickly took the heads of the other two vampires, who were still clinging to life, before throwing the sword to the ground.

Kaleb remained silent as he watched Ethan dust himself off, but he couldn't help the gasp that escaped his throat when Ethan turned and looked directly at him. And just like that, he disappeared into the night.

CHAPTER 27 - *Alexa's Choice*

Without a word, Lucias entered the room and grabbed Alexa by the arm, which she didn't fight against; she was just praying he was taking her to Ethan. She had been hit by his pain several minutes earlier, which robbed her of breath and knocked her to her knees. It took several attempts and nearly all of her concentration to shield herself, and even that only lessened the pain; she could still feel it and knew she needed to help him somehow or he would die.

Lucias pulled her down the hallway and stopped in front of a door where his son was still standing.

"Has he been freed?" Lucias questioned.

"Yes, Sire."

"Excellent," he said turning to Alexa. "You can go in and join your husband now. I should warn you; he is probably in a bit of pain at the moment, so try not to mind the screaming," he said with a wicked sneer.

Alexa's hand was shaking as she reached for the metal door which Kaleb had already unlocked. She pulled hard, barely moving the heavy door, but the small crack broke the soundproof seal and she could hear Ethan's pained moaning. She tugged harder and Lucias put his hand up, preventing her from opening it further.

"On second thought, we should make sure you are properly attired to greet your husband before you enter," Lucias whispered against her ear, sending panic through her at the thought of being separated from Ethan after being so close to him.

Before she could protest, Lucias reached up and ripped the robe from her body, leaving her completely exposed.

He put his hands on her shoulders and spun her around to face him as he slowly looked up and down her naked body. Fighting to keep the contents of her stomach down, Alexa swallowed hard, then stood up straight and lifted her chin defiantly.

Lucias chuckled with amusement at her little effort to appear strong. "You know, this ensemble needs something," he said gripping his chin as if he was trying to decide what. "Ah, yes; I know," he said, as he reached out with both hands and scraped across the tops of Alexa's exposed breasts as she screamed out it pain.

He smiled with satisfaction as blood began to run from the wounds, while Alexa struggled to contain her fear. "Perfect; now you may go," he said, waving his hand dismissively as if he were shooing away a fly.

He nodded to Kaleb, who grabbed the door and pulled it open just wide enough for Alexa to enter. She peered into the room cautiously before she saw Ethan lying crumpled on the floor. The sight of him looking so broken removed all of her fear for herself and she rushed towards him, only to be stopped dead in her tracks as he roared, "GET AWAY FROM ME!"

It felt like days had passed while Ethan lay there on the floor as Lucias' poison burned through his body like molten lava. It didn't help matters that he could barely breathe, due to the broken rib that had punctured his lung and was not healing due to the injection. He needed blood; a lot of blood, and quickly.

He fought with everything he had not to scream out in pain, refusing to give Lucias the satisfaction; but he couldn't help the occasional moan that escaped his throat.

When he heard the click of the lock, he swallowed hard, trying to separate his mind from the pain in preparation for whatever torture they had in store for him.

It was several moments before he heard the door move, and then it hit him. The smell of fresh blood filled his nose and strength flooded back into his body as the beast fought to get out. He pushed up on to his knees as another wave of scent hit him and he froze. In that single moment, the fear that had been chasing him around his entire life had finally caught up to him.

He clung to that fear, as he fought the bloodlust inside him that was growing more powerful by the second and roared at her to get away from him.

Ethan jumped up and rushed to the other side of the room, putting as much distance between himself and his wife as was possible.

When he finally dared to look at her, he groaned loudly as the sight of her naked, bleeding body further incited the beast within.

"What can I do?" she whispered, still frozen by the door, as she watched her husband and felt his pain through their bond.

He pinned her with his stare and she gasped when she saw his eyes, the irises glowing red. "Stay away from me!" he growled.

"What did they do to you?" she asked, quietly taking a tiny step towards him. She looked down and saw the deep purple of his broken ribs, knowing that it should have been nearly healed by now.

"I am infected," he replied shakily, as he continued battling the beast.

"You need blood," she said, taking another step towards him.

He let out a sound that was akin to a whimper. "Alexa, please; do not come any closer. It is all I can do to keep the beast contained," he said through gritted teeth. "I just have to make it a couple more hours."

"And then what?" she asked, already knowing his response.

"It will be over, and you will be safe," he whispered, as he slid down to sit on the floor; with his face and palm pressed against the wall, like he was anchoring himself to it.

"You mean you'll die," she said angrily. "No, Ethan; I can't let you do that." She took several more steps towards him and he jumped to his feet.

"Damnit, Alexa!" he roared, "I'll kill you; do you understand that?" His body was shaking violently from his pain and the effort to restrain the beast with her so close and the smell of her blood surrounding him.

She closed her eyes and swallowed hard as she reinforced her shields against his pain, knowing the time had come.

Opening her eyes she whispered, "Yes, my love. I know that I must die to save you. I made that choice a while ago."

Alexa nervously followed Ethan's mother through the door to her parlor.

Josephine sat on the cream striped sofa and patted the seat next to her. "Please sit down; I won't bite," she said with a small chuckle. It was funny coming from an actual vampire.

Alexa did as requested and Josephine took both of her hands and closed her eyes. They sat like that in silence for several minutes, before she opened her eyes and stood.

"You are a very strong woman, Alexa. That is very clear. I am going to share some things with you that will be difficult to hear, but I need for you to know. Perhaps I am being selfish, and for this you must forgive me; but I love my children and I would do anything in my power for them. As a mother, I am sure you understand." she said, looking to Alexa as if asking for permission to continue.

Alexa remained quiet and nodded.

"My son has told you of the prophecy, yes?" Again, Alexa nodded.

"He has brought you here, to me, because he wants me to tell him it has changed or that there is a way to change it; one part in particular."

"What part? He said you don't know how Chloe ends the war or who wins, right? How can he know we would even want to change it?"

"I was afraid of this," Josephine said as she began to pace. "He has not told you what happens to you. If I tell him he cannot change it, he will try to drive you away. But something he does not understand is that, in certain matters, fate will find a way. You could leave here tonight and go into hiding, but somehow, you will both end up exactly where you are supposed to be, exactly when you are intended to be there. Except, then you will have lost the time that you could have had together. You would both live in misery, separated from one another, from the other halves of your souls, only to end up in the same place in the end."

She took her seat next to Alexa again and took one of her hands as she stroked her cheek with the other. "This is very difficult. I know that we have only just met, but I have already seen how happy you make my son, and for that I love you like a daughter."

Alexa's eyes welled up with tears as Josephine took a deep breath. "Please understand; I do not know exactly how long you will have," she dropped her hand from Alexa's face as tears gathered in her eyes as well. "You are going to die before the war is over."

Tears spilled over Alexa's lashes. "I cannot begin to imagine how hard this is to hear, but there is more you must know. You will have to make a choice when the time comes. Ethan can survive, but you will have to force him to," a small sob escaped her throat. "He will have to take your life to save his own. If he does not, you will both perish."

Remembering Josephine's words, Alexa's eyes filled with tears. She thought of Chloe, how she would miss the sweet sound of her laughter and the warmth of her embrace. She tried to picture her all grown up, to see what she would look like in her wedding dress someday; praying that, no matter what happened, in the end Chloe would be safe and happy. For those last few stolen moments, she pictured her daughter's future knowing that this was as close as she would get to seeing it.

And then she stood up straight, wiped the tears from her face, and took once last deep breath for courage before she walked across the room to Ethan.

She stumbled when she felt his pain spike as he continued to struggle to contain the beast that was consuming him. It was so acute that he could no longer speak, or even try to keep her away. He tried to turn away from her into the wall, all the while feeling it growing bigger inside of him. It was like there was a separate entity sharing his body, a parasite eating away at who he was in order to make room for itself to grow.

Alexa placed her hands on his trembling shoulders and laid her cheek against his back. She whispered against his skin, "Ethan, I love you. Even now, I wouldn't change it. I wouldn't trade a single moment of my time with you."

She couldn't see it and she wouldn't, but even with the beast taking control, a lone tear streaked down Ethan's cheek at her soft words.

"You can survive this, my love; you must, for Chloe," Alexa said with conviction, as she bit down as hard as she could into her own wrist and pushed it under Ethan's chin next to the wall.

His battle was lost. The small part of who he really was, her husband, her mate, which remained, was shoved into a corner of his mind as the beast bit down into Alexa's injured wrist, the force of it breaking her bone. He pulled on her blood harshly; his primal side, growing impatient with the slow flow of blood from her wrist, turned and tore into her neck.

As she felt her life starting to slip away, so did the pain. She used the last bit of her strength to raise her hand to his hair, wanting to feel its silky softness in her fingers one last time. A single tear slid from her eye as a final picture entered her mind. She saw Chloe again on her wedding day, this time standing with her father, both looking up at the sky as a gentle rain started to fall.

THE END...

The Fate Series

Choices of Fate - Book 1

Redemption of Fate - Book 2

Absolution of Fate - Book 3

For more information on titles by S. Simone Chavous
please visit

www.ssimonechavous.com

Acknowledgements

Writing *Choices of Fate* has been an amazing experience and looking back over this long journey, there are many people that I need to thank.

First of all, I want to thank my wonderful boyfriend, Brian. Without his love, support, and encouragement, none of this would have been possible. I believe wholeheartedly, that one must know great love to write it. You are my Ethan, I love you baby!

To my girls, Cami and Isabella, you gave me the strength and motivation to do something that, not so long ago, felt beyond my reach. Having both of you in my life has shown me that I can achieve great things and seeing your beautiful, smiling faces every day reminds me that the sky is the limit. I hope someday, when you are both facing the inevitable trials of life, you can look back on this accomplishment, and know that you too can realize your dreams and that I will always be there to help you along the way.

To my mother Wanda, who when I said I wanted to write a book simply said, "I know you can do it and you will be great at it." I love you mom.

Deb, thank you for taking such good care of my little pork chop and giving me time to write.

My dear friend Yuli, thank you from the bottom of my heart for reading all of my first drafts, one chapter at a time, providing invaluable feedback and pushing me to keep cranking them out.

My wonderful neighbor Jill, you provided early encouragement being one of the first people I shared my idea for *Choices* with, a shoulder to cry on when I needed it, and even the inspiration for your

345

namesake character. You are the best neighbor and friend anyone could ever ask for.

To my best friend, Paula, you have been there through many of the ups and downs in my life over the last twenty years, this journey was no exception. Whether it's been a day, months, or even years since we've talked, I always know we can pick up right where we left off. Your friendship means more to me than I could ever say.

Ashley Truelove of Lookin' for a Bookin', you are too awesome for words! I am so grateful for all of your help getting the word out and look forward to working with you in the future.

To Kathy Krick of K² Editing, what can I say? We started this crazy journey into the self-publishing world together. You've been patient and supportive, not only in editing *Choices,* but also as a friend. Though we've never met in person, I know I can always count on you.

All of my other friends and family, April, Rebecca, Gregory, Kendall, Charlie, Ruth Ann, Melvin, Melisa, Michelle, Bryan, I love you all!

To all of the bloggers and reviewers that stay up way too late reading, reviewing, and going above and beyond to help authors, only to get up in the morning and go to work, thank you from the bottom of my heart.

And last, but certainly not least, I want to thank all of my fellow authors, especially R.L. Mathewson, Felicity Heaton, Caris Roane, Molly McAdams, Abbi Glines, Amanda Stone, Erika Ashby, Gail McHugh, Monica Murphy, and Kim Karr. You have all inspired me in some way, either through your own amazing stories or some much needed words of encouragement.

About the Author

S. Simone Chavous spent seven years as a tax accountant before deciding to pursue her true passion as an author. *Choices of Fate,* the first book in the Fate Series, was her debut novel. She lives in northern Indiana with her boyfriend, two beautiful daughters, and their rambunctious vizsla, Lily.

To learn more about S. Simone, please visit:
www.ssimonechavous.com

or connect with her on Facebook at
www.facebook.com/ssimonechavous